P9-AQI-772

HERE IN THE DARK

ALEXIS SOLOSKI

FLATIRON BOOKS
NEW YORK

This is a work of fiction. All of the characters, organizations, and events portrayed in this novel are either products of the author's imagination or are used fictitiously.

www.flatironbooks.com

Library of Congress Cataloging-in-Publication Data

Names: Soloski, Alexis, author.
Title: Here in the dark / Alexis Soloski.
Description: First edition. | New York : Flatiron Books, 2023.
Identifiers: LCCN 2023018589 | ISBN 9781250882943 (hardcover) |
ISBN 9781250882967 (ebook)
Subjects: LCGFT: Theatrical fiction. | Detective and mystery fiction. |
Novels.
Classification: LCC PS3619.O4374 H47 2023 | DDC 813/.6—dc23/eng/20230428
LC record available at https://lccn.loc.gov/2023018589

Our books may be purchased in bulk for promotional, educational, or business use. Please contact your local bookseller or the Macmillan Corporate and Premium Sales Department at 1-800-221-7945, extension 5442, or by email at MacmillanSpecialMarkets@macmillan.com.

First Edition: 2023

10 9 8 7 6 5 4 3 2 1

For Ada and Thom, “My sunlight! My springtime!”

The critical profession, in fact, is cruel in its nature, and demands for its efficient discharge an inhuman person like myself.

—**George Bernard Shaw**

HERE
IN THE
DARK

CURTAIN RAISER
Playing Dead

I am seven years old. I am in the dark. I am wearing a blue velvet dress and black buckled shoes. I am sitting, so still, in a chair much too big for me. I am watching.

In front of me, one man lunges toward another with a knife. Blood blossoms on a white shirt, the stain opening like a flower, as the second man crumples to his knees, then to the ground. The first man stands above him, smiling thin and sharp. Then he turns that smile to me.

I can't swallow. I can't breathe. My fists grip the armrests, every knuckle white.

"Don't worry," my mother says softly. "He isn't dead. You can see him breathing. Look at his stomach: it's going in and out. See? It isn't real. It's only a play. But you're real." She gently unbends one of my hands and covers it with her own, whispering a litany she has whispered many times before, her head so close to mine that her lips brush my ear. "These are your fingers," she says. "This is your hand, your palm, your wrist, your arm . . ."

But this time I can't hear her. Or I won't. Instead, I watch the shirt, the blood, the knife, the smile. I know the man will come for me next. I move to stand. I want to run. But I collapse back into my too-big chair.

I faint.

Curtains fall. Curtains rise. A second act, twenty-five years later. My mother is dead and I sit in the dark so often now. I watch stabbings, shootings, strangulation. Worse.

"Death," says the Duchess of Malfi in a play I adore, "hath ten thousand several doors for men to take their exits." I believe her. I keep count.

As I watch, I swallow. I breathe. My lungs empty and fill, my stomach swells and subsides. Chairs fit me better now. I don't wear velvet dresses or buckled black shoes. I certainly don't faint.

Instead I sit, here in the dark, and I slide my pen noiselessly along the lines of my notebook. I have learned to flick the pages with a minimum of rustle. I have learned to write without light.

I am attentive. I am discerning. I am very nearly happy.

I became a theater critic.

Of course I did.

1

NUMBER WITHHELD

When the phone rings, on a damp November Wednesday, I'm in the bath. I have just returned from the bank, depositing the check—overlarge, on thick, cream stock—from the executor of my aunt's estate and arranging its disbursement. I had not seen my aunt in years, had barely corresponded with her beyond compulsory birthday and Christmas cards. Death came for her punctually and without prelude, which must have met with her approval. Though she may have preferred a place more fit and private than the parking lot of a Hannaford on a late afternoon in May, just before the dinner rush. A heart attack, proof at last that she had a heart at all, her body falling in a way, I was told, that set off her car alarm. She would not have liked the noise. I had not expected an inheritance. But as it happened, she divided her fortune—a small savings account, a smaller civic pension, the proceeds from the sale of her house—between me and a local wildlife charity. She had always favored birds over people, and in this I could not blame her. Though I don't really care for birds.

I do not need her money. But taking it seemed easier than any alternative. So I listened, a close-lipped smile mortared to my face, while an adviser at the bank, a sweaty, pink-cheeked white man in a striped tie that I would swear in any court was a clip-on, lectured me, in a voice like a leaking faucet, about funds and bonds and certificates of deposit.

"Let's just do whatever is most safe," I finally told him. Because it was not what he wanted to hear. And because I am safe about some things.

My aunt, however distant—she lived in New Hampshire, which in New York City terms might as well have been the moon—was the last person in my world who knew my mother, the last person but one who knew me as I was before. I might have received her death as an invitation to step more completely into the small life that I have made for myself or to step into some new larger one, unburdened now. To live, at last, in full. And some part of me—yearning, wild still—must want that. But when the news of her passing reached me, I stepped nowhere except along my typical routes, into assorted theaters and then back to my apartment with an occasional low-lit bar to vary the scene. The executor also sent me two yellowing photo albums, which showed my aunt and my mother as kids and then adolescents and then young women—long limbed, freckled, alive. I paged through them once, then shoved them onto the tallest shelf of the closet, where they have remained.

If I were the sort of person who allowed myself much in the way of an emotional life—in daylight hours, anyway—I suppose I would have felt lonely, orphaned, unmoored. Instead I applied myself to the notebook page and the laptop screen as I never had before, writing and rewriting until each paragraph glittered, diamond bright and twice as sharp, which was only slightly sharper than my usual. This is the curse and blessing of the critical instinct, the irrepressible impulse to report the truth of a work of art, no matter whom that truth offends. These shows invited me. They invited criticism. They should have been finer, sturdier, more plausible. They weren't. And here I was to tell them so, angling for the magazine's chief critic's job with every quip and censure.

That job has stood open for two months now, ever since Crispin "Crispy" Holt, scion of a wealthy Boston family, who fled Princeton as soon as he had his first taste of the Living Theatre (and some extremely high-grade LSD) and had written for the magazine for decades, finally announced his retirement. Rumor has it he shipped his inherited wealth to some Caribbean tax haven, where he can enjoy flashbacks and the occasional cabana boy in tropical ease. I can't confirm this rumor. As a female who lacks a four-octave range, I was beneath Crispy's notice. But for Roger, my editor, I am a sort of protégée, a local girl made something better and more clickable than good. I was certain he would tip me for the job straightaway. Instead he alternates my columns with those of the other junior critic, Caleb Jones. Caleb has a newly minted dramaturgy MFA, a retina-scarring smile, and the aesthetic discernment of a wedge salad. Me, I have taste for days. And a brisk, prickly style. Roger will see sense. Eventually.

On this morning, the adviser eventually presented me with a stack of papers and I initialed and signed, initialed and signed, then handed back his pen (I have better ones at home) and drifted out onto the pavement and up the five flights of stairs to my apartment. I poured a drink, because my aunt did not approve of drink and because I have been drinking more lately—I have to, the pills don't work the way they used to—and ran a very hot bath, to feel something or nothing or both at once, tipping my head back until water filled my ears and the city went quiet and remote.

But that cell phone ring—the shrill factory setting I have never bothered to change—sounds, then stops, then sounds again, reaching me even here. Scam callers rarely phone twice. It could be Roger, I tell myself, needing me for some final query or to workshop some display copy. So I move to answer it.

Drops skitter against the porcelain as I stand, wobbly legged, bracing myself against the wall until my blood pressure evens, shaking the red-black spots from in front of my eyes. Wrapped in a thin towel, I shuffle to the living room—I live in a studio, so really, it's the only room—and reach into my bag for the phone. I've missed two calls from the magazine. The main desk, not Roger's extension. I dial and Esteban, our receptionist, answers.

"It's Vivian," I say, lowering my voice toward the gothic. "You rang?"

"Gorgeous," he chirps, "where you been?"

"East Tenth. Roaming the halls in my satin peignoir and mourning your loss to womankind."

He giggles at a pitch that would shatter crystal. He knows my apartment isn't large enough for halls. He also knows that I don't own a single peignoir.

"Poor bebita," he says. "Well, maybe I got you a consolation prize. A man keeps calling for you. Has a sexy voice. Like very sexy."

"You didn't give him this number?" I say, wrapping the towel more tightly.

"Tch, bebita. Credit. Please. Tried to tell him your email, but he says he wants to talk to you."

"Ten to one he's a publicist."

"A sexy publicist."

"Absurd. Impossible. Against every natural law."

"Maybe, bebita. But he is your problem now."

He gives me the man's name, David Adler, and his phone number, which I record sulkily in the nearest notebook, my dripping hair dotting the page like tears. I smile my way through "Thanks" and "Talk soon" and then let my face slacken as the call ends. Having fumbled into clothes, I slouch into the armchair, balancing the laptop on my thighs. I search my email for "David Adler," then repeat the search in the trash folder. It returns no results. So he isn't linked to any recent play or musical. At least none I've heard of. Which must make him an untried director or a junior publicist set on me reviewing some show so far off Broadway that the subway runs out of track. My uninterest is profound. You can see only so much failed theater and live to tell.

Yet I think of what Roger keeps saying. How he would prefer more sympathy in my reviews or, failing that, a warmer relationship with the artistic community. He calls it the "Let's Not Be Such a Withholding Bitch, Shall We, Kiddo?" plan. Roger has been to sensitivity training. The training did not take.

Warmth is not my forte. As far as the rich palette of human experience goes, I live on a gray scale. Aristotle said that drama was an imitation of an action. I am, of necessity, an imitation of myself—a sharp smile, an acid joke, an abyss where a woman should be. For a decade and more I have allowed myself only this lone role, a minor one: Vivian Parry, actor's scourge and girl-about-town. I don't play it particularly well.

Except when I'm seeing theater, good theater. When I'm in the dark, at that safe remove from daily life, I feel it all—rage, joy, surprise. Until the houselights come on and break it all apart again, I am alive. I know myself again. Here is a dream I often have: I'm walking the streets of Times Square and I've lost the address of the theater I am meant to attend, so I keep wandering, usually in the rain, faster now as the time moves closer to curtain, wet through, up one block and down the next, just wanting and wanting, without remedy, without end.

The profession of theater critic isn't especially necessary or exalted. Here is P. G. Wodehouse on reviewers: "Nobody loves them, and rightly, for they are creatures of the night." But it is the only thing I am good at. The only survivable thing. And I want to practice it with more choice in what I see and what I don't, more space to take in art through ear and eye and strange neuronic tangle and make sense of what results, more opportunities to feel real, even for just a few hours at a time. I am firmly in my thirties now, older than my mother was when she had me, and I would welcome some confirmation that I have not wasted my life. That I was right to choose to have a life at all. Full benefits wouldn't hurt either. So if a call is what it takes to get the job, I can make it. With Roger's advice in mind, I tap in David Adler's number, confident in the blocker I've installed on my phone. On his screen all he will see is "Number Withheld."

He answers before the first ring has finished.

"Hello," I say. "This is Vivian Parry. You've been trying to reach me?"

David Adler isn't a publicist. Or a director. He's a media studies master's student with a breathy tenor—a clarinet with a broken reed—that I find entirely resistible. His thesis, he tells me, centers on critics—their influences, their preferences. He's eager to include a theater critic, especially a female theater critic, especially a younger one, there are still too few women writing, aren't there? He has read my work for years and please will I meet with him? Please can he interview me?

I can hear the need threading his voice. Aching. Ugly.

If David Adler is a scholar, not an artist, then he's of no use to me. But just as he can hear me inhaling to refuse, he adds that he's putting together a panel at the Performance Presenters conference in January and he'd love to enlist me for that, too. *American Stage* has promised to publish excerpts.

So I bite back that refusal, like an epileptic chomping her own tongue. An interview and a panel stint that invite me to explain my relationship to art, that link my rigor to my love for the form, these could help convince Roger that I'm the woman for the byline. So I suggest a time the following Tuesday. He asks me for a location and I name a nearby patisserie, shaping my mouth into a smile so that the words don't come out too clipped. He needs material. I need exposure. I'm familiar with this transaction. Most arts journalism mirrors it. Counterfeiting eagerness and basic human decency makes it seem less tawdry. I end the call as quickly as I can, returning to my laptop to translate the experience of the play I saw last night—an early Fornés drama—into argument and image and evidenced claim.

The day darkens without my noticing and by the time I click send, there's barely time to swipe my lips with something dark and matte—cheap costuming—and detour to the corner store for a milky coffee and a bag of salted plantain chips that I sip and crunch as I race-walk to the train. Then it's down into the subway and back up again into the lights and billboards of Times Square, a place so fake it makes theater seem more real by comparison.

Shouldering past tourists, sidestepping ticket holders, I lunge for the theater as if I'm cresting finish line tape and make my way toward a waiting cluster of lip-glossed press agents, their shining, home-straightened hair already curling in the evening's mist. One of the women separates herself from the group and presses an envelope into my hand. I grin to keep from flinching. Her name is Kerry. Or maybe Sharon. I can name every Shakespeare comedy in first folio order, but I can't tell these brunettes apart.

"Just the single ticket, ri-ight?" she says, that last syllable soaring toward the marquee.

"You be-et," I echo.

Time was, every play I saw, I saw with my mother, my hand in hers across the armrest, and then an ice cream after, where we would talk through all the parts we liked the best. When I was small, I would fall asleep on the car ride home and she would carry me to my bed, so that I couldn't tell where the show ended and I began. In my dreams, I would imagine myself back in the theater, playing all the parts. But I don't act anymore. Not onstage. And now I always go alone.

"I gave you the aisle, just in case you need to escape," the press agent says. She looks as though she would like to wink at me. But winking gives you crow's-feet.

"You know me so well," I say, turning toward the doors and leaving the smile behind.

A velvet rope parts and I'm beckoned in, past the crowd. My bag is checked, my ticket scanned. A first usher hands me a *Playbill*, then sends me down the aisle to a second usher, who directs me to a seat that I could have found myself. I greet colleagues—hunched and flustered or jolly and brazen—as they pass me, chatting about what we have seen. But my attention always returns to the stage and its closed curtains—waiting, wanting.

I stand and sit several times, letting latecomers take their places, before I settle myself with notebook and *Playbill* and pen. The preshow music cuts out, the lights dim, and except for the beeps and chimes of phones powering down, the room goes sweet and mute and I remember how many thousands of nights in how many thousands of seats I have sat just like this, hushed and expectant. This evening's play, midcareer Noël Coward, doesn't invite and won't reward my ardor, but I will give it anyway until the lights come up and I cram myself back into my body and stumble up the aisle, still poised between this world and the other. But now, here—finally!—the curtain parts. My gaze goes soft, my lips part. I'm away. I'm home.

The rest of the week passes, as most weeks do, in a swirl of emails and previews and deadlines and drafts and edits. A paper cup of coffee wakes me in the mornings, an icy shot of vodka tucks me in at bedtime, and in the hours between I read or I write or I walk until afternoon creeps toward night and I can button myself into something borderline presentable and head for the theater again, again, again. Weekends are just like the weekdays. But weekends are easier. Matinees mean that I can lose myself twice in one day and the hours in which I have to pretend to be a person are fewer.

On Saturday, I'm escaping my evening show—a sex comedy, impotent—when a press agent, a man this time, corners me near the exit.

"So," he says, sucking in his cheeks in a way that suggests impertinence and fish, "what did you think?"

I make my face go broad and blank, a prairie made flesh. "What can a person even say?" I tell him. Then I feint left, dart right, and take the 2 to Tribeca to meet Justine at a party in some painter's loft. His work involves pouring acid at various strengths onto sheets of matte metal, so "painter" isn't quite the right word and Tribeca is always at least a little wrong, but I go anyway, as Justine is to be refused—as casting directors and the men who do crowd control at sample sales have learned—strictly at one's peril. Greeting us at the door, the artist offers cocaine from a vial on a chain around his neck. Justine accepts, rolling her eyes as she sniffs from the tiny spoon, once, twice.

"Does he seriously not know the eighties are over?" she says as we lay our coats on a sectional. "And that I wasn't even, like, alive for them?"

"Well, he does live in Tribeca," I tell her.

Later, when the party has thinned to the point of transparency, she disappears up to the sleeping platform with him, her black hair swinging like a pendulum as she climbs the ladder. I wave, though she can't see me, and spend a few more minutes finishing the second glass of upmarket pinot noir I've allowed myself. Then I take the screeching cargo elevator down to the sidewalk, mottled with new rain. I turn toward Canal Street, stretching my hand out for a taxi as I walk, watching the streetlights turn my fingers sodium yellow and ghostly. I hear someone behind me, shoes clicking against the cobblestones half a beat after my own. I spin around, whipping hair into my eyes, but there's no one, nothing—only street and shadow and the false pink promise of the corner Lotto sign. Then a cab shrieks around the corner, its headlights blinding. I hail it and give my address in a voice that's too high, too quick. Hands fisted, eyes shut, I force myself not to stare out the back window as it speeds me home.

On Monday night, with most theaters dark, Justine, wearing heels more than usually vertiginous, somehow climbs my stairs. We order in Thai food and the deliveryman tries to engage her in some tonal language. "Sorry," she says. "My parents raised me very fucking wrong. English only. And high school French." Still she tips him more than she can afford and we poke around the cartons for a while before I mention tomorrow's interview with the grad student, David Adler.

"Look at you so famous," she says. "Mommy's little head case all grown up. You see these?" She gestures with a chopstick in the general direction of her eyes, moist now. "Tears of fucking joy. Now. To business. What are you wearing?"

I offer an elegant shrug meant to convey an unconcern with clothing as a social signifier. Justine seethes as only a person who insists on wearing slingbacks to a fifth-floor walk-up can.

"I can't believe this," she says, wrenching open a final dresser drawer. "You don't have any fucking clothes."

I gesture to the pile that now covers my floor. "With respect—"

"But they're old." She reaches into the wardrobe's depths and tugs at a paisley dress. "Prehistoric."

"Don't touch that," I say, slapping her hand away. She knows better than to handle my mother's things.

By way of apology, she peels off her own black cigarette pants, throwing them my way.

"Won't you need those to get home?"

"Pants are overrated. Wear your black boots, a blouse, and that maybe-Hermès scarf I gave you," she says. "And mascara. Babe, do you even have mascara?"

"Somewhere?"

Justine looks as though she might weep again. Unlike me, she can conjure tears at the drop of a hat. I have seen her. The hat was a Stetson. To console her, I unearth a bottle of bourbon I've hidden under the sink and pour Justine several fingers over ice, plus a smaller glass for me, before heaving my window fully open and joining her on the rusting fire escape. She pulls out a vape pen, inhales and exhales, letting the smoke spiral past the sagging power lines and the ivy sprouting from the cracks in the concrete.

"This interview," she says, "it's about . . ."

"Critics and how we got to be this way. Influences, standards and practices, who hurt me such that this is the life I have chosen."

"Funny," she says. "Not funny. So nothing personal?" She takes another hit.

I make a top-to-toe gesture. "Like I do personal. Barely a person here."

"I know it, babe. State-of-the-art defenses, you. Fort Knox in a B cup." She scrutinizes my chest. "B minus. But seriously—" For just a moment she lets the mask drop, the mask that's truer than her face by now, and someone younger and less certain looks out at me. "You don't think he'll ask about . . ." And I can see her flailing for the word. Which gives me a queasy sensation. Justine never flails.

"About before?" I say. I'm trying to make it sound casual, but it comes out clipped.

"Yes," she says. "Sure."

"How could he? Those records aren't exactly public domain. And I don't use that name anymore. How would he know to ask? Besides," I say, pausing to swallow and grimace, "I sprang fully formed from *The Portable Dorothy Parker* and a shoebox full of *Playbills*. You know that."

"Yeah, but, you know what Faulkner said about the past, right?"

"That it isn't dead? That it isn't even past? Of course. It's in his only play."

"It's just that it's been on my mind lately," she says, exhaling through pursed lips and looking down to the concrete below. "I don't even know why. And I worry about you, okay?"

Considering that one of us has nearly aspirated twice on her own vomit in the last decade and that this person isn't me, her worry seems misplaced.

"I'm fine. Top drawer. A stock photo suggesting joie de fucking vivre." I gesture toward her empty glass. "Speaking of living your best life, want another?"

When I return to the fire escape, she's busying herself with her phone and she doesn't meet my eyes.

"How's the bad doctor?" I ask, dangling my legs into the void.

The bad doctor is an internist she met at an underground supper club in Bushwick. They chatted over homemade absinthe, and at the evening's end, he wrote down his number on a prescription pad. "I get great samples," he said. Maybe he uses that line on every girl. It worked for Justine.

"He's fine," she says, zipping her phone away into her crossbody bag. "I mean uncool and almost forty and possessed of some very fucking antiquated ideas about whether I should sleep with other people, ideas that I am obviously choosing to ignore, but basically fine. Incidentally, he's also big on this Percocet-style thingy that's supposed to be maybe not quite so totally addictive and fabric-of-society destroying and he slipped me a couple of packets."

"And?"

"Like a choir of dry-mouthed angels, babe."

"Share?" I ask. But I don't have to.

She pulls a silver box from her pocket and places a yellow pill on my tongue, lifting her glass to my lips. I let myself lean into her and she leans back into me, with her scent of oud and smoke and sugared almonds, and within minutes I can feel it coming on, a lowered safety curtain between the world and me. As it twines around the bourbon, I feel sleepy and warm and slow. Then I feel nothing at all.

I must have put myself to bed, because I wake beneath my duvet in a reasonable state of undress, my head pounding like a speaker with the bass turned up too high. Some lingering dread, like the sticky feeling of having walked into a spider's web, tells me I've had my usual nightmare. Though sometimes I have other dreams. Sweeter ones. Dreams that I'm onstage again, enfolded in the glow of the lights. Loved. Known.

I scoop water from the sink, swallow some aspirin, bundle into my coat, and totter to the corner store, returning with a large, sloshing coffee. I put myself back to bed, laptop open before me, reading up on a Danish theater director I'm set to interview later in the week, cutting and pasting anything borderline useful from her past press. In an idle moment, I search for David Adler. The engine returns more than a million hits. I scroll through lawyers and admen, a novelist and an electrician. No academics. Which seems odd, but not that odd. Maybe he uses an esoteric spelling or has some allergy to social media, an allergy I share.

At twenty to two, I run a brush through my hair and swipe a Coty tube—another inheritance from my mother, reserved for special occasions—in the general direction of my lips. I never do find the mascara. I unlock and lock the trio of bolts securing my door and descend the stairs into the November street, ducking beneath bare trees.

Upon reaching the bakery, I stand on line until a hand grasps my shoulder and that clarinet tenor says, "Vivian?"

I turn sharply, hand raised in defense, to find a man around my own age or maybe a few years younger, huddled in a blue parka. Dark hair curls over a pale forehead, across the frames of his horn-rimmed glasses, and down to long sideburns. He's smiling at me, tentatively, hopefully, with a mouth too wide for his face.

"Are you David?" I say, leaning away slightly. "How did you recognize me?"

"Well, there's the illustration on the magazine's website. And then I found that picture of you from the Critics' Circle ceremony last year."

I know the picture he means: my little fox face half turned away from the camera, gray eyes gone red, like a night creature surprised, in the flash's blaze. I've always meant to find a way to untag it.

"I see," I say. "Shall we order?"

I ask for a macchiato and a slice of quiche. David shoulders in, pointing to a chocolate croissant and paying for it all with a rumpled $20, dropping the change into a tip jar with a sign that reads, "I Was a Liberal Arts Major. Help."

While I wait for the drink, he picks out a table, seating himself in the chair that faces the door, which is my usual move. I like to know my exit routes. From a threadbare canvas bag, he extracts a composition book, a pen with a chewed cap, and a minicassette recorder, an item I've only ever seen in thrift stores. He catches me looking as I sit opposite.

"I used digital for a while," he says with a slight shrug. "But I found that I missed the aura that the material artifact provides."

Academics. So unpretentious. To think that Justine gave up her pants for this. I thought it would take me at least a few minutes to regret my choice to meet with him. I thought wrong. He pushes a button and a red light turns on, the tape rotating in its spools. Then he opens his notebook, shielding the page with his hand, a technique I use, too. There's something in that mirrored gesture—or maybe it's knowing that I'm at the wrong end of the table or that I'm the one who ought to be asking questions—but I go dizzy for a moment and I have to lower the ceramic cup so that the macchiato doesn't spill.

The panel, I remind myself. The article. Taking a deep breath, I ready a persona that's warm, witty, friendly, like a less obviously alcoholic Dorothy Parker, a gentler variation on my usual act. I can play it for an hour.

"Okay," I say. "So just what are you and your thesis adviser clamoring to know?"

"Yes," he says, taking up the pen. "Right. And thank you. Really. You have no idea how much this means to me, to my research." Something in his voice has changed, sharpened, like a guitar string twisted one revolve too tight. He must be nervous. I must make him nervous.

"I've only just started doing these interviews and so I'm sorry in advance if these questions aren't the most pertinent or in, like, the best order. I'm still figuring out this human subject thing. So be gentle, okay?" He smiles so wide I can see his gums.

"Gentle?" I say. "Sure thing."

"Okay, great. Let's get started. First up, how did you become a critic?" he asks.

I have told this story often enough. So I give him the rehearsed speech, the prepared shrug, the studied laugh. I tell him how I studied theater in college and then moved to the city the minute I graduated, making just enough as a legal proofreader to rent a studio apartment with a two-burner stove and a four-foot bathtub. I barely saw theater back then. Barring the occasional rush ticket, I couldn't afford it. In February of that first year, my aunt heard from a friend that the magazine was looking to hire fact-checkers. I came in and took the test and they hired me. A few months after that, Roger Walsh cornered me in the office kitchen. The chief critic, Crispin Holt, was out sick and his usual fill-ins had already left for Labor Day and there was a David Mamet premiere that wouldn't review itself, although I'm absolutely sure David Mamet would have preferred it that way.

"Roger had heard from someone that I'd majored in theater," I tell David Adler. "Or maybe I just had that look? That damage? Roger asked me if I wanted to go. And I did want to go. Even to David Mamet. And I was either too green or too gutsy, but afterward I wrote exactly what I thought of the show, which went mildly viral. That led to another assignment and then another and by the fall I had come on as the junior critic. The rest"—I pause here, making an on-and-on gesture—"is no one's idea of history."

"And that's where you've stayed?" he asks.

That stings—a spider's bite—whether or not he means it to. Because at twenty-two, the title of junior critic felt precocious. At twenty-seven, reasonably impressive. At thirty-two, like a bouquet of roses in the dressing room of a show that closed just after opening, the bloom is very much off. "Please," I say. "I'm still in the place with the two-burner stove and I get excited whenever a Sophocles revival comes to town. Obviously, I fear change."

"Do you?" he says, staring at me through his glasses, glasses that have not been glare-proofed.

The question feels too much like one a therapist might ask, one several therapists have asked. So I bat it away. "It's either that or the fact that there are vanishingly few jobs for young women with strong opinions on Gertrude Stein."

"Ha," he says. It isn't exactly a laugh. Just the syllable pronounced. As the sound dies away, I notice he hasn't so much eaten his croissant as deconstructed it, layer by layer, a laminated flaying. He continues: "You said you studied theater?"

"Yes," I say. "I wrote a senior thesis on metatheatricality. All those plays within plays. Couldn't get enough, I guess."

"Maybe I have it wrong, then. You weren't an actress?"

I work to keep my voice light—a cloud, milk foam. "Yes, as a kid. School plays. The few musicals that would have a pitchy alto like mine. Community stuff."

"But not in college?" He has leaned in closer. Too close.

"Oh, a bit in college," I say. My heart has started beating faster now. This is what Justine had worried about. What I had dismissed so casually. I choose my words carefully, working to steer him away from the past and back to the present. "And the less said about it, the better. I wasn't especially good at it. But that training, it helps with reviewing. A person has to know how hard it is to make theater—the contingency, the collective effort—to write about the form with any understanding or compassion. So I find that experience quite useful."

"Compassion?" he says, an eyebrow quirking. "Is that a core value for you? Nice. Now about your time as an actor, I found this." He turns a page of his notebook and unfolds a sheet of paper, and even though I haven't seen it in more than a decade, I recognize it immediately. It's a printout of an article from my student newspaper, a review of the *Hamlet* we did my junior year.

"This is you, right?" And there's no point denying it. I can see my picture next to the text. The girl in the black-and-white photo looks younger, of course. She is paler, thinner, hollowed out beneath the eyes. Still, it's a decent likeness.

"How did you find this?" I ask.

"I'm a graduate student," he says. "We're trained in research. Is it okay if I read a section?" he asks. He doesn't wait for my answer. "Here it is," he says. "'Not even in death does Beatrice Parry, a junior in the theater program, appear lifelike.' Harsh. And I guess you went by Beatrice then? Anyway, would you agree with that description?"

I would. I would agree that I was not lifelike then and that I have not been lifelike since. But I never let myself recall the devastation of those rehearsals and the blank, white days that came before the opening and after. My stress hormones have rushed in now—breath coming shorter, blood singing. And I want to run from here—plead some excuse or leave him with none, slip back out through the door and find myself, minutes later, curled beside the fizzing radiator inside my apartment or bellied up to the bar at the Polish place around the corner, sinking my daily vodka early, working to forget. But I steel myself. The job. Roger. The panel. I give him a gunpoint smile. I stay.

"Agree?" I say evenly. "Of course. There's a reason I switched my concentration to dramatic literature. I was never much of an actress."

That isn't exactly true.

It isn't true at all.

But it's the lie I tell myself, eight shows a week.

"So now you know why I became a critic," I say. My smile has widened, every tooth a sham pearl. "I couldn't hack it as an artist. You got me! But as much as I enjoy revisiting the scene of my greatest failures, you wanted to discuss my current work, yes? My influences, my methods?"

"Your influences. Your methods," he says. "Yes, Vivian. Let's go on to that. And I wasn't judging you. I hope you know that. Just establishing context. Probably it's good that you got out early. Not everyone is meant for a spotlight." He reaches up to brush the hair from his forehead, sending pastry flakes spiraling to the floor, and for just a moment, the glare of his glasses subsides and I see something behind his lenses, something that looks less like nervousness and more like arousal or excitement. Can he really feel this way about a thesis, about context? But then the hair flops back again.

So I tell him: how I choose what to review, how much research I do before and after, if I've ever changed my mind about a play. (Once, I tell him, an Edward Albee tragedy.) I offer up some stories just for fun—the time a Wall Street wifey spilled her sippy cup of chardonnay and ruined all my notes, the time an actor in a musical I'd publicly detested cornered me in a bar and I had to literally crawl out the back. I list my favorite playwrights and then, as though I'm letting him in on a secret, my least favorite.

He scoots his chair forward. "But the playwrights you mention, the ones you love, they've all been dead for, like, a century at least," he says. "So I'm so sorry and no offense, but how can you critique new works if you don't even like them?"

"I do like them. It's not my fault if no one has managed anything as good as *The Ghost Sonata* in the past year or two."

"But what about new forms? What about truly experimental work? I'm thinking of an essay you wrote a couple of months back. You said the theatrical avant-garde was like, basically dead?"

"Well, it basically is," I tell him. "For centuries there were rules and customs to transgress. Back in the day—way back—even adding a second actor was an absolutely wild choice. But by the time you've done away with character and plot and place and time and clothing, what's left to get out in front of? There's no vanguard anymore, there hasn't been one in decades."

"Really? Nothing? Like in your whole lifetime?"

"Really," I say. "Nothing."

"But that essay you wrote, something must have triggered it, right?" he says, his voice climbing toward the pressed tin.

"Yes. Probably. But I see so much. Let me think." I close my eyes a moment and then force them open again. "Okay. Right. It was some devised piece at the old synagogue on Eldridge. Collective creation. Beyond derivative."

"I read that review. It was a participatory piece and you wrote that you refused to participate. Was that fair to the work?"

"I participated in that I watched and listened. I shared space and breath. That ought to be enough. Did you see it, David?" I ask.

"I did," he says. And I believe him. Because when he answers, something in him softens, unfolds. His face takes on an expression almost holy, and I wonder if that's how I look when I'm in my plush seat in the dark, ravished by a show.

"And you participated?" I ask. "You confided in the actor assigned to you?"

"Of course," he says. "Why didn't you?"

"Because I'm the critic," I say, that stress response surging again. "Not the subject. Whatever the show is about, it isn't about me." The café has begun to feel far away, the distance across the table immense. I notice, as though from above, that my teeth have begun to chatter, that I have to press them together to still the rattling. I don't love the turns this conversation has taken. How I have failed as an actress. How I have failed as a critic. David Adler's contention that I lack the aptitude to perform the only task that makes me feel reliably human. Surely I have supported the community enough for one afternoon.

"Thank you so much," I say, bracing myself to stand. I'm angling for the exit, so I'm all charm again. A walking four-leaf clover. A rainbow without end. "You're so kind to take the time. I know we didn't especially get into the 'woman critic,' 'female spectator' of it all. But it's so boring to see these things as a binary, don't you honestly think? And we've had such a thorough chat. And so well researched! I'm sure you have everything you need."

"Oh, okay," he says. "Are you sure? Because maybe—"

"No," I say. "Thank you," I say, overenunciating the words as I reach for my coat. "I'm on deadline, as always, so I really do need to leave."

"Okay," he says, switching off the recorder and repacking his bag. "Of course. No problem. I'll call you when I have the information about the panel."

"I prefer email."

"Email it is," he says.

"You have my address?"

"Of course I do. And you're right, Vivian. Thank you. I have everything I need."

He stands then, grasping one of my hands in a kind of valedictory clinch that sends a wintry shudder up and down my arm. And in that moment, I observe several things. The eyes behind his glasses are a deep brown, almost black. Twin pools. The darkest I have ever seen. And there's a flash of something behind those eyes, something cool and sharp, unyielding as a dagger point. The anxiety, that flappy smile, they've fled. He is seeing me. Really seeing me. As I am. Not as I pretend to be. Looking into that face, so close to my own, I realize something more: David Adler has been acting this whole time. He's pretending to be a person, too. And he's good at it. Better than me.

"Bye, Vivian," he says. "Be seeing you."

Before I know it, my hand is loosed and I'm half falling against the table and he's out the door, walking at speed toward Avenue A, nearly colliding with a man—beefy, like an upside-down triangle—in a red baseball cap, and then walking again, or no, running now, across the street and into the bleak greenery of Tompkins Square Park and then gone from my sight.

2

OTHERWISE ENGAGED

Two weeks later, on the Monday after Thanksgiving, I stop by the office to firm up an article for the winter arts preview. It's auspicious that Roger has asked me, rather than Caleb, to write the theater feature. Or that's what I tell myself. I make my way through the cubicle labyrinth until I spot the white head of Roger, devouring a pastrami sandwich stuffed twice the height of his open mouth. He swallows and waves at me to sit.

"What about my brilliant story idea where you ask the Rockettes what they wear underneath those skimpy outfits?" he says, dabbing at mustard. "I'm sure I can get an extra page for the accompanying pictorial. Okay, okay. You can stop the feminist death stare. We'll give Radio City a pass this year. Anything else?"

I pull out my notebook. "What about a piece on special effects in seasonal shows? How designers create fog and ice in overheated theaters, what they put in those machines that make it seem to snow."

"What if we had a scantily clad Rockette playing in said snow? Hey, ouch. I guess this insubordination is what comes of teaching all you women to read and write. But yeah, sure, go ahead. And there's a tight turnaround on this one, did I mention? Our editor in chief, from his East Hampton vacation home and in his infinite fucking wisdom, moved it up a week. So type fast, yeah?" He leans back in his allegedly ergonomic chair, inserting a thumb into each of his suspenders. "How was your Thanksgiving, kid?"

"Ate kung pao shrimp. Streamed *The Amityville Horror*. The old one. I thought it would make me feel better about having no home to go to."

"Can you cut it out with the orphan thing? How many times did I ask you to come to our place? You know Cheryl loves having you by. Speaking of . . ." He bends forward and opens the half-size fridge he keeps beneath his desk, extracting a foil-wrapped package. "There's a couple slices of pecan there and one of apple crumb. Cheryl remembered you have some ancestral hatred of pumpkin."

"It's not that I don't like it," I say. "It's just that it never tastes like my mother's."

"Sharper than a serpent's tooth, you know that? Sure, sure, don't say it, that's why you get the page hits. But could you enjoy something once in a while? Or pretend to? When was the last time you saw a show you actually liked?"

"The year was 1606. *King Lear* at the Court. That last scene still kills me."

"Cute, kiddo. But that last piece got more of those angry comments about you and the community."

"The community could put on a better quality of play," I say. "But I am trying, Roger. Trying in any way that doesn't fatally compromise my integrity. There's that panel I mentioned. And speaking of—" I'm about to ask about the head critic job, about when he'll decide, when Roger realizes he has an editorial meeting and blunders toward the conference room like a midsize bull going badly off course at Pamplona.

"I'll need that weather story by Monday first thing," he says over his shoulder. "Fourteen hundred words. Clean ones. Send a memo to photo tonight. And try to take it easy. Easier. Okay, kid?"

He has gone before I can move to stop him. And I'm alone.

As I'm leaving the office, Esteban bars my way. He's wearing a short gold kimono over dark jeans and more eye shadow than I would ever dare. He kisses me on both cheeks, then runs a hand through my hair, sucking his teeth at the split ends.

"Tch. Bebita, when you gonna go to that stylist I recommended?"

"Never. Lunch? Ramen?"

"Can't. That whore Trish is out pretending to be sick again and no one's on to cover the phones. But I was just gonna call you. Some girl phoned, all upset. Like really upset? Like she needed a horse tranquilizer? Like yesterday?"

"Don't we all?"

"Said she has to talk to you, gorgeous."

He hands me a neon sticky note. Gritting my teeth and remembering the sting of Roger's exit, I dig for my phone and tap in the number as I walk down the stairs. Maybe I can't give the community exactly what it wants. But I can return the occasional call.

"Hello," says a female voice, strained and low.

"Hello, this is Vivian Parry. I had a message to phone you."

"Yes, yes! You are Vivian! Okay, yes!" She speaks with a graveled accent, from somewhere I can't place. Somewhere in eastern Europe, maybe. "I have his calendar. Today only and . . ." I hear the sounds of a deep inhale. "Sorry. . . . Okay. Do you know this man, David Adler?"

"David Adler?" It takes me a second to place the name. I have barely thought about him since our strange interview. I am good at forgetting unpleasant things. I have successfully blocked every revival of *Annie*. "Yes. I do know him. Not well. But I met with him. Briefly. He spoke to me about a research project."

"When is this?"

"About two weeks ago. Tuesday. In the afternoon."

"Yes. His calendar says this. That you have this meeting, two p.m. What time is he leaving?"

"Around three. Maybe a little earlier. I'm not sure exactly. And I'm sorry, forgive me, but who are you? And what is this about?"

"My name is Irina. David, he is my fiancé. Next month is our wedding. But he is gone. He is disappeared, okay? And you are the last person to see him."

Irina asks if I'll meet with her, and even though I'd like very much to be back home, my public face stored for later use, out of curiosity or confusion or motives more opaque, some shared loneliness calling out across the 5G network, I find that I agree. She suggests a chain coffee shop on Second Avenue. I tell her the color of my hair—light brown—and of my coat—gray. She scurries toward my table twenty minutes later.

A woman around my age, Irina wears a baggy black skirt and an even baggier sweater—as shapeless as a mud puddle. A wisp of dark hair slips a fluffy pink beret, framing a face so mouselike it's a wonder she doesn't have whiskers. Her skin is snow, her eyes red rimmed, promising further tears.

"You are Vivian?" she says.

"Yes," I say.

She looks toward the counter. "Do you want coffee?"

I shake my head. "No. I've had too many cups already. Just tell me what you need."

She sits opposite and with a sniff and a swallow, she begins. Apparently, she and David became engaged four months ago. She waggles her left hand, showing off a princess-cut sparkler half the size of a scone and impossible on the salary of any grad student I've ever met. She describes the Brighton Beach catering hall they've chosen for the reception and the dress she's bought from Kleinfeld. "All nonrefundable," she says.

"But what happened to David? You said he went missing?"

"We have a meeting on this day he is seeing you," she says, lowering her head toward the hands now curling and uncurling in her lap, "a cake tasting. David, he has the sweet tooth. But he is not come and he is not answering his phone. In the morning, I call to his roommate. His roommate says that he is not come home. I go to the police then, but they tell to me a person must be gone for longer, okay? So I wait—two days—and then I go again to the police and this officer, this man, most unkind, he tells to me that I cannot make a report, that I am not family, and that if David is gone, it is because he does not want to marry me."

A lifetime spent waking up to Irina's pink eyes might make braver men bolt. But as though she can hear my thoughts, she cries out, "It is not true! When he proposes to me, when he gives to me this ring, it is a great surprise. I tell to him, it is too much, it is too soon, but we are meant for each other, always, he says, for all of our lives. Okay?" She hides her face in her baggy sleeves as more tears flow.

Onstage, I see people weep so often. The close-up version is wetter, messier. It turns my stomach, already roiling from the smell of sugar syrups and singed coffee. "I'm sorry," I say, angling my eyes away. "But I'm not sure how I can help you. I don't really know David Adler. I met him only that one time. What is it that you think I can do?"

"Yesterday, David's roommate, he finds the password for David's computer. It is put with tape to his desk." She makes a muddled gesture with her hands. "To, how do you say it, the backwards?"

"To the underside of his desk?"

"Yes. The underside. Okay. My father, he does not allow David and me to live together. Not before we are married. So David has a roommate and the roommate, with the password, he looks inside David's computer. The searches, they are all erased. But the calendar, it is not erased. And the calendar says he is to meet with you. So okay, what please is this meeting? Tell to me what you remember."

I have decent recall, a necessity in my line of work, which involves bringing the show to the page days after having seen it. But Irina, twitching opposite me, needs better than decent. So I risk an old acting exercise, a sense memory trick. Just this once. Smelling the coffee all around me, I think back to the coffee I drank with David Adler, and at first nothing happens, all I can see are the green and browns of this café. But then I feel something inside me loosening, opening, and I can picture that other table, that piece of spinach quiche, David Adler sitting so far away in front of me.

I tell her everything I can recall. That we met on time. That he wore a parka, blue or maybe green, that he never took it off. I tell her that we spoke for an hour, about theater, about my writing. That he ate a chocolate croissant. Well, he didn't eat it, not exactly. But that detail I leave out. I also don't mention the look behind his eyes or that wintry sense I had that he was playing a part, playing it so well.

When I mention the chocolate, she makes a little moan, like someone—me, it seems—has just poked a purpling bruise. "He loves chocolate. Always. For my birthday, he brought to me this great box of chocolates and he ate them all." She dabs at her eyes. "After this meeting, did you see where he went, the way?"

"East," I say, "toward the park. Oh, and he bumped into someone. Or nearly. A man taking up half the sidewalk."

"A man! What is this man?"

"Sorry, no one. Just some muscled-up guy in a red baseball cap."

"Red?" she says, her voice hitching. "This cap, you say, it was red?"

"I think so. I'm not sure. That's all I can remember. I'm sorry," I say. I nearly mean it.

Irina lets out a breath, slowly, grudgingly, as though she would take it back if she could. She shuts her eyes tight, a single tear escapes. Then she opens them. Her face is sterner now. "Okay," she says. "Will you do for me this one thing more? When the police tell to me these terrible things, my father, he hires a private investigator. So you will call to him, okay? To the investigator?" She stands and rummages in her purse for a business card, which she places in my hand, leaning in, her wet, pink eyes inches from my dry ones. "You are a smart girl. Yes. And a good girl. This is true, okay? You will help?"

"I'm sorry," I say. "I don't think—"

"You think he has no love for me. That he leaves me before this wedding because he has no love for me. But he is not a man like this. He will die if I am to leave him. Many times he says this. Now I worry that he is dead already."

I know what it is to be left by the dead. I know how life can give way in the face of that. Because I have lost someone and I haven't lived through it. Not really. So I take the card and I promise to call. She begins to cry in earnest then, still awkwardly upright, bumping the table with her hip as the tears fall. I look away until she quiets. When she speaks again her voice is low, insistent.

"No," she says. "David is not dead. I will find him and then we will marry. And we will eat cake. So much cake. He loves cake. Always."

Back at home, I slide a piece of pecan pie onto a plate and put the rest of Cheryl's bounty in the fridge, empty except for ketchup and duck sauce packets, crusted jam jars, a shriveled lime, a paper bag with grease spots, its contents otherwise unknown. I have heard of New Yorkers who turn off their kitchen appliances and use them to store shoes. I've thought about it, but I don't have all that many shoes.

I curl into bed, switch on my laptop, and nibble at the pie. Or try to. Even the smallest bites stop my throat. Eventually, I set the plate on the floor and find the business card Irina gave me. Ridiculously, my hand trembles as I hold it by a corner.

I know what I ought to do. Flush the card. Have my rationed drink. Take half of a thumb-severed pill or, failing that, a whole one. Regain my knife-edge equilibrium. Whatever quiets the pity that I feel, the wisps of sympathy, the stomach-turning excitement. Whatever stops me from wanting to involve myself in this situation, to play any further role. Because even if I make my living by deliberate disconnection—by sitting apart, in judgment—the desire to act, to participate, has never entirely left me. And I know what happens when I involve myself. When I allow myself to feel without limit. Bad things. Dangerous things. Things it might take stronger pills, or something much worse than pills, to quell.

Yet that desire remains. And now curiosity has joined it. What was David Adler doing with me at the café, exhuming my past in the way that he did? And where did he disappear to hours later? And how and when and why did he learn to playact his way through the world so well? And was any of what he showed me—the nervousness, the excitement—remotely real? I consider myself a superlative judge of theater and life and the crucial differences between. But David Adler has shaken that certainty like a cheap souvenir snow globe. To do my best work I need it settled again. Without what Aristotle called the scene of recognition or what the therapists I'm occasionally required to see will insist on referring to as "closure," my mind won't rest. So maybe I allow myself to accept a very small role. To make myself a part of something in daylight hours.

I look at the card: a thin rectangle in a shade of soured milk, two corners creased. The card says: "Jake Levitz, Licensed Private Investigator." Below it there's a phone number and a fax number, but no email address, which makes me think Jake Levitz must be very old or a real crank and quite possibly both.

Before I can decide whether to call him, my phone pulses with a text from Justine. She asks me if I have a play booked for tonight, and when I reply that I do, a rare Monday performance, she texts again, telling me to meet her afterward at a new bar in Greenpoint. She promises me that the bartender is a friend of a friend and she's almost completely sure we can drink for free or nearly free and could I possibly wear something sewn by tiny, starving third world hands sometime this fucking century and also she thinks she left her earrings here and can I bring them. (There are sentimental tragedies shorter than Justine's texts.) I don't have the energy to deny her, so in many fewer words I agree.

Then I wrench myself back to work—making a list of snowy holiday shows, sending a flurry of interview requests with "time sensitive" in the subject line, spending a dangerously amusing fifteen minutes reading the FAQs and safe-handling instructions for a theatrical snow machine. Apparently, you're supposed to point it *away* from your body. After a quick soak and the barest drop of vodka and the selection of the 1980s corduroy shirtdress that Justine will loathe, I'm out the door and angling for the F train that takes me to the noise and thrum and billboard commotion of midtown and then to the door of the theater, where after those few simple rituals—the giving of the ticket and the taking of it, the bestowal of the program and the unnecessary steering to the aisle seat—I lose myself and find myself for 110 intermissionless minutes.

The play tonight is Racine's *Phèdre*, that neoclassical update of a classical tragedy, and through it all, the betrayal and the deception and the death and the terrible desire that can barely be spoken, that can never be filled, I am rapt. Phaedra dies by her own hand, driven mad by forces beyond her control. The young man dies, too. And when the lights come up again, tears are streaming down my face and I don't know whom I'm crying for—Phaedra, myself, Irina, anyone.

Forty minutes later, in Greenpoint, I slide past the suspect pharmacies, the fluorescent-lit 99¢ stores, the sticky window of the doughnut shop, now shuttered. I buy a buttered roll at the corner deli, and since I haven't had a pill and barely anything to drink today, I promise myself two rounds. Three if the bartender has a heavy hand with the ice and mixers.

The bar is the usual industrial reclamation project: sheet metal tables, salvaged wood walls, Edison bulbs. I find Justine toward the back, toying with the cherry that garnishes her manhattan. She introduces me to the two men she's met: Moritz, a photographer originally from Berlin with the architect glasses to prove it, and Ray, a lighting designer in a safari jacket.

When she tells them that I'm a critic, Ray favors me with a snaggle-toothed smile and says, "So you're the enemy, right?"

"Sure I am," I say. "Thinking up ways to ridicule your spotlights and specials even now. But maybe a vodka gimlet will make me feel a little more generous?"

"On it," he says.

Moritz leaves to smoke a cigarette on the patio and I draw in close to Justine. "A designer?" I say. "What are you thinking?"

"I'm an actress and you tolerate me," she says.

"That's different. I knew you before. You're grandfathered in. Grandmothered. But if I keep on like this, I won't have anyone left to review." Really, you only have to sleep with one up-and-coming director—well, two, or possibly three, memories of a particular Tuesday remain hazy—to learn that you shouldn't mix business with what passes for pleasure.

"So take the photographer. But just so you know, babe, I'm making a literal fucking sacrifice. This could have meant new headshots."

"Who says I want to take anyone?"

"Come on. It's been ages since you had a boyfriend. And yes, I'm using 'boyfriend' as a euphemism. Now shut your vodka hole. They're coming back."

Ray hands me a lowball glass and I dip my tongue into the shivery mix. True to her word, Justine launches a frontal assault on Ray (not a euphemism, she has tits for days) and I manage a stilted conversation with Moritz, who offers me a German-accented lecture on how much he hates American cameras. Another round and I'm willing to hate them, too. Sometime after midnight, Justine and Ray slip away. Moritz asks if I'm ready to leave, so I shoulder my bag and we move into the cold.

I turn in the direction of the subway, but he grips my arm and leads me around the corner, out of reach of the lights. He pushes me against the brick wall of an old butcher's shop and kisses me. I can taste the tobacco on his tongue. I like it. It reminds me that there's at least one bad habit I haven't taken up. He kisses me harder, pressing his hips into mine, wrapping my hair in one of his fists as he tilts my head back.

"We will go to my apartment," he says.

"No," I say.

"Then you will take me to yours."

"No."

He tightens his grip on my hair. "Then where do we go?"

I'm tired of talking. And my mind keeps flashing to the conversation with Irina, the business card waiting for me at home. I don't want to think. I need not to feel. So even though I'm not especially attracted to him, I deepen the kiss, taking his lower lip between my teeth, pushing my body against his, and then he's scuffling, one-handed, with his belt, and tugging down the waistband of my tights, and then I'm only my body, but also I'm outside my body, a white-noise hum creeping up into my ears. My lids close and I surrender to the roughness of the brick until even that starts to seem very far away. I don't feel the cold anymore. I don't feel anything. Later, at home, there's blood in my underwear. And it's my period or it isn't and I can't bring myself to care. It looks like someone else's blood. I throw the underwear away and I put myself to bed.

3

P.I. SCHOOL

On Tuesday, tucked up in bed with two ibuprofen working against what turn out to be period cramps, I write up the review of *Phèdre*, marveling again in the calibration of the tragedy, how catastrophe sounds in that very first line, how every choice is inevitable and terrible, right and calamitously wrong. I draft and then I redraft until the sentences gleam, until anyone reading it will feel themselves at that theater, in that audience, watching the horror unspool. I also manage a few thankless paragraphs on the musical version of *Old Yeller*, which I had seen, under protest, on Sunday. (Two words: *rabies ballet*.) I send the column off, already anticipating Roger's praise. "See," I type into the subject line, "I can like a thing." And then, out of the goodness of my shriveled heart—and for other thornier reasons—I retrieve the P.I.'s card and make the call.

"Levitz Investigations," comes the growling answer. The man sounds like a bulldog with a hangover. A small bulldog.

"Hello," I say. "This is Vivian Parry. I was asked to call you. A woman named Irina—" I pause as I realize I don't know Irina's last name. "Irina," I repeat. "She gave me your number. It's regarding the disappearance of a man named David Adler. I had an appointment with him on the day that he apparently went missing. We didn't spend long together—maybe an hour, maybe less—and we spoke only about my work. So I can't imagine I—"

"You're the critic chick?"

"Yellow and feathered," I say.

"Cute. Looks like you were the last gal to see him. So, yeah, we should talk. Why don't you come by the office this afternoon?"

If I'm lukewarm on phone conversations, I'm even less enthusiastic for in-person ones. So I offer a brisk lie. "It's a busy day and I'm on deadline. Can't you ask me your questions now?"

"Nah, you always do face-to-face when you can. It's the first thing they teach you at P.I. school."

"There's a P.I. school?"

"What are you? New? Come around three. It's fifteen Pell Street. Top floor. The buzzer's broken, but you can force the door if you put some shoulder into it."

Canal Street judders with cars and people and the cries of hawkers peddling rambutan and dragon fruit, the bristling red-pink skins jabbing at the gray sky. In a Hong Kong bakery with steamed-up windows, I bag a pork bun off a tray, tearing with my teeth at the pillowy dough as I leave. Under my thin-soled boots, I can feel the rumble of the subway, a reminder of other streets beneath the one I'm walking, other stories, other worlds. Quickly, ignoring the cramps, I make my way down Mott to Pell, a narrow lane where tongs bloodied one another a century ago.

The P.I.'s building houses a Malaysian restaurant at street level. A cook on a smoke break glares at me and flicks his cigarette too close as I shove the glass door open to shrieks of grinding metal. The stairs, swathed in a stained runner the green of penicillin, creak at every step; sections of the banister have crumbled away. I've streamed the occasional black-and-white noir, so I'm half expecting a smoked-glass door with Sam Spade lettering, but instead I find a cheap wooden one, splintered around the knob. I knock and the growl from the phone invites me in.

The front room doesn't look much like an office. There's a futon covered in a greasy sheet, a ragged rag rug, a pot displaying a ficus long deceased. Behind a dusty wooden desk sits the P.I., a white man stranded somewhere in his sixties. With his fat, stubbled cheeks and unruly graying ringlets, he doesn't look much like a P.I. either. More like a cherub gone to seed. On his desk, a stack of creased manila folders abut a glass ashtray where a dozen half-smoked cigarettes molder. Nearby sits a take-out container from the Malaysian place, a single noodle lurching tentacle-like over the side.

Jake Levitz hauls himself out of the chair, and before I can stop him, he swims his hand forward, pressing the rough, nicotine-stained pads of his fingers against mine in a boneless shake. Then he waves me toward the futon. "Sit. Glad you made it. It's Vivian, right? You go by Viv?"

"Only under duress."

"Okay, Vivian it is. Call me Jake. You want something to drink? I've got water and . . . nope, I finished all the pop. Just water."

"I'm good," I say, lowering myself gingerly to the sheet.

"You want a cigarette?"

"I don't smoke."

"Yeah, I'm trying to cut down." Jake gestures to a pharmacy bag on the shelf behind him. "Got the patches. Gonna start wearing 'em." He opens one of the folders, hefting a pencil in his pudgy fingers. "So. Vivian. Let's do this. You met with David Adler two weeks ago, on Tuesday?"

"Yes. Around two in the afternoon. He said he wanted to interview me for a project on critics and how we develop our practice, our style. It was research for his thesis, he said. We met at a patisserie near my house."

"What's this patisserie called?" he asks, clearing his throat wetly.

"La Religeuse."

"La what?"

I spell it for him. Slowly.

"So what all did he ask you about?"

"Theater, mostly. My favorite playwrights, my favorite plays. Boring if you're not in the business."

"I go to plays," he says, tapping his pencil against the paper.

"Do you?" Of course he does. He takes his aged mother to a matinee musical every spring. With a stop at Junior's for cheesecake after.

"Yeah, saw the Beckett one-acts at the East Side last month. You go? You like 'em?"

This surprises me. "Yes, I did. *Rockaby*, especially."

"Me, I love that one with the mouth. Crazy! So anyway, you and the subject—that's what I call Adler, the subject—you meet at this café, you eat some pastry, you praise Melpomene—"

"You know the Greek muse of drama?"

"Lady," he says, raising his eyebrows in my general direction, "I know all kinds of stuff. Stuff that would knock your bobby socks off. Never know what'll come in handy on a case. That's what they teach you in P.I. school. I once broke open a fraud ring just 'cause I knew who won the sixty-nine Series."

"Who?"

"Mets in five. Back to your pastry date. David, how'd he seem to you?"

"Seem?"

"Yeah, you know. Appear. Act. Behave."

I can hear Hamlet in my head: "Seems, madam! Nay it is." Because I don't really know how to answer this question. Do I describe the David Adler who interviewed me or the man I caught a glimpse of as we finished?

"Nervous?" I say finally. "Or that was how he seemed at first. He said something about how he hadn't done a lot of interviews before. Human subjects were a new thing for him. He had a chocolate croissant. Is that relevant?"

"Could be. Could be."

There's something else I ought to tell him, some further detail, but my mind has shelved it just out of reach. "By the way," I say, "where was he enrolled? I tried to look him up online."

"Some school in New Jersey is what I heard. Not sure which. Though I guess I should probably talk to his dean or supervisor or whatever. Came to the city to finish his master's whatchamacallit. Thesis. Hey, that reminds me, funny story about New Jersey." He leans forward in his chair. The metal makes an affronted screech. "Last month I went out to Secaucus on a case. There was this escort, see, and she had this one john—No, on second thought, I shouldn't say more. Might offend your ladylike sensibilities."

"Who says I'm so ladylike?"

"Never seen someone sit on a couch while trying not to actually touch it."

"Nicely observed. They teach you that in P.I. school?"

"Lady, there is no P.I. school."

"Maybe I'm just trying not to get period blood all over your sheet."

He sits back—the chair screams—and raises his hands in a gesture of surrender. "Okay. Point yours. So Davey, he seemed nervous to you, huh? He say anything about himself? About what was going on?"

"No. I don't think so." And now it's my turn to sit forward. "What do you mean 'going on'?"

"Patience, ladylike. We'll get to that. What was the subject wearing?"

"A sweater. Black, I think? And glasses. And he had on a green parka with fake fur around the hood."

He reviews his notes. "Yeah, that checks out. Though fiancée says the jacket's blue. He take any calls while he talked to you? Send any of those texts or snapgram thingies?"

I tell him that David Adler never took his phone out. That we spoke for an hour, less.

Jake scribbles a note. "So that last puts him at the café around two forty-five, two fifty. You think any of the staff would remember him?"

"No. You order at the counter and bring the food to the table yourself. I can't imagine he made much of an impression."

"Didn't shove an éclair down his pants or nothing?"

I find myself smiling, genuinely. "Not that I recall."

"Figured. Still, I gotta ask. And when you were done talking, you see where he went?"

"Into Tompkins Square Park. Or maybe just through it."

Jake closes the folder. "All right," he says, lighting a cigarette. "You want to know a little more about the subject?"

"Please."

"You didn't hear it from me. Disclosing information pertinent to the investigation, not a good look. But bouncing ideas off a pretty girl, it's one of my favorite methods."

"As long as you don't try to bounce anything else off of me."

He laughs. Or possibly he coughs. "Nice one, ladylike. So our subject wasn't having a red-letter day when he met you. Unless maybe that letter was F. F for 'fucked,' if you catch my meaning. While he was finishing up his degree, he had a side job working as a programmer for Luck Be a Lady. You know it?"

I shake my head.

"Online casino. Opened recently. Not one of the major players, but some big money behind it. Owned by one Boris Sirko. That last name sound familiar? No? Well, guess who shares it? Sweet Irina, the girl who gave you my card. Boris is her doting daddy. Little Davey, our subject, he's making a pretty smart play seeing as how his fiancée just happens to be the boss's daughter. But here's the thing: Davey is good at his day job, maybe too good. Someone's written a code that games the Luck Be a Lady roulette program. Makes it land on red more often than it should. And the site muckety-mucks think that this someone is Davey. So a couple hours before your pastry rendezvous, he gets called into the big office and he gets fired. Sirko has a couple of security thugs search his desk, 'cause they think he's got the code saved onto some disc or drive or cloud thingamajig. They go through his computer, they go through his phone. They don't find it. So they haul him out—probably with a preview of the bodily harm to come if he ever sets his size ten foot there again—and give him a nice kick in the ass for severance.

"But here's another thing," he says. He's breathing heavier now; his cheeks have reddened. "I've been asking around a little. Seems like Davey wasn't so great at programming after all. No way was he good enough to write code that would skim all that cash. So either someone put him in the frame for it or he paid somebody smarter to make that program for him or there never was such a program and Sirko had other reasons for wanting him gone. But that's between you, me, and this dead plant, ladylike."

"That doesn't make any sense," I say. I've scooted so far forward on the futon I'm nearly falling off. "If he'd just been escorted from the office that morning, why would he go to the café and ask me whether I prefer Ibsen or Strindberg? Why wouldn't he just cancel?"

"Got me, ladylike. Maybe he was just going through the motions. Some people do that when they're really stressed. Switch to autopilot. Go about their day. Anyway, what's your answer?"

"Strindberg. Always. But if Sirko wanted David Adler gone, then why would he pay you to find out where he went?" But even as I'm asking, it starts to come together. The filthy office, the cluttered folders, the ex-ficus. Jake Levitz is just the sort of P.I. you hire if you're trying to placate your grieving daughter, but you don't actually want her missing fiancé found.

"Says he doesn't want his daughter to worry," says Jake, steepling his fingers like some deconsecrated church. "No way is he gonna let her marry that schmuck, that's my guess, but he doesn't want her up nights wondering what happened to him. Interferes with her beauty sleep."

It would take a very long sleep to turn Irina into a beauty. "So what do you do now?" I ask. "Do you have a lock on David Adler's cell phone? Are you monitoring his credit cards?"

"You see too many movies. Police can access all of that if they get a court order. Maybe. Me? Not so much. I'm calling around to his friends and relations—known associates, we call 'em—targeting his usual hangouts. My niece, smart kid, helps me out with internet stuff, social whatchamacallit, although it doesn't seem like he went in big for that. So far: zip. I could dust the entirety of Manhattan for prints, I guess, but Sirko's stingy when it comes to my hourly, so instead I made some flyers. Maybe you could put up a couple near your café."

He reaches into his desk drawer and extracts a sheaf of papers, tilting them toward me so I can see a fuzzy photo of David Adler, eyes a smudge behind his glasses, and the legend "Have you seen this man?" And I wonder if I have. Or if I saw only what he wanted me to see.

"You like 'em?" Jake asks, hauling himself to a standing position. "Made 'em myself. I'd better put up a few more. Come on, ladylike. I'll walk you out."

I rise from the futon, momentarily light-headed, and then move out onto the landing, where I begin a creaky descent. Jake huffs behind me, pausing to lock the door and light a cigarette. "Was I of any help today?" I ask him.

"Probably not a lot. Case turns on that croissant, I'll cut you in on my bonus, okay? Not that I picture Sirko as the bonus-giving type. He's dicking me around on fees already. But if you remember anything else, ladylike, you call me."

"I will," I say.

We've reached the street door and Jake waddles ahead of me, wrenching it open in a manner almost gallant. "Hey, ladylike," he says, catching his breath, "lemme know if you ever need a date for one of your shows."

"Sorry," I say. "I always go alone."

On the walk back to my apartment, I pull my coat close around me and duck my head against the wind. Every so often I daydream of moving somewhere clement, somewhere I wouldn't spend five months of the year trying to keep my teeth from chattering like a paving crew's jackhammers. But the dreams pass. Some people aren't meant to thaw. And if they have theater in Florida, I don't want to see it.

I sort through what Jake's told me, but the story won't cohere. Does the accusation of embezzlement explain David Adler's nervousness? Does it explain why I thought he was acting? That steel behind his eyes, was that the real David Adler? Or was it some muddled fear response? Bewildered, I do what any self-respecting journalist would. I veer into the nearest bar. I have rules about when I'm allowed to drink and where and how much and several bylaws relating to garnishes. Mostly I follow them. But at the moment, I just want something to stop my hands from shaking.

I order a vodka rocks. Then I do what I do on those very rare occasions when I am stuck on a story. I call my editor.

"Roger," I say. "Have I got a lede for you."

"Please tell me it's the one about that new burlesque club."

"No nudity, but listen." Having already told him about the panel, I now detail my hour with David Adler, my coffee with Irina Sirko, my recent and dubiously hygienic visit to Jake Levitz's place of business. By way of conclusion, I take the last bitter swallow of my drink and signal the bartender—stocky, tattooed, wearing a porkpie hat indoors—for another. "So what do you think?"

"Relax, Viv. It's weird. Sure. But this is New York. Weird happens. Last month our car wouldn't start. Turns out that rats had crawled inside the hood and eaten a chunk of the engine. They left behind some chicken bones. Look, you did what you could: you talked to his fiancée, you helped the P.I. You want to know more, you can ask the people at *American Stage*. Probably he was exactly who he said he was, doing the best he could given the circumstances, and once he slowed down and caught his breath, he headed out of town for a while. If it's upsetting you, let it go."

"Roger, when have I ever left a show at intermission?" The bartender brings my drink and reaches over to raise the volume on a K-pop playlist.

"Where are you?" Roger asks. "Seoul?"

"Yes, Roger. I hopped a Korean Air flight this morning. But I'll be back in time for the curtain on the Brecht show. The conversation with the investigator, it rattled me, okay? I stopped into a Chinatown bar for a stiffener."

"Jesus. What time is it? You said you were cutting down, kid. We talked about this."

"You said you'd stop calling me 'kid.'"

"I need you on the ball. Go home. Sober up. And drop the girl detective thing, okay? Focus on a Pulitzer for criticism instead. Be sure to tell the committee you owe it all to me."

"Is that what I need to finally get the job?" I say, wincing even as I ask.

"Working on it, Viv."

I finish my drink and wend my way slowly north, letting my mind empty against the lowering gray of buildings, sidewalks, and sky until I'm gray, too, a walking shadow. But thoughts of David Adler remain. So I buy a chopped cheese sandwich at a corner store and sneak it into the reading room of the library on Second Avenue, hiding the wrapper, and most of the sandwich, somewhere in the self-help section. And then, chasing down the only leads I have and vodka-numbed just enough that I don't question why I am chasing them at all, I search my phone for the Performance Presenters website and find the name of the director of operations and events, Faye Timms, a woman I remember from a work dinner a few years ago—white-blond hair, skin like crepe paper, a high-necked blouse that buttoned at the back. I compose a brief email, saying I'd been contacted about participating in a critics' panel and am wondering if she has a date for it yet. Then I settle in with a collection of Shaw's music criticism. A ping tells me that Faye has responded. The conference doesn't have a panel like that scheduled, they haven't run one in ages. Would I like to propose one for the year following? Do I have a moderator in mind? Would I like to moderate it myself?

Barely trusting my fingers, I send a brief note telling her I must have been mistaken and that I'll think about her suggestion. I hit send and move back farther into the library, looking up the number for *American Stage*. Typically, I would email or text, enjoying the distance the screen provides. But nothing about this this feels typical and I want answers as quickly as I can get them. When the receptionist answers, I ask for Ron Diaz, the managing editor, a man I know from Critics' Circle meetings past.

"Ron!" I say when the call connects. "It's been too long." I'm making my stage whisper sound cheerful, sociable, like a tiny brass band. "I'm so sorry I couldn't do that festival coverage for you, but you know me, I'm a hothouse flower. I wilt beyond city limits."

"That's okay, Viv," he says. "We'll find something for you one of these days. Something local."

"Perfect," I say. "Can't wait. And listen, this might sound certifiable, but a man, this grad student, he approached me saying that he was putting together a January panel, something about critics and why any sane person would want to become one. Anyway, he said that you had promised to publish excerpts and I just wanted to make sure it was all legit before I agreed." Which is of course what I should have done in the first place.

"Honestly, that doesn't sound familiar," Ron says. "But let me check. What's the man's name?"

"David Adler," I say as neutrally as I can.

"David Adler," he says, drawing out the syllables, and I can hear insectoid clicks as he enters them into a keyboard. "No," he says. "I don't see anything like that in my email. And I'm looking at the planning memo for the February issue and there's nothing about a panel. Are you sure he said *American Stage*?"

"I thought so," I say. "But I must have had it wrong."

"Do you think he could have meant *Theater Year* or *Journal of the Stage*?"

"I'm sure that's it."

"Or maybe this is how he gets nice girls to talk to him about dramatic structure."

"Ron!" I make myself laugh, the tinkle of shattered glass. "That is a very specific kink! Anyway, appreciate you. Hate to run, but I've got a very early curtain. Talk soon."

There is no early curtain. The show won't start till eight. I leave the library and in the hours left to me I walk from block to block to block, pouring myself out into the evening, letting the streets take me where they will, walking fast enough so that I won't have to think about David Adler, about how little that he told me was true. Near Penn Station, a child in a red raincoat catches my eye. Which is when I remember what I meant to tell Jake Levitz, about the man David Adler nearly collided with as he sped toward Tompkins Square, about Irina's surprise when I mentioned the man's cap. Jake Levitz told me about how Sirko's security thugs searched David Adler's office that morning, about how they roughed him up afterward. That man on the street, that man in the red cap, was he one of them? Was he following David? Was that why David ran? Could that man have seen us together? Should I have mentioned him to Irina at all? I don't notice I'm shivering until I'm inside the *Mother Courage* lobby and the shaking finally stops.

Caleb's there, stringing for one of the websites, bar mitzvah–ready in a sweater vest, collared shirt, and bow tie, his brilliantined hair reflecting the light in oily rainbows. I try to slide by, but he catches my eye.

"Hey, Vivian!" he says with a voice like congealed syrup. "Your piece on the Coward? Savage. Loved. I mean, I could never write like that. But I'm so glad that you can. And aren't you just so excited for this? I know what they say about the alienation effect, but I always feel so close to Brecht, don't you?"

I fumble for something light to say. "Sure I do. It's why I had this ring made: WWBD. What Would Bertolt Do?" I'm in my seat before he realizes I don't wear a ring.

I retrieve my notebook and wait—tensed, like a tightrope walker about to take the first step—for the lights to fall. The curtain opens, a folk song begins to play. And for a moment I worry that the feeling won't come, that the worries of the day will stand in the way of transcendence, transport. But there it is, that interior click. The sense of being lifted out of myself and into the characters' lives. So as much as it upsets me to agree with him, Caleb's right. I don't feel alienated. I feel soothed and whole, happy even, as I watch the coins accumulate and the children die. I don't think about my own mother. I don't think about David Adler. I barely think about the play—that will come later, alone, when I pull the thing apart and put it back together again on my laptop screen. But while the show goes on I sit, held close by the dark, and I feel what it might be like to be alive.

4

RHETORICAL QUESTION

Back at home, I slug a single icy vodka and then brush my teeth and put myself to bed, though I stay awake awhile, eyes open and glittering in the lightless room, replaying the show scene by scene by scene, as the radiator gurgles wetly. In the morning, after a few more ibuprofen and the largest coffee the bodega can serve without a permit, I settle in for several hours of writing and revising. I put myself back into *Courage*'s wagon, fumbling toward a terrible survival, then I take myself out again, braiding emotion and analysis until it organizes itself into tidy paragraphs. Yet as soon as I've clicked save and send and celebrated with a handful of dry cereal, thoughts of David Adler crowd in.

I remind myself what Roger said, that I should give up on the girl detective act, that I should concentrate instead on writing my way into the job I have dreamed of, the job that would give me some sense of belonging, of permanence. But a theater critic reviews performances and David Adler's act nags at me. Because I failed to see it as an act until it was too late. Because it bordered so closely on my own. I don't know if what he showed me was art or life, and I want to know—so that I can judge it, categorize it, put it aside, and continue on to the next show. And yet I shouldn't risk involving myself further. Not for a man I never even knew. Besides, how would I begin? Happily, before my mind can tie itself into further hitches and knots, it seizes on one of Brecht's best lines: "Food first, ethics later."

Under a gunmetal sky that threatens snow, the first of the season, I step out from the building's vestibule and wander through Tompkins Square Park, its grass brittle, its basketball courts untenanted, stray candy wrappers silvering the paths and spiked bushes. A few yelps sound from the playground and the dog run, but even these seem hushed, cushioned by the low-hanging clouds. The park is the public space that screened David Adler from my sight, and even though weeks have passed, I find myself looking for him, startling for a second as I catch a flash—blue, red?—from the other side of the Temperance Fountain. I look harder, but the flash has gone. Breath comes hard for a moment, so I bundle myself into a bench, clutching my knees to my chest, conserving heat. The paths and trees recede until it all looks like a stage set—artificial, illusory, the sort of thing you could pull apart in minutes with just a single sledgehammer and a screw gun clicked on reverse.

Before I slip away any further, I grip the bench's arm as hard as I can, the icy metal biting back into my fingers, substantial and firm. *These are your fingers,* I tell myself, *this is your hand.* But just as I'm starting to steady, I get that sick-making sensation of being watched. I check the fountain again and then swivel my head, owl-like, left, then right. Scanning the grounds, my eyes snag on a scattering of old clothes at the base of an elm tree maybe twenty feet away and almost immediately I realize that the pile isn't just clothes. There's a figure lodged inside the brown and blue folds, a man, seemingly, though something about the angle of the body registers as profoundly wrong. He isn't passed out. He isn't asleep. He isn't sunning himself on this sunless day.

I push up from the bench and step warily toward the tree, aware now of the gravel under my feet, the cold air circling my throat like choking hands. Approaching the body, I see that a hooded sweatshirt covers the face like a monk's cowl. This couldn't be David Adler, could it? The clothes are all wrong, and besides, he went missing weeks ago. Tompkins Square isn't the best maintained of the city's parks, but a body couldn't linger here so long unnoticed. Even the rats would protest. Still, I can taste acid as I bend down for a better look, a finger and thumb grasping the lip of the cotton hood and gingerly pulling it back.

As the face spins into focus, I see that it's him. It's David Adler.

Horror comes for me then. Holding me so close that I struggle to breathe. But as I'm willing myself to inhale, I realize it's a trick of the eye or the mind. The man on the ground has black hair razored close to the skull and wrinkled, yellowed skin, like the peel of a shriveled lemon, with a white scar extending upward from his top lip, which has curled away from stained teeth as though it has some better place to be. I've never seen him before in my life. In his life. With numbed fingers, I scrabble in my pocket for my phone, shuddering when it slips from my hands and bounces off the man's leg. I crouch to retrieve it and dial 911. As I wait for the connection, I hear a heavy, rasping exhale, clawing at the mouth as it escapes. I look down at the body, revolted, confused. Then I realize that the sound has issued from my own throat.

"Hello," I say when the dispatcher answers. "I'm in Tompkins Square Park and I want to report a death." As I speak, I raise myself to stand, my heart hammering as though it wants to break a rib. And then, without warning, a wave of black washes over me, sucking me under, forcing me to the ground, where I land so near the body that our arms almost touch in some awful, botched embrace. I hear the phone bleat as it lies on the sere grass beside me: "Ma'am, ma'am? . . . Ma'am, are you there?" Then I'm gone again.

The paramedics find me sitting up, hugging my knees. They cluster around the body, holding a wrist, prying an eyelid upward, making an obvious death official. Then the larger one, a thick-necked, power-shaved white man, with a flame tattoo licking up from his collar and singeing his right ear, turns his attention to me, asking if I'm feeling dizzy.

"A little," I say. "I blacked out when I found the body."

"Duane," he barks at his colleague, "get the blanket. This one's in shock."

"No, really. I'm fine now. I have a thing where I faint sometimes. I was on my way to lunch when I went into the park, heading for the diner on B, you know? And I skipped breakfast so I must have been light-headed already and then I saw him and—" I can hear myself, my voice splintered, cracking. But I can't seem to slow my speech or lower my pitch or manifest a character more in control. Because a story is unfolding in front of me and I have no way to sit outside of it, pen in hand.

"Shhh," the other paramedic, a man with midnight skin, tight braids, and a dancer's gait, says. "It's okay. We got this." He wraps a crackling silver blanket around my shoulders, gently, like a mother girding her child against the cold, then leads me back to the bench I had sat on earlier.

"You're not one of those vegans or raw foodies, are you?" he asks.

"What? No."

"Hang on."

He lopes away, returning a minute later with a coffee thick with half-and-half and a chocolate-glazed doughnut.

"Eat it," he says. "You need the sugar."

"I really don't think I'm in shock."

"Eat it."

"Is it organic?" I wait for irritation to cloud his face before I bite in. "Kidding," I say.

We smile at each other. Then I remember what's beneath the tree and I stop smiling.

"Detective's here already. He's going to want to talk to you. You feel up to it?"

I steady myself with another gulp of coffee. "Sure."

The paramedic leaves. A woman in uniform winds shrill yellow police tape around the tree where the dead man, now sheeted, lies.

"Ms. Parry?" says a voice. And I see that a man in a navy overcoat has sat on the bench next to mine and angled his knees toward me. A turned-up collar frames a face the reddish brown of expensive loafers. He has an ethnicity I can't place, with startling blue eyes and a sharp nose like the beak on some bird of prey. A bird of prey in a striped tie.

"Ms. Parry?" he repeats. "I'm Detective Paul Destine. I'd like to speak with you. Do you mind coming along to the station?"

I think of every police procedural I've ever read or seen. "Am I under arrest? Do I need a lawyer?"

"If you want one," he says, opening his hands. "But no, ma'am, I don't see you as a suspect. Your presence is voluntary."

"So why the station?"

"It's warmer there and I need to take your prints. For purposes of elimination."

"Okay," I say. I return the blanket to Duane, nodding my thanks. The detective, Destine, walks me to the station, a yellow brick building, its windows studded with air conditioners, and leads me to a desk where a uniformed cop, his features squashed in the middle of his face as if they're on the run from his ears, takes my fingerprints while I try not to recoil from his touch. I'd expected some sort of scanner, but he simply presses all of my fingers into an ink pad and then rolls them one by one onto a sheet of stiff yellow paper, which he has me sign. Afterward, he hands me two desiccated wet wipes, which don't do much to swab away the black.

Destine leads me down a hall painted a suicidal taupe and opens the door to a shabby room with several folding chairs surrounding a wooden table. A mirror occupies the upper half of one wall. He straddles a chair and places a legal pad and pen on the table's surface.

I point to the mirror. "Is that so other detectives can observe the interview?" I ask.

"Yes."

"Is anyone there now?"

"Doubt it."

Unease scuttles crablike up my spine. "Can you check?"

He does a fantastic impression of a man trying very hard not to roll his eyes. "Check for yourself," he says, pointing toward the hallway. "First door on the left. Should be open."

It is. I step inside a narrow room. On this side, the glass wall appears thick and tinted yellow, which makes Destine's skin look darker, his eyes brighter and more piercing. He glances toward the mirror, and even though I know he can't actually see me, it feels as though my clothes and skin have gone transparent.

When I return to the room, Destine pulls out a chair for me. It would seem gentlemanly if he weren't also smirking.

"This isn't a formal interview," he says. "So it won't be recorded."

"Informal's fine," I say, flashing on the last interview I gave, the mini-cassette whirring in its plastic casing.

"After we get the ME's report, I'll need you to return and sign an official statement. Will you be in the area for the next couple of weeks?" I nod and withdraw my hands into my coat sleeves to warm them.

"I'm not really the vacationing kind."

Destine flourishes his legal pad. "Name?"

I give it to him, along with my age, my address, my phone number, my occupation. I tell him what brought me to the park. How I caught sight of the body. How I called the dispatcher.

"Did you know the deceased? Had you ever seen him before?" he asks.

"No," I say. Yet even as I speak, I remember how my brain superimposed David Adler's face on the corpse. I flinch and I can see Destine clock it. So I swallow and make my face a little sterner. "Never."

"Did you touch the body at all?"

"I moved the hood of his sweatshirt away from his face, to see whether or not he was breathing."

"So we shouldn't expect any of your prints on the body, Ms. Parry? No DNA?"

I like the sound of his voice, brusque and cool and slightly amused, as it coils around my name. "I blacked out while talking to the dispatcher and I fell. My hand might have hit the body on the way down. I told the paramedics as much."

"Do you black out a lot, Ms. Parry?"

"It's a good color on me," I say. There's another answer, a truer one. But jokes, as several therapists have told me, are a way to distance and deflect. Something about this man makes me reluctant to allow him any closer.

"Oh, Ms. Parry. Snappy. I like that. Anything more you want to tell me?"

I shake my head. "Do you know who he was? The dead man?"

"A wallet was found on the body, but we can't release the name until the family has been notified. You can check the crime blotter in a day or two or I can have one of my officers call you."

"And do you know how he died?" I ask, my voice fracturing on that last syllable.

"I have a pretty good idea," he says, setting the pen down. "An overdose, probably. We've had reports of bad heroin from one precinct over. But that information has to wait, too. Anything else?"

"No, thank you. That's all."

"Well, thank you, Ms. Parry," he says. "You're free to go."

I shift my weight to stand when a further question occurs to me.

"Wait. As long as I'm here, there is just one thing more: Have you ever worked on missing persons cases?"

"A few. Does that have anything to do—"

"It's not related. But I was wondering, if a man disappeared, someone my age, say, would you investigate it?"

"Is this a rhetorical question, Ms. Parry?"

I think he means hypothetical, and it isn't, not at all. But I nod anyway.

"So this rhetorical guy, he's on the ball? He's not slow or impaired or anything? There's no psychiatric history?"

"Let's assume not."

"And he's a citizen?"

"I think so. Canadian at the outside."

"I mean, is he a good guy, in general, not dealing drugs or running with a gang?"

I think of what Jake Levitz told me. About roulette, about the program and the possible embezzlement. "Good enough," I say. "No gang involvement."

"Then he's not missing. This isn't an airport paperback or some network show, Ms. Parry. Men don't go around getting disappeared. Probably there was a situation he wanted out of, so he left. You can look at the stats if you want to. Missing men aren't really missing. A guy like this, either he takes off under his own steam or . . ."

He's been looking up and away, but suddenly he turns his icy eyes full on me, and even though I'm not guilty of anything, it doesn't feel that way. I know how his sentence ends. But still I have to hear it. "Or what?" I say.

"Or he's dead. Because he killed himself. You sure we're talking rhetorically here?"

I nod and I stand up from the chair. Then I faint again.

When I come to, I'm out of the interview room and stretched on a scratchy sofa with a scratchier acrylic blanket thrown over me. I sit up, which triggers a wave of nausea. I thrust my head back down between my knees.

"Doing your yoga routine, Ms. Parry?" a voice says.

Gingerly I lift my gaze and see Destine watching from the doorway. He must have carried me here. "Just light-headed," I say.

"That's a lot of passing out in one day. You should get that checked."

"I have," I say as crisply as I can while staring at my own vagina. "It's a blood pressure problem. Neuropathic postural tachycardia syndrome. It triggers when I stand up too fast. It's nothing serious. But I'm supposed to avoid stressful situations and there are some support hose my GP wanted me to wear." My GP also wanted me to give up alcohol and pills. I found a new GP. I didn't mention the fainting.

"Is this a stressful situation?"

This time when I raise my head it stays raised. "You mean everyone else finds corpse discovery and police interrogation so soothing?"

"You talk a good game, Ms. Parry. I could listen to you all day. But since I've just seen you collapse on the floor of my interview room, maybe you want to try straight answers for a change. So, a simple question to get us started: You need a glass of water?"

"Maybe a soda? I'm short a few electrolytes."

He leaves and returns a few minutes later with a red-flavored sports drink. I sip it slowly and when it's half-finished I gather myself to leave, but Destine blocks my path.

"I can't let you go," he says.

"You mean I'm under arrest?"

"I mean I let you go and you pass out crossing the street on the way home and suddenly my department's being sued for negligence. And I am many things, Ms. Parry, but I am not ever negligent. You have someone who can pick you up? Family? Boyfriend? Spiritual guide?"

I take my phone out and call Justine at the SoHo fetish-wear boutique where she picks up occasional shifts. As Destine watches, I tell her I'm at the police station and that I need someone to come and get me, and she says that one of the other salesgirls owes her a huge fucking favor, so she'll come and bail me out as soon as she can get the register covered. I tell her I don't actually need bail. She seems disappointed.

Destine takes me by the ladies' room, where I run some water over my face and pinch my cheeks until they're less ashen. Then I'm led to a set of folding chairs near the front desk. Destine hands me his card. And then he puts a hand on my arm, the grip too tight.

"Call me if you think of anything else."

"Anything else about a dead man I've never seen before?"

He shakes his head and walks away. "Smart answers, Ms. Parry. Very smart. You ever feel like giving different ones, you let me know."

The folding chairs aren't all that comfortable, but by the time Justine comes to collect me, I'm sprawled across three of them, fast asleep.

I want a drink—badly—but Justine, in a slashed coat and thigh-high boots that make a favorable impression on the officers at reception, tells me I need to eat something first. When Justine assumes the role of the sensible friend, even I start to reassess my health and well-being. She pulls me into a noodle shop with thick rubber mats covering the floor and plunks me into a chair while she gives an order to the counterman. She returns with a pot of tea and pours me a cup, stirring in two packets of sugar.

"Drink it," she says.

"I hate sugar in my tea."

"You need it for the shock, babe."

"Everyone says I'm in shock," I say as I stir. "I'm not shocked at all. I'm blasé, unmoved, very nearly bored. I see dead bodies all the time. I'm used to it."

"That's onstage. This is different."

"Not very," I say, taking a sip and grimacing.

"Entirely."

And of course she's right.

The counterman brings our bowls and we gather spoons and chopsticks from a jar on the table. Justine rasps hers back and forth, removing the splinters. I don't bother. In the bowl I see thick, pallid noodles and chunks of meat that might be duck, bobbing in an oily broth. As the liquid settles I can also see a reflection of my face, fragmented by the food and the ripples. I close my eyes and lift some noodles to my lips. They go down more easily than I'd expected, slippery, salty, blood warm.

"How's the chow fun?" Justine asks.

"Uproarious. No, really. It's good. Thanks. I haven't eaten today, except for a doughnut a friendly neighborhood paramedic gave me."

"Viv, oh my God, you can't keep fucking doing that."

"Well, as it happens I was on the way to a balanced lunch when I chanced upon a dead body. Which put a dent in my meal plan, you know? But this from the woman who used to describe two shots of Jack and a quaalude as a three-course dinner? You're giving me nutritional advice?"

"Yeah, well, I don't have your blood pressure thing. You want to start fainting again?" She catches something in my expression. "Oh my God. You did. You motherfucking fainted again. For fuck's sake, Viv." If I didn't know that Justine reserves her wrath for tourists who walk three abreast on the sidewalk and women who can't pull off a bold lip, I would think that she was angry with me.

"Tons of people faint when they see a dead body," I answer her. "Even world-weary sophisticates like me. And I'm taking care of myself the best I can, okay?" Which is true. And unencouraging. I don't want to talk anymore, so I raise the bowl and take small, slow sips, letting the liquid gently scald my tongue. Then I put it down. "I'm really tired. Let's forget the drink. I just want to go home."

Justine sighs and spears a wonton. "Three more bites for mommy, then I'll walk you."

As we leave the restaurant, exhaustion sets in. It's all I can do to button my coat. I check my watch and I'm surprised to find it's only five thirty. I have a show to see tonight, a comedy about generational trauma at a theater above a garage in the financial district. I can just about manage it if I sleep for an hour beforehand. Outside, the clouds have cleared and the temperature has tumbled. The broken streetlight in front of my building crackles as it sends out its starved yellow glow. Justine helps me up the stairs, letting me rest on the third-floor landing. My knees ache. They always seem to ache on the stairs now. I wish I could tell myself that I am too young for joint pain. But the joints argue otherwise.

By the time we reach my door, I know I can't make it down and up these steps again tonight. While Justine puts the kettle on, I write an email to a press agent claiming food poisoning. Then I call Roger, giving him an edited version of the truth and telling him I'll need to delay copy for a day or two. I decline to tell him about the nonexistent panel, the *American Stage* article that never was. There's only so much you can burden an editor with at any one time, especially without a good kicker. Justine pours the hot water into two mugs and adds generous slugs from the bourbon bottle.

"Strictly medicinal," she says. "I suppose cloves are too much to hope for?"

"I think that podcast guy I dated left oregano?"

She wrinkles her nose. "No thanks." But she does find a jar of crystallized honey and excavates a few spoonfuls. As I blow on the drink, she says, "Okay. Spill. What was it actually like?" She sips. Her lipstick bloodies the mug's rim. "Were the eyes open? Was it horrible?"

Like a lot of people with a middle school goth period and a subsequent flirtation with suicide, Justine has a passion for the morbid. It is not a passion we share. Especially today. "Yes," I say. "Unspeakable. So glad you asked. And thank you for this sad approximation of a toddy. Now go home. Or at least shut up. I just want to sleep."

"Want a tuck in?" She reaches into her purse and rattles a bottle. "From the bad doctor. They're like Ambien. Only better. I took one the other night and it was like nine-hour anesthesia. Fucking amazing. He said something about weird dreams. But I don't think I dreamed at all."

I put my hand out for a tablet. "Whatever. I have weird dreams already."

She closes my fingers over the whole bottle. Pills are, after all, our love language. "Take it," she says. "There's like a dozen in there and I can probably get more. Call it an early Christmas present."

"You always know my size," I say.

I see her to the door and snap all the locks closed. I swallow the dull green pill, then strip down to my T-shirt and climb into bed. I'm asleep almost before my head hits the pillow. Until I'm startled awake, reaching out suddenly for a body that isn't there. I don't know what time it is, but the quiet suggests a very late hour. Or a very early one. Then I hear it. Footfalls thumping above me, a noise like thunder. Which wouldn't seem so strange, except that even in this narcotized state I know this: I live on the top floor. There's no one above me. And our tenement isn't the kind of place that runs to a roof deck. I dismiss it as a side effect, some auditory hallucination. And then I let myself sink back down to sleep.

5

SNOW-BLIND

When I was a kid, I felt everything and I felt it so much. I'd cry over a bruise, a slight, a story in a reader. I would journal until my hands ached. Once, I sobbed over a tree, a sugar maple gone crimson with the fall's first chill, because I knew how soon those leaves would spiral to the sidewalk and crumble into dust. My mother held me close and whispered to me that it would be all right, that new leaves appear in the spring, that what departs returns to us. She was wrong, of course.

Theater never makes that promise. A performance lasts an hour, two. That's all. Clap. Stamp. Shout "Encore!" until you're gasping and blue. It does no good. This particular instant of actor and audience won't come again. Not really. Not the same.

Me, I make few efforts toward permanence. There's the magazine. And the studio apartment. And Justine, the one person who knew me, if only from a distance, in my life before. But in the present, when anything or anyone else tries to hold me down or too close, I know the drink or the pill or the blocked-number code to shake myself free. Because I need to feel less now.

Yet this morning, when I remember yesterday—those clothes, the wind-chapped face beneath the tree—I am anything but numbed. My heart beats at some furious pace and I'm sweating in the steam heat. Through the window, cracked as always to counter the radiator's punishing sizzle, I hear an ambulance on its way to some fresh emergency. Another cold corpse. Another weeping fiancée. Or maybe it's coming for me. I can recognize the sweat and elevated pulse as a trauma response, a physical manifestation of an emotional expression that any licensed therapist would think appropriate. Appropriate for anyone else. Because I know what happens when I feel too much. And antipsychotics are no one's idea of fun. Not even mine.

The dead body has nothing to do with David Adler. I know this. But somehow my mind has twinned the two catastrophes. I wish I'd never returned his call, never sat for that interview, never phoned Irina or met with Jake Levitz. I have risked too much, thrust myself too close. The dead body is my recompense. Before I can second-guess myself, I find Jake's business card, also Destine's, and I shred them both, throwing the paper confetti into the toilet. Then I swallow half an Ativan, practically my last, run a scalding bath, and scrape a rough washcloth over each limb, sloughing memory away.

Toweling dry, I make some resolutions: No more pushing my body to the point of collapse. No more involving myself in calamities that don't concern me. So what if David Adler was fired? So what if Irina can't return that Kleinfeld dress? These are not my problems. I am going to live calmly and quietly and unexceptionally, safe in my critic's remove. I'll sweat over a great lede. And over nothing else.

At the bagel shop on Second Avenue, at a window seat, laptop open, I force down a lurid amount of cream cheese and send a note to the press agent of last night's play, switching my booking to this evening. I schedule more plays, ensuring I won't have a free night. The cognitive behavioral therapist I saw for three sessions emphasized distraction as a useful coping mechanism. Here's hoping an Ionesco revival counts.

Outside again, I notice that Christmas decorations have surfaced along the street—cardboard Santas leering from store windows, snowflakes hung like suicides from every lamppost. The East Village on a winter afternoon has a slapdash ugliness the other seasons disguise—tenements and high-gloss condos, dive bars and boutiques, all jumbled together on gum-scarred streets. It's a personality disorder of a neighborhood, which is probably why we get along. Underground, in the subway, I let the L train speed me away to Eighth Avenue. Then I'm propelled back up the stairs, through the jostle of the gallery goers and tourists, and north and west until I reach a warehouse in the Twenties with a sign on the door that reads "Jack Frost Associates." I ring the bell and hear it echo in some cavernous space beyond. A rasp of metal on metal sounds as bolts unlatch and the door swings wide and a man stands there, filling the doorway, impossibly tall, then lurching past me onto the sidewalk, where he stretches out his arms and neck to meet the cold.

"Sorry," he says, turning back toward me. "We've been soldering all morning and it's hotter than heck in there." He wipes sweat from his forehead with a checkered bandanna and smiles at me. He's a white guy, maybe mid-thirties, cavalierly muscled, with shaggy hair that can't make up its mind between blond and red, wrinkles at the corners of his eyes, and a spatter of freckles below. "You're from the magazine?" he asks.

"Yes," I say, "Vivian Parry. And you're Jack Frost?"

"Call me Charlie. From the email, it sounds like you're here to see some snow."

"I am."

"Okay," he says, opening the door again and ushering me inside. "Can I take your coat?"

He can. As soon as the door closes, dry heat prickles my skin and sends sweat beading at the nape of my neck. As I shrug out of my top layer, I follow Charlie into the core of the warehouse—a riot of boxes, vacuum tubes, a forklift, and several workers, a couple of them bare chested, including one bent over a welding torch. My nostrils flare at the smell of singed hair.

"Sorry. I know. It's like the equator in here. A problem with the pipes. Do you want snow only or the whole weather shebang? Like rain and fog and all? We're working on a lightning effect, but it won't be ready till sometime next year."

"I'd like to see all of them, please. All the ones you use in the theater."

"Sure," he says, beckoning me toward a repurposed Ping-Pong table. "Step around. Let's start here."

Leaning on the table, he opens a laptop, its cover scarred with band stickers. I ready my pen. "So you probably know this already, but the cheapest thing to do when you need a storm effect is not to use any effects at all," he says. "Just have the actors pretend they're in a storm. Let the words do the work. Blow winds and crack your cheeks, right? Next step is sound, which can mean everything from rolling a cannonball across the floor to a thunder machine in the wings to some fancy speaker setup. Then you add lights, blinking, flashing, stark, dim, whatever. In Elizabethan theaters they used to create lightning effects with gunpowder and fireworks. Which explains why Elizabethan theaters burned down a lot." He laughs and I echo him.

"Yeah," he continues, "not recommended. Okay, so we have acting, sound, lights, and then more recently, projection design. I've programmed a couple of sample sequences." He clicks the program on, loosing whorls and swirls, and as our heads crowd together at the screen, I smell the sweat on him and another scent, too, a sweet, citric tang—like oranges, like sunlight.

When the program ends, Charlie takes me over to a metal arch fitted with pipes and tubes of varying thickness. "When you're ready to move into real stuff, rain's the easiest. You take a length of PVC pipe like this one and you poke holes into it. How wide and how many determine the intensity." He points to a drain in the concrete floor. "You rake the stage to ease runoff, build gutters below, and make sure wardrobe has plenty of shoes with good traction. Let's start with a drizzle."

He flicks a switch on a control panel encased in plastic. A whirr, a rush, and then a light spray, cooling my skin. I move away, sheltering my notebook. One of the female techs, a woman, square faced, Latinx maybe, with a buzz cut and a "Performance Artists Do It Live" T-shirt, runs into the spray, frolicking spaniel-like as the drops blur her glasses.

"Awesome," she says.

"Corinne's always trying to turn the workplace into a wet T-shirt contest," says Charlie, loud enough for her to hear and with affection. "She says it's freedom of expression. I say it's harassment."

He switches the setting from drizzle to downpour and Corinne flees.

Once the water drains away, he takes me back beneath the arch and shows me a snow cradle, operated by a hand crank, which makes a quiet chuffing sound as it releases a flurry of plastic flakes. Then he demonstrates a more advanced model, triggered remotely. At first just a few flakes spiral down, but soon a blizzard swirls around me, loosing slivers of plastic that settle in my hair and the crease of my notebook.

"Yeah," he says, "it's not much good for snowballs, but you line up three or four across the stage and you can get a pretty good storm going. Especially if you place a couple of these beasts in the wings." He points to a squat machine with a tube emerging from it, like a cubist's vision of an elephant. He directs the tube just to the left of me and flips it on. Wind gusts out, thick with more plastic flakes, forceful enough to make the ends of my hair rise and dance.

"But here's the big show," he says, pointing upward to a small metal box facing into a round fan. "Theatrical snow that actually feels like snow. Or sort of like it." He sets the machine whirring. "Just don't try and catch any on your tongue. It's ninety percent water and the other ten percent is basically harmless, but it tastes like laundry soap."

He flicks a switch and then, as promised, snow eddies around me, piling at my feet, melting as it slides over my skin. I bend down and try to gather some into my hand, but it glides through my fingers, slippery, strangely warm.

"It dries fast and doesn't leave a residue, so no danger to the kick line," Charlie says proudly.

"I've never seen an effect like it," I say. It seems so right for the theater, nature rendered safe, predictable and temporary. Looking past the machine up through the skylight, I see that snow—real snow—has begun to fall outdoors, and I can picture these other, wilder flakes alighting on cars, coating concrete, blanketing the city's wounds and scars like so much gauze. Charlie pushes a button and the machine grumbles to a stop.

We move to fog devices then, a small handheld sprayer and a larger one on wheels. He switches the larger one on and almost immediately a sickly murk, with a smell like rancid baby powder, rolls out, tangling with our feet and then rising. "There's a compressor if you want your fog to stay *Phantom of the Opera* floor level," he says. "And there's a haze machine, but honestly that's more for nightclubs."

"That one we can skip," I say. "You said in the email that you had a new machine for mist?"

"Oh, yeah!" he says. "We've been tinkering with it for months now and I'm semi-obsessed. It's not so different from the fog, but it's thicker and heavier and wet on your skin. Right now it dissipates too much in an open space, but we'll get the mix right eventually. It's in a side room. Come on."

He takes me back the way I entered and through a door to a small room with a single table supporting a compact gray contraption with a short hose and a pebbled plastic exterior. Charlie turns it on and at first it only hums, but soon a mist unfurls, not the powdery gray of the fog, but a brilliant showy white, like bleached bone. I glance over at Charlie smiling, but within seconds mist surrounds him. That white smile disappears first.

Down the length of my arm, I watch my fingers fade away. Then even my upper arm blurs. My breath goes fast, shallow. To calm myself, I bring a hand to my face. "These are your fingers," I whisper. "This is your hand." But I can feel the tendrils of mist sliding down into my nose and throat with every tooth-clenched inhale, filling me up, whiting me out from the inside. Part of me wants that. The disappearance. The not being. Wants it so much that if I don't leave the room right away, the wanting might never stop.

I can't see the door, but I stumble to where it might be, hissing as I scrape my knuckles on cinder block, feeling along the walls for the handle, until hands grasp mine.

"Hey," says Charlie. "Hey." He keeps one arm around me as he silences the machine. Then he half pulls, half drags me a few steps into the hall, where I sit down abruptly with a mortifying "Oof" and stay seated, head bent, arms ringing my knees.

"I'm sorry," I say. "The air. I couldn't—"

"It's all right," he says, kneeling beside me. "Can you breathe okay now?"

I nod.

"I don't know what happened," he fusses. "Maybe Darren messed with the formula and didn't tell me. It's actually even safer than the fog. Or it's supposed to be. Do you have allergies? Or asthma? Is your throat swollen? One of our guys, Joel, he used to work as an EMT. I can get him for you."

"No. I'm fine now. Really." Or I'm not. But it's nothing an EMT can fix.

"Okay," he says. He takes the bandanna from his pocket and wipes his forehead. "Is this where your nice, friendly feature story turns into some kind of blistering exposé?"

"Like you're the practitioner who's tried to smother a critic."

He smiles then, and blame mirror neurons, but I smile, too. "Okay to do the formal interview now?" I ask.

"If you're up for it."

"Of course," I say, uncurling and pushing up to stand. "But I've had about as much weather as I can bear. Is there a café close by, maybe? Or a quiet bar?"

"There's a place right across the street that's usually pretty empty about now."

We enter the kind of red-velvet nightspot that looks impossibly chic at two a.m. and deeply depressing twelve hours later. At the bar, I collect an orange juice for Charlie and a vodka tonic for me. I don't usually drink this early, but I tell myself that the sugar in the tonic will help my nervous system recover. I almost believe it.

We settle ourselves on a banquette the color of dried blood. I perch my recorder on a table furred with dust, turn it on, and ask him how he got involved in theatrical effects (a double major in drama and engineering), what's his best-selling product (the machine-operated snow cradle), and the difficulties of making winter wonderlands indoors. By the time I'm downing my second drink and he's describing an avalanche fiasco during a grad school production of *When We Dead Awaken*, I realize I'm nearly enjoying myself. At the end of the interview I shake his hand without flinching, feeling the strength of his grip, the calloused fingers. And I wonder, for a moment, what it might be like to be a real person, to inhabit my body in a real way.

"All right," I say, replacing the recorder in my bag. "I'll transcribe this before my show tonight. Appreciate it."

"What are you seeing?"

"*The White Plague.*"

"No way! I love Čapek."

"Seriously?" I make a mental note to stop underestimating the theatrical taste of everyone I meet.

"Yeah, for real. *R.U.R.* was the first show I ever designed in college. Hey, you don't have an extra ticket, do you?" he asks.

"I only have a single," I say. But then I hear myself add, "If you really want one, I can email the press agent and ask for another."

"Oh, yeah! Definitely. But only if it's not a lot of trouble."

"It's a free ticket to a low-budget show by an obscure Czech author. How much trouble can it be? I have your number in my email. I'll text if it's a go."

He sees me to the sidewalk and then reenters the warehouse while I weave my way downtown, feeling a few last flakes of real snow against my cheeks, softer and colder than the ones from Charlie's machine. I'm not sure why I promised Charlie a plus-one. Dizziness from the mist, maybe. Or making good on the morning's resolutions. Or because he saw me, however wrongly, as real, as whole, as a person worth caring for. Besides, what harm can a ticket do?

Or is that what Mrs. Lincoln said?

I switch my phone back on and I'm preparing to text the publicist when I notice the alert for a voice mail message. What kind of a monster still leaves voice mail messages? When I play it, I find out. A monster named Paul Destine.

I look at the phone, at the hand holding it, at the smears of ink still staining the whorls of each finger. They look like someone else's fingers. I hit the call icon.

"Detective Destine, please," I tell the officer who answers. "It's Vivian Parry returning his message." The phone bleeps and I hear the tuneless strains of a jazz saxophone. Then Destine is on the line.

"Ms. Parry?"

"Yes."

"As I said, we've contacted the family of the deceased, so I can release that name to you now if you want."

"Want" isn't the right word. But I don't have a better one. "Go ahead," I say.

"Vinnie Mendoza. Thirty-seven years old. You know him?"

"I've already told you I don't."

"Well, you've got a shared line of work. Sometimes he worked as a barback at the Jigger—"

"I drink there, Detective. I wouldn't call it an occupation."

"Ms. Parry, if I may, he also picked up stagehand jobs at the theater on Fourth and B."

I know the place. It's a former Catholic school with an elaborate proscenium stage where the assembly hall used to be. If you close your eyes and listen closely, you can still hear nuns thwacking pupils with a handy missal. I've never met any of its stagehands.

"Like I said yesterday, I've never seen him before. My job doesn't often take me backstage." Then a darker thought occurs to me. "Why are you telling me this? You said it was an overdose. Was it something else? Did someone do this to him?"

"If they did, Mr. Mendoza probably wouldn't have noticed. The examiner confirmed fentanyl. Plenty. And I'm only going by the collapsed veins and the puncture marks he showed me, but if someone spiked Mr. Mendoza, that someone was around a lot. Any more questions?"

"No, that's all right. Thank you."

"Nothing rhetorical?"

"Thank you, no. Not today."

"You take care, Ms. Parry," he says with a rasp I might almost mistake for a laugh. "Come by the station when you can and sign that report. Meantime, you keep warm."

I press the button to end the call. Then I text Charlie: Sry called press agent and show sold out. And then another text: Thnx for snowstorm! I cringe slightly as I key in the exclamation point. But I imagine that's how someone who actually felt contrition, who felt anything, would write it.

I turn back into the wind, letting it sting my eyes until they tear. Then I shrink my gaze until it holds only the gray square of pavement just ahead of me and I start the cold walk home.

6

THE ACTOR'S PARADOX

I was a sophomore theater major when I first encountered Diderot's *The Paradox of the Actor*, a debate in the form of a dialogue. One side holds that a performer truly experiences all of a character's pain and pleasure. The other counters that actors fake these feelings: On the surface, an emotional whirlwind. Inside, complete detachment. At the end of the dialogue, Diderot takes this latter opinion, deciding that the best actors feel nothing. All mask. No face. I didn't like his conclusion back then. I was too susceptible, too sensitive, too eager to lose myself in a role, and too alarmed when I succeeded. I've grown harder since. I like it fine now. And it's how I play this single, undemanding part: myself. For colleagues, for publicists, for the men I meet and rarely see again, I'm as convincing as I have to be.

But for my psychiatrist, Dr. Barlow, who rents a bijou office in a grand edifice just off Riverside Drive, this brittle mask won't do. I have to show her not only the carapace, but also a glimpse of what she actually wants to see, the quivering creature under it. That's an act, too. But a tougher one, a double role that demands a more complete identification with the character. I dare it only during these quarterly fifty minutes on her extremely comfortable sofa. Why dare it at all? Because I miss acting, real acting, like a parched lawn misses rain, like a baby misses the breast. And because she's the one with the prescription pad.

On this Tuesday morning, after a late night spent negotiating the edits on the winter arts feature I had filed first thing Monday, I enter a foyer twice the size of my studio and glide along the marble floor. I sign in with the doorman, his coat buttons gleaming like the brass door handle he'll polish as soon as I've walked on. In the waiting room I murmur my name to the receptionist and settle in with a glossy magazine. As I page through it, a woman in a robin's-egg-blue coat emerges from an inner door and hurries past me, mouth narrowed, limbs tensed, blinking so as not to cry. Dr. Barlow, stingy with the refills again.

When I hear my name, I enter that same door and shuffle down the short, carpeted hall into her office, removing my coat with care and arranging myself on the beige leather sofa as soft and buttery as brioche. Only then do I initiate brief eye contact and a limp smile. Dr. Barlow pats her nimbus of natural hair, adjusts the glasses joined to a beaded chain, and smiles back. A scarf—bright yellow, nearly the same shade as the police cordon—drapes loosely across her shoulders and down her chest.

"How have you been, Vivian?" she asks in her husky voice, pencil hovering above a matching legal pad.

"Okay? I guess?" I say, letting my eyes slip away. I like to begin with shyness, a certain reserve, then gradually increase eye contact and uncross my arms and legs until she believes we've established rapport. It's a beautiful mutualism. She gets the satisfaction of having created a therapeutic bond with a reticent patient. I get my scrip. And if I'm lucky, something else—a sliver of what it was like to lose myself in a role, to wonder if I would ever come back.

I sink into the couch a little more and begin with a clipped rhythm, pitching my voice softer and higher, letting it rise at the ends of most sentences. "Work's fine? I guess? I've been eating better," I say. "Maybe not three meals? Not every day? But I'm not working through lunch like we talked about. And I've cut back on coffee, too." I pause there, seeing if she'll mouth the baited hook.

"You have?" she says. "And why is that?"

"I haven't been sleeping well," I say. Which isn't true. The pills Justine gave me make the world retreat within minutes. Oblivion on demand. But that's the thing about privilege. A person gets used to it so quickly. So I want more. In a bottle with my name on it and at least three refills.

"Do you have trouble falling asleep or staying asleep?"

"Both? I guess?" I raise my eyes to hers, just for a moment, then drop them back to my lap, a choreographed sequence set to an internal eight count. "And I've been having nightmares." This, at least, is genuine. Though the pills ensure I sleep so heavily that I don't usually remember the details.

"Is there a particular nightmare you have often?" She sits more forward now and her voice has a purr to it, like a cat before it pounces.

"It's more like a picture? A face?" It isn't.

"Do you know whose face it is?"

"Sort of? I mean I didn't know him, but . . ." I trail off and I let her see my eyes dart to the box of tissues on a stand near the sofa, though I don't reach for one. Not yet. I offer up these next words like a benison, a gift with all its ribbons frilled: "I found a body."

"A body?" she says, her head and torso canting toward me. "Do you mean a dead body, Vivian?"

"Yes," I say. She's enjoying this and I'm enjoying it, too, basking in the fullness of her attention. "It happened a week or so ago? I was going out for lunch and I cut through the park near my house and he was under a tree?" I inhale shakily, bringing my hands to my face. I dare a lip quiver. Too much?

Dr. Barlow doesn't seem to think so.

"Take your time," she says. Her voice is calm, a mountain lake unrippled, but she has scooched to the edge of her seat. "This must be painful to recall."

"It is?" I say. I hold the pause as long as I dare, then let her see me compose myself. "He'd overdosed. That's what the police said. I had to go to the station. They took my fingerprints? I didn't know the man, I just found him. But I feel . . ."

"Yes," says Dr. Barlow.

"I feel—I don't know—guilty somehow? Like there was something I should have done. Even though he was dead hours before I got there. Like maybe I could have saved her?" I didn't know that I would say "her" before I said it. And it makes me break character for a moment, because

I'm not sure whether that syllable was a genuine slip or a brilliant improvisation. Either way I know Dr. Barlow won't let the error go unparsed.

"Her?" she says, and oh, that lake has ripples now. "Didn't you say you'd found a man?"

"Yes," I say. "Sorry. Him. I meant him." And now I do reach for a tissue, holding it in front of my face like a veil.

"But you said her," she prompts. "An interesting substitution, don't you think?"

"Is it?" I say. "I don't know." But I do know. And there's no avoiding this next part. So I let the character, this sad and cringing version of the self I used to be, talk on. "Maybe I was thinking of my mother? I've always felt like somehow if I'd been there—"

"Look at me, Vivian," says Dr. Barlow.

I shake my head.

"Please," she says.

I raise my wet eyes to hers. And then the moment comes, the one I hope for, when I've gone so far into the role that I can trust the words and the whirlwind to their work. I am in it and without it. Observing myself from above as a few tears come. The pleasure is borderline erotic, almost unbearable.

"From what you've said about your mother and this man in the park, there was nothing you could have done in either case. A burst appendix, an overdose, you can't hold yourself accountable. You can grieve those losses, but you can't make yourself responsible for them, all right?"

"It's just—" And the tears come faster now, sluicing down one cheek and another, the sentence unfinished. I take a stuttered inhale. "Okay-ay," I say, the word a kind of wail. "You're right."

"Are you angry with me, Vivian?"

"No-o," I say with genuine surprise. "Of course not. Why would I be?"

"Because I asked you to take better care of yourself, to eat lunch even on your writing days. If you hadn't agreed to try, you wouldn't have found yourself in the park."

Even sunk so far into character, I have to smother a smile. Psychiatrists, always pulling focus. "No," I say. "I'm not mad at you."

"Well, I would understand if you were."

"No," I say, drying the tears. "Not at all. I think you're really helping me. I'm eating better and I want to sleep better, too. But with these dreams . . . I can't . . . I don't—"

I break off then, but the set of her lips tells me I have to continue. "Isn't there something you can give me for that? To make me sleep more soundly? Not for always. Just until the shock of finding the body fades and I'm not so scared all the time."

"Do you mean sleeping pills?"

"I guess so-o?" I say, letting my voice quiver until it's practically vibrato.

Dr. Barlow has taken up the folder on the side table that holds my chart. She's flipping the pages and frowning. Never a good sign. "I'm sorry, Vivian," she says. "But I don't think I can. Sleeping pills are contraindicated in the case of anyone who's suffered a major depressive episode."

"But I've been fine for a decade," I say, wide-eyed, pleading. "More."

"Have you really?" she says. "You're surviving, yes, but judging by what you tell me and what I observe as an intermittent lack of affect, I would argue that depression remains, however well you're disguising it. Right now the pills on the market have too many side effects. And we don't want you to risk ending up in a facility again, do we?"

We do not. And I am wondering, not for the first time, why *we* don't see a doctor with a freer hand with the prescription pad. But I know the answer. Not every doctor lets me perform. Not every doctor appreciates my performance, appreciates the talent I have cut out of myself in my determination to stay alive, however thin and limited this life is. I want her approval. I want her applause. And in these strange weeks since I met with David Adler, since the boundaries between theater and life went fuzzy at the edges, I want her pills. Which she won't give me.

"Isn't there anything that will help me?" I say. The character, that susceptible girl, has slipped away. There's nothing to do now but put my everyday mask back on and endure the rest of the therapeutic hour.

"You can use an over-the-counter sleep aid and see if that works," she says, sitting back. "Or melatonin. Try not to exercise or work on your computer for at least an hour before bed. I find that a cup of chamomile tea often helps."

If I could scald Dr. Barlow with a cup of it right now, it might help enormously.

"Failing that, your Ativan has sedative properties, so try taking half a pill in the late evening—a whole one, if wakefulness persists."

"Okay," I say, imploring, "that's good advice. It makes sense. But in that case, can you increase my prescription just a little? Because I don't think the pills are working as well as they used to. And it's not like the other symptoms of anxiety have stopped. Maybe once I'm over this, I can work on that. Try meditation again. Or talk therapy. But I just need something to get me through in the meantime, until the nightmares stop."

Dr. Barlow is shaking her head like a plump metronome. "I understand," she says. "And I'd like to do that for you, but Ativan carries a risk of dependence, which is why we keep your dose low and encourage you to spread it out. Your use of alcohol and recreational drugs suggests that you're possibly prone to addiction—"

I can barely bother with even my usual mask now. My voice slides down to somewhere low and cold and vicious. "I told you that my use is occasional, not habitual. I was being honest with you. I don't see why you should punish me for that."

"Vivian, I'm not punishing you, but with your history, as I've told you before, you shouldn't be using at all. Even the Ativan poses a slight risk. So let's keep on with the present dose."

I grit my teeth and manage something like a nod.

"But perhaps this is an opportunity to reconsider insight-oriented therapy. This association of the man with your mother, it suggests unresolved issues. Wouldn't you like to move on from that? I'm sure I could find time for a weekly appointment. And if your anxiety worsens, we can always try antidepressants again."

My jaw is clenched so tight it's a wonder I can speak at all. "Yes," I say. "It's so good to know we have that option."

She keys in my usual scrip. I murmur a farewell and leave, the tissues crumpled in my pocket, souvenirs of my failed performance. I guess I'm not the actress I used to be.

To clarify: It wasn't acting that landed me on the psych ward. Not exactly. And it wasn't my mother's sudden death, at least not right away. After the funeral, which fell during the fall break of my junior year, I spent an unspeakable week at the house with my New Hampshire aunt, a woman incapable of consolation, deciding what should be donated and what sold and what stored, because it never occurred to her that I might need time to mourn before dispensing with my mother's worldly goods. Then I returned to school. This was a time when I enjoyed attracting attention to myself, so I performed the grief I felt, heading to class with eyes raccooned and hair disheveled, speaking with the kind of graveled seriousness that the occasion demanded.

In the evenings, when classes ended and dinner had finished, I went to rehearsal, crossing the campus in the glimmering dusk and entering a dusty, black-painted room. Acting, back then, was delectation, adventure, escape. From elementary school on I could lose myself in a role, throwing off my real identity like yesterday's clothes, trying on finer garments. And even though I didn't think much of my everyday self—a girl never as fascinating or dynamic as the parts I played—there was comfort, such comfort, in knowing that at the end of each show I could rehang the costume and swab the stage makeup away and find myself again in the mirror of my mother's congratulations, her jasmine-scented embrace.

I've never really known my father. My parents split before I was a year old and he sped across the country and toward a new family. For a while there were dutiful conversations and the occasional card, which even as a child I knew his wife had selected. But eventually those stopped, too. He didn't know when I passed my driving test or received my college acceptance letters or graduated high school. He never came to a single show I starred in and he didn't attend my mother's funeral. I'm not sure anyone thought to invite him. Still, I never felt his absence as a lack. Because my mother never allowed for it. When my mother was alive I lacked for nothing.

She was young enough when she had me that we more or less grew up together, in a cottage, in a cul-de-sac, in the sort of polite New England town where everyone carries tote bags from the local PBS affiliate and grows their own tomatoes in a backyard plot. We had our fights in my teenage years, but not many. What I remember most is how happy we were—tritely, indescribably.

When she looked at me, I knew exactly who I was.

In the weeks after her death, during those rehearsals, I fell back on all my usual techniques, creating a history for my character, speaking in the character's voice, walking with her gait, fluttering my hands as I imagined she would. But something had changed. At the end of the night I found myself unready or unwilling to lay the character aside. Simply put: I didn't know how to return to myself. Or I did know. And I didn't want to. I couldn't be the girl that my mother had loved. Because being that girl meant living with the pain of her loss, a pain so great that I thought I might die, too.

Life went blurry then. Only the lines I spoke in that windowless rehearsal space, only the actions I committed in the service of the play, felt clear, felt real, better than real. Anything else—ordering a coffee, speaking in seminar, attending a party in the dorm—seemed false, forced. The fainting spells, which had troubled me as a child, returned. I'd rise from a prone position and the world would go black. I didn't resist it. The world felt so strange and empty then, I was glad to be out of it.

I still went to my classes, wrote my essays, attempted a social life, but I couldn't shake the certainty that it was all some elaborate pose. The browning lawns and weathered buildings seemed stage sets, the Frisbee throwers and vegan protesters minor characters. I lived—if I lived at all—for those few evening hours of rehearsal. Did I mention that we were rehearsing *Hamlet* and that I was playing poor, mad Ophelia? That still kills me. Or it nearly did.

I heard her lines in my head; I heard them all the time. Lying in bed, daydreaming in class, swirling food around my plate in the dining hall, I heard her words echoing until my mind clouded and my body became a set of rag-doll limbs and there was nothing to do except as the play suggested, to meet loss with death.

No, I didn't try to drown myself. Brooks where willows grow aslant weren't a feature of our campus life, no matter what the brochures suggest. So when the feeling overcame me that I was growing as crazy as my character, that my tether to the world had raveled, and that whoever I had been was now a person—another person—lost to me, I swallowed a bottle of tequila (forgive me, I was younger then) and handfuls of my roommate's painkillers. I went to sleep.

As suicide attempts go, I don't think mine would score very highly: negligible difficulty, poor execution. My roommate, Kate, found me splayed on my bed not twenty minutes later. I'd like to think I looked romantic—a doomed maiden in some Pre-Raphaelite painting—but as Kate later told the other girls on our floor, I'd already vomited on my shirt and across the duvet.

College lore has it that should your roommate kill herself, you're guaranteed a 4.0 for the rest of the semester. Kate could really have used the boost, but instead she called campus health services and I spent the next hours with a tube down my throat, enjoying a friendly round of gastric lavage.

That I hadn't left a note should have spoken in my favor, but the doctors refused to believe that I'd swallowed those pills by accident. (This was before I learned to lie more convincingly to mental health professionals.) Some feature of my affect—or its absence—made them wary. They kept me in the campus hospital for forty-eight hours until they could ensure that my liver had rebounded, and then, with the New Hampshire aunt's consent, they transferred me to a state medical center with a psych ward.

I remember how, in that first hour, the door closed with a metallic thunk and something came awake in me and I screamed and I thrashed until they dosed me with a sedative and put me to bed. When the sedative wore off, I clawed at my arms until they bled, shrieking that they weren't really mine. They restrained me then and gave me an antipsychotic, which put me into a perpetual doze. Flowers appeared at my bedside, so I may have had visitors, but mostly I recall the stuttered convoy of doctors—the white coats the same, the face hovering above the collar always different. In my few lucid periods, they elicited as much of my history as I could offer—my mother's death, my rehearsals, the growing sense of unreality. Doctors don't rest until they have outfitted you with a diagnosis, and mine was depersonalization disorder, a syndrome in which the patient experiences a loss of identity, a disconnection from her life experience. I couldn't argue it. And while I knew that my mother's death had hastened this particular break, I wondered if maybe I'd had this disorder all along. If that was why I could disappear into a role so easily, because there had never been that much of me to vanish in the first place.

I couldn't heal from a disorder like this. Not truly. Not entirely. But I could learn to live with it. To convince the doctors of this, I reduced my repertory—playing the grieving daughter, the recovering patient—without committing to any role too deeply. After a few weeks, when they no longer believed me a danger to myself, they graduated me to an SSRI, which numbed me somewhat less than the lithium and a bit more than a blithe afternoon inside a meat locker. Merry Christmas to me.

I improved and improved, or that's what I pretended, and soon, just before the new semester, an assistant dean came for a meeting, as did my aunt. In the sun-streaked office of the lead psychiatrist, we discussed my options. My aunt wanted me to withdraw, but I maintained that the structure of courses and extracurriculars and the promise of an on-time graduation was what I needed most. And everyone could see that my aunt wouldn't make much of a caregiver. Eventually we all agreed that I could reenroll—making up the work I had missed on a relaxed schedule, taking a summer class if needed—provided I participated in weekly group therapy sessions at the campus hospital and also met with a psychiatrist on an individual basis. I agreed, of course. I would have agreed to almost anything that let me flee the pulverized food and crunching sheets and too-bright lights. Days later, I returned to school.

News of my attempt must have traveled. This time, teachers and classmates greeted my return differently. A professor's eyes would dart away from mine as he devised a new due date for a paper I'd missed. A former friend would talk animatedly about a party she was planning only to break off awkwardly when I set my tray down. Kate requested and received a housing transfer.

Rehearsals posed other problems. From the first day back, it became clear that Ophelia was a part I couldn't play, at least not in the way I had played it before. Committing too strongly to the character risked another depersonalization episode, a second painkiller rendezvous. So I hit my marks and spoke my lines, but without passion or affect, barely able to raise my voice above a monotone. Which earned the review David Adler discovered. The critic wrote that I was lifeless. It was true.

After *Hamlet*, I didn't act anymore. At least, not in pursuit of any degree. With the approval of the department heads, I switched my concentration to dramatic literature. Offstage, however, I continued to perform, but without risk or investment. I taught myself to chatter in a way that sounded credible, to laugh as tunefully as I could manage. In the mirror of what was suddenly my single dorm room, I practiced smiles until I found one that looked almost natural. I didn't know how to live, but I hadn't made up my mind to die, and this mask bought me the time and distance I required. At the tops of my papers, I began to use Vivian, my middle name. A name my mother had never called me.

No one suspected the charade. No one except Justine. She was part of the therapy group the dean insisted I join. I had seen her in a few of my theater lecture courses, rows away. We had crisscrossed at auditions. But she was a year below me, a sophomore to my junior, and we had never been cast in the same show. She was silent during most of the sessions, so much that I had wondered, shamefully, if English were difficult for her. But when the therapist finally insisted she speak, she told a fluent, tearful, and expletive-laden story about childhood sexual abuse followed by adolescent promiscuity, an STD scare that wasn't really a scare, and an unfortunate encounter between her wrists and a straight razor, which went a long way toward explaining her predilection for short skirts and long sleeves. At the end of that meeting, we rode down in the elevator together. As it reached the ground floor, she said, "I need a drink. Are you coming?"

"I can't," I said.

"Why not?"

"It's these pills I'm taking. You can't mix them with alcohol."

"What did they put you on?"

"Prozac," I said, keeping my eyes on the glowing buttons.

"Prozac? You can totally drink on Prozac!"

"Are you sure, because they said—"

"Please," she said as the elevator dinged and we exited into the lobby. "I've taken all of them. And seriously? Don't ever let them put you on anything with 'lex' or 'fex' in the name. That shit's impossible to get off of. But the only ones you really can't drink on are the ones with the black box warning about how they fuck with your liver. Prozac isn't one of them, babe. Trust me. The *Physicians' Desk Reference* is literally my bible. Except I actually believe in it."

I hesitated. Then I remembered what she'd confessed to that night and reasoned she didn't want to be alone. Besides, making up another excuse felt too effortful. "Okay," I said. "Maybe just the one."

"But that's the loneliest number," Justine said, voice like creamed honey, leading me to the nearest bar and smiling to the bald man outside, who waved her in without checking her fake ID or mine. Some people have perfect pitch, some can calculate vast sums in their heads. Justine, I would quickly learn, can get into any bar she likes. She had a bourbon and Coke. I ordered a vodka and orange. I liked sweeter drinks then, sweeter anything. I remember arranging my face into a sympathetic pout and asking, as softly as the background music would permit, "Was the session tonight hard for you?"

She smirked at me over the rim of her glass. "Oh, that's fucking adorable. You're pretending to care."

"No, I—"

"You don't. I can tell. I watch you in the room sometimes and you're nodding or you're biting your lip or you're looking so sad. But it's just playing pretend. Don't worry. I don't think anyone else notices. It's just that I've seen your shows. You did that same lip-biting thing in *Hedda Gabler* last year."

"I'm sorry," I said. I'd flattered myself that my role-play in these sessions was better than that. That no one could penetrate it. So it threw me—what little of me remained—that Justine had seen through it from the start.

"And you're right," I went on, swiveling the straw in my drink. "But it seems impolite to stare blankly while everyone's tearing their hearts out of their chests and parading them around the room."

"Don't apologize. Everyone else in there makes me literally sick. They just want their boring pointless lives back."

"And I don't?" I said.

She looked at me straight on, eyes like twin spotlights. "No. And neither do I."

"But all the things you said in there, about wanting to find a safe place . . ."

"It's just what they want to hear. If I say it every so often, then they'll leave me alone. Which is what *I* want. You, too, right? You don't really want to get better. You barely want to live at all."

That somehow she would see me, the whole of me, there, in that dark bar, it was too much. The bar itself seemed to recede and I held on as tightly as I could, gripping the table with one hand, bringing the glass to my lips with the other, reciting my silent litany: *These are your fingers, this is your hand, your palm, your wrist, your forearm, your—*

"It's okay," Justine said. "You don't have to answer. But you should want to live. Until thirty, at least. After that everything's basically downhill. The problem is, babe, that you aren't having any fucking fun. And fun won't start until you get off those pills."

"But—"

"I know," she said, downing the last of her drink in one luxuriant swallow. "You wuv your widdle pills. They make everything so nice and blank and neutral. Like it's Wednesday, but forever. And you worry that if you really truly actually feel something, the feelings won't ever stop. But they will. You just have to control them. Measure feelings out. Show them whose bitch they are. Speaking of, this bitch needs another drink." She held up her hand, signaling the bartender.

"I guess I have been a little bored," I said.

"Well, obviously. Go off the pills slowly, taper down. Let your psychiatrist know. Tell him—it's a him, right?—that you think you're ready. He'll probably be pathetically proud. But after a week or two start talking about anxiety. Tell him you're not having it all the time, just when you have a paper due or when you run into someone who used to be a friend. That cunt roommate, maybe."

"She's not a cunt."

"She absolutely is. Anyway, you'll get a prescription for diazepam or lorazepam, something to take the edge off. You won't need to take it every day, just when things get too fucking intense. It's like a chemical fire curtain."

"Are you sure? They had me on a tranquilizer before. Lithium. All I did was sleep."

"Lithium? Seriously?" She seemed impressed. "They must have thought you were extra crazy. The pills I'm talking about are way more fucking chill. Best part: they won't mess with your orgasms and"—she took a sip of her freshened drink—"they work even better with a little booze. Along the way you'll learn to control, to compartmentalize. It's really not that hard."

I should have known better than to take pharmacological advice from a teenager with razor scars. I didn't.

The advice worked, though not in the way Justine intended. I don't get my kicks from champagne. Or sex. They're what I use to keep the world at a comfortable distance. If I have fun now, it's only in the dark, only at the theater. That's when I feel—for two hours' traffic—like an actual human, the grown-up version of the girl who used to share an armrest with her mother.

But back then, I had questions. "It sounds okay," I remember saying, swirling the ice at the bottom of my drink. "But if you have it all figured out, then why are you sitting here with me? Admittedly I don't have a great sense of what constitutes a good time, but I know I'm not it."

She sipped her drink. Then she gave me her sword-point smile. "Because I've been thinking lately that if there isn't one person in my life I can be honest with I might actually go a little crazy. Crazier. So congratulations. I picked you. But don't worry. I'm only interested in honesty on very fucking rare occasions. Tonight's one of them. Can I tell you a secret, babe?"

I nodded.

"A lot of what I said in group was true. I was molested and I did sleep around. I still do. And I've spent enough time on therapists' couches to understand how the one thing probably relates to the other, though I'm not really looking to stop. It works for me. But here's the thing: I didn't try to kill myself because I was so frightened or hopeless or any of that other absolute shit."

"So why did you do it?" I asked, leaning closer.

"Just to see if I could."

Leaving Dr. Barlow's, shoulders slumped, torso practically parallel with the sidewalk, I stop into a bar. It's hours earlier than my usual first drink, but the rules I have held so dear no longer apply. Not since I sat with David Adler. Not since I found that body. Maybe even before that. As far back as early summer. I am outgrowing this life, these rules. Or they are outgrowing me. Downing the drink, I check my phone. There's an email from Roger, which includes some angry comments, found on a chat board and forwarded by Caleb, about a review of the family dramedy that ran late last week. (The kicker: "If these characters share DNA, couldn't they at least share the same play? Million-dollar idea: A 23andMe, just for genre.") Would I care to respond? No, I think as I drain the last of the vodka, I would not.

Out of the bar, onto a train and off it again, I plod east, straight into the wind, cheeks burning, then swing into the pharmacy for my typical prescription and out again, the bag rattling in my hand. As I turn onto my block, I notice a large man exiting my building at speed. Pilfering packages, maybe. Or chased away by one of the old Slavic women on the third floor. He passes me, and from under the hood of his windbreaker, I see, for just an instant, a streak of red, the brim of a cap. A coincidence, I tell myself, a fluke. But still I grip my keys more tightly, the barbs sticking out between each finger. I let myself in and slam the door closed behind me, then hurl myself up the stairs, ignoring my knees, my calves, my breath. Three locks unlocked and I'm inside, and it's only after I've drunk some water at the sink and rummaged in the cabinet for cereal dry enough to abrade the roof of my mouth that I see it, a folded piece of paper shoved beneath the door, a note from the management company, I assume. But the management company has never addressed me this way, in red permanent marker and with just two words, an imperative impossible for any theater critic. But I don't think that these words are about the theater. They're about the man who went missing. Or just possibly the man I found.

Here they are: STOP LOOKING.

7

LITTLE GLASS EYES

In the days after I discover the note, show openings crowd in, the pre-holiday rush, which means that I can busy myself every night. Barring the occasional coffee run, I spend the few sunlit hours indoors, huddled back against the pillows, laptop balanced on my thighs. These reviews take all day—I make them take all day—which saves me from thinking about anything else. Like a note. Or a body. Or a man who was maybe never there at all. As the cursor blinks, I spin inchoate images into paragraphs. I trace lines of argument, turning them around like skipping ropes, hopping this way and that until they no longer trip me. I let description thicken and thicken until it's all just cream. Nothing that I write is generous, none of it consoles. But this is the fault of the art, I tell myself, it's not mine. I can't pretend goodness or genius or truth where none exists. And yet something miserly has crept into my writing, something cruel that I can't soften no matter how many revisions I put myself through. Despite my hunger for the chief critic job, my critical instinct won't allow it.

Unfeeling. It's more or less my brand by now. Modus vivendi, too. And yet every night I hope for that click, that mimetic embrace, that rush of real emotion. I keep my eyes fixed below the proscenium arch. I look and look. But only in the dark. Where no one else can see me. I don't look for David Adler.

On a frigid Saturday without a matinee, Justine rings and I buzz her in. She canters upward, a coffee in each hand, and pushes past me, as I note her strange ability to make even woolly tights and a puffer coat seem sexy. Arranging herself on the bed—she knows better than to attempt the armchair—she tears the lid from a coffee with her teeth. I reach for the other and she pulls it away.

"Oh, did you want coffee, babe?" she says, fluttering her false lashes innocently. "These are both for me." She takes a sip from one and then opens the other and sips from that, too. "I can feel it working already. Mmm, nectar. But if you really need caffeine, put on your Sunday clothes and pretend like you enjoy my beautiful fucking company."

"It's Saturday," I say.

"I was quoting *Hello, Dolly!*, fuckface. Now pretty please do a decent approximation of a functioning human and get dressed."

"Fine," I say, slipping off my pajama pants and reaching for a pair of jeans. "I enjoy your beautiful fucking company. I adore it. I couldn't love it more if it came with a lifetime supply of triple-filtered vodka and a double date involving a young, gym-ripped Edmund Kean. Can I have my coffee now?"

"Sure," she says.

I taste it, then grimace. "There's sugar in it," I say.

Justine smiles. "Told you they were both for me, babe. If you want something drinkable, come outside and keep me company. I want to go to the flea market."

"It's too cold for the flea market."

"That just means it'll be less picked over."

Accepting the inevitable, I struggle into a sweater and boots.

"I haven't slept all night," she says, nudging a discarded *Playbill* with her toe. "I had an audition yesterday afternoon for that new production of *Winter's Tale* at Stage Right."

"Which part?"

"Paulina. Shakespeare's boss bitch, extremely my type. But then they asked me to read for Hermione. I hate Hermione, a victim who spends literally a decade and a half in hiding and then reunites with her abuser. Like, yay, happy ending! On the other hand, she has an absolute shitload of lines. The cold read went well, so I went out to celebrate. I called you," she says, working her lips into a pout, "but your phone was off. I had to go out all alone."

"I'm sure you weren't alone for long."

"Yeah, well," she says, hustling me toward the door, "I met some guys who do installation art with random building materials and they dragged me out to some loft party in Queens."

"I'm sorry?" I say, reaching for my coat. "I could have sworn you said Queens."

"I know, right? I've survived a night in an outer borough and lived to tell. It was sort of a drinks thing, but around two it turned into a dance party and when that got boring we went up to the roof and built a fire and watched the sunrise and then one of the guys took me out for blueberry pancakes. I fucking love pancakes."

"Are you going to see him again?"

"Of course not. He lives in Queens."

I lock every lock, then beeline to a street cart for a coffee that won't send me into insulin shock. Past the park, a handful of vendors have set up stalls in a disused parking lot, tables piled high with clothes and knickknacks, pages of vintage magazines riffling in the winter wind. My fingers go numb from the cold, and while Justine eyes a nightie here, a cameo there, I shove them into my pockets and let the rest of me go numb, too, let the stalls and the vendors and the curios recede until it feels as if I'm back in the theater's dark, watching a scene through a lit scrim. This is the self I like best—chill, distant, unloving and unloved.

Eventually, Justine finds a dress she wants to try on. She strips off her jacket and is about to unbutton her shirt when personal feelings about frostbite and public nudity demand I turn away. Suddenly, the hairs on my arms stand on end as I feel eyes rake over me. I turn and see a white man with a drooping blond mustache staffing a table to my right. He isn't the one watching me. It's his stock, an assortment of taxidermy animals. Their little glass eyes stare out at me, and in a raccoon with bared teeth, I can see my own eyes reflected back—glittering, impassive. I reach out a hand and brush the claws of some rodent, hunting that shrill spike of pain as a point jabs against my finger.

"You like the ferret?" the man asks.

"Sure," I say.

"I do 'em all myself," he says. "Right in my living room. I wash 'em real good, soak 'em in alcohol, stuff 'em full, and sew 'em right up. Bet you can't even see the stitch. The ferret's sixty bucks. But I'll take fifty. I trapped him right here in the Village."

I replace the animal on the table. "Thank you," I say. "I have all the ferrets I require."

I veer toward the other end of the market, to a card table piled with paperbacks. I'm running my finger along the green spines of some old Penguin mysteries when, once again, there's that prickling sensation at the back of my neck, a warning that I am being watched. Then there's a hand on my shoulder and I nearly scream, indifference shattered, but it's only Charlie, swathed in a navy peacoat with shining buttons, smiling his burnished grin.

"Hey," he says. "I didn't mean to startle you. I just wanted to thank you for the article. The online version was great and I picked up a print copy yesterday, which was even better. My mom bought like eight. We've already had a couple of extra calls about our effects."

"I'm glad," I say, recovering what composure I can. "The photographer did a nice job." Charlie's picture took up nearly a page, a frisky shot that showed him pointing a fog hose at the camera, biceps flexed. Should someone commission a "Men of the Theater" calendar, expect him to book March.

"*You* did a nice job. Really. Our marketing guy wants to use some of your lines on our site." He points to the book in my hand. "You like mysteries?"

"Depends," I say, setting the book back down. "Do you live around here?"

"Yeah, I'm over on Sixth between C and D. Me and a couple of the guys from the workshop are restoring this building—"

He might have told me more, but Justine appears at my arm and his speech falters. This is how most men respond to Justine.

"I bought the dress," she says. "It won't be so terrible once I raise the hem." She turns to Charlie. "I like to wear skirts short enough that the whole world's my gynecologist. My name's Justine."

"Charlie," he says. "And you're making me sorry I never stuck with premed."

"Charlie designs theatrical effects," I say. "I interviewed him for that piece on stage snow that just ran. Justine is an actress."

"Are you working on anything now?" he asks.

"I'm up for a part in *Winter's Tale*."

"That's a great one. I've always had this idea for how they could do the statue. . . ."

I wander away, content to let them trade notes on tragicomedy, but Charlie takes a step toward me.

"Hey, I was just wondering, do you want to grab lunch or something? When you're done here?"

"Oh, thanks," I say. And I'm about to invent a load of laundry that desperately needs the delicate cycle when Justine interrupts me.

"Absolutely," she says. "We'd love to. We're starving."

"What about those pancakes *we* had?" I ask, mouth tight like a freshly stretched drum.

"That was hours ago. And in another borough."

Justine says she's happy for Charlie to choose the place and that we eat everything, even though neither of us eats much of anything. Charlie leads us to a building on Second Avenue and then down a linoleum hallway lit with buzzing fluorescents. He shoves open a heavy glass door and we find ourselves in a Ukrainian café that smells of dill and stewed fruit. A grandmotherly woman in a peasant blouse ushers us into a booth with patched benches in a doubtful shade of prune. Justine slides into one side and then places her bag beside her so that I'm forced to share a bench with Charlie. We've only just received menus and water tumblers when Justine stands again.

"Oh my God," she says. "I completely forgot. I have an appointment and I'll be brutally fucking late if I don't get the train right now."

I'm immediately suspicious. Justine is rarely forgetful. Or punctual. "What kind of appointment?"

"Hair."

"But you just got it cut."

"Waxing. Hair waxing."

"Can I talk to you for a second?" I squeeze out of the booth and we huddle near the restaurant door. "Want to explain the less than competent subterfuge?"

"Are you dumb or new or still just totally fucking anhedonic?" she says, making her I-can't-even face. "Babe, all this guy wants to do is gaze at you passionately over stew or whatever. I'm in the way."

"I'm not interested in passion. Or stew."

"Could you maybe just try and have a good fucking time for once?"

"I don't like good times."

"Tough," she says. "Because I like them for you. I'm leaving."

"Wait!" I say. "Do you have a way to get more of those sleeping pills? My shrink won't give me a prescription. Apparently my history is a semaphore with all red flags."

"I'm seeing the bad doctor tonight. I'll ask."

Then she's through the glass door and gone. As I reverse back to the booth, I contemplate making a similar excuse, but I see Charlie sitting there, looking boyish and sweet and a little forlorn. Some tendril of the nice girl I used to be surfaces and I slide in across from him, along vinyl so stiff and grooved it resembles a long-play record. Then I do what I have to. I pretend it's a scene. I'm a girl on a date—a little nervous, a little giddy. I laugh. I smile. I make a show of asking his advice about the menu. I try not to think that this is who I might have been, in a different show, in a different life.

As I counterfeit, I push some cabbage around the plate in a way that resembles eating and I keep Charlie occupied with cheerful questions about his work, which he answers between bites of sausage. The performance goes over well, at least until I press for even more details about confetti cannons. Then Charlie shakes his head. He smiles at me, kindness crinkling the corners of his eyes. "Hey," he said. "I didn't take you to lunch so we could do another interview. That first one was great. But this time I thought we could just relax."

If he wants me to relax, I'll need something stronger than cabbage. "Sorry," I say. "I overdosed on caffeine this morning. I'm maybe a little wired."

"And not that hungry," he said, pointing to my nearly full plate. "Do you want to take that to go?"

"Not really."

"Do you mind if I bring the meat home for my cats?"

"Of course I don't mind. You have cats?" Of course he has cats.

He pays the check and insists on walking me home, steering me past the postbrunch crowds with ease, shortening his long, swiveling stride until it matches my own. When his shoulder forces a gentle collision with mine I can feel his heat on my skin, even through coat and sweater and shirt.

We're on Avenue A and nearing my building when we pass a magic supply shop called the Mystery Box. The logo on the window shows two disembodied hands wielding a handkerchief and a wand. Charlie doubles back.

"Do you know this place?" he asks.

"I've passed it plenty. But I've never been in."

"I was a kid magician," he says. "Did it for years, talent shows, birthday parties. Then I turned sixteen. Got interested in girls. Hung up the top hat. But I still like to check out the stock once in a while. Do you mind?"

Before I can refuse, Charlie puts a gentle hand on the small of my back and propels me through the open door and past the velvet curtain that hangs beyond, plunging me into a room that resembles a bordello for the dead: black walls, display cases skirted in purple plush, red lampshades casting a sanguinary glow.

Charlie chats with the owner, a squat man with bright eyes and unnaturally pink cheeks, wearing a lopsided toupee. I mill around, pausing before a glass cabinet that holds a straitjacket Houdini allegedly escaped from. The sight turns my stomach, conjures a hazy memory of straps during my time on the ward, and I retreat, sliding into a folding chair set against the store's back wall and gripping the edges of the seat. *It's all right,* I tell myself. *These are your fingers. This is your hand—*

Charlie reappears at my side, one arm curled behind his back. "I've got a surprise," he says, grinning.

I bring the room back into focus and arrange my mouth into something like a smile. "Is it a rabbit?" I ask.

"No," he says. "Check this out."

He whips his arm around and reveals a small knife. The blade gleams bleakly in the shop's low light.

Before I can stop him, he sinks it into his chest, level with his heart.

I would scream, but my throat has closed and my mouth has stilled and as I move to stand, blackness rushes up and over me. A wave. A wall. A mountain of night. I fall as though I'm stabbed, too.

When my eyes open again, I'm back in the chair with Charlie kneeling at my feet and the store owner, his toupee now even more askew, bending over and offering me a murky glass of water.

"Are you okay, miss?" he asks in a voice that squeaks like new tennis shoes.

I'm not. But I nod and busy myself with small, regular sips.

"I am so, so sorry," says Charlie. "It was a stupid joke." He picks up the knife and I inhale sharply, turning my head away, not wanting to see. "Vivian, please. Look at me. It's okay. I promise."

Reluctantly, I shift my gaze back. "It's a trick knife," he says. "A theater prop. Stage combat stuff. That's why I thought you'd like it. It only looks like metal. It's actually plastic. The blade retracts into the handle." Carefully, he rests the point of the knife against the flat of his hand and I watch as the blade slides slowly, noiselessly, into the grip. He releases the blade, then vanishes it again.

"It's just a trick," he says. "An illusion."

Tentatively I reach for the knife. My hand is shaking; I still it. Charlie lays it on my palm and I close my fingers over it, then point it downward and press it into my thigh, like Portia in *Julius Caesar*. There's no incision, no pain, just a soft, dull pressure as the handle drives into my leg. At the base of the handle I notice a small latch.

"What's this for?"

"Stage blood. You fill the reservoir and when the knife fully depresses, the liquid releases. That way you don't need blood packs."

I laugh in a way that isn't exactly mirthful. "Good effect."

"No, it was stupid. I'm sorry. I'll put it back."

"No," I say, "I want it. I'm buying it."

Outside I accept Charlie's arm as we walk the last two blocks to my building. He keeps glancing over at me, brow furrowed in concern. "Don't look so anxious," I say. "I'm fine. Really. I startle more easily than I should."

"But you fainted."

"I'm the first girl who's ever swooned in your arms? Charlie. Impossible."

He doesn't look any less worried. I try to leave him at the door, but when I mention I'm on the fifth floor he insists on walking up with me. And I consent. Because I want to numb myself again, to forget the fainting, the fright, the horror of what I believed was another loss. A pill takes thirty minutes to kick in, and alcohol—unless it's the sort of moonshine that might blind you—doesn't work more quickly. Sex is the fastest way to stillness that I know.

"Come in," I say. "Do you want something to drink? There's a bottle of wine somewhere."

"It's a little early for me," he says, smiling as he notices the poster of *The Changeling* near my bed.

"But it's Saturday. We could have begun at ten a.m. with eggs Benedict and Bloody Marys. When you think about it, we're actually late."

"All right," he says, falling into the armchair before I can warn him. "You've convinced me."

I locate the pinot noir in my dresser drawer, nestling cozily among some sweaters, and slosh generous amounts into mismatched tumblers, then hand one to Charlie. Careful not to spill, I arrange myself against the pillows on the bed.

"Don't suffer in that chair," I say. "I picked it up at the vintage place on Ludlow and as soon as I brought it home all the springs committed suicide." I gesture to the pillows next to me. "The bed's much more comfortable."

He looks uncertain. Which is expected, but also very boring.

So I widen my eyes into a pair of perfect, blinking orbs and attempt something that passes for distress. "Charlie, that thing in the store. I feel so silly about the way I acted, but the truth is, I'm still a little spooked. Would you hold me?"

"Oh," he says. "I mean. Sure, yes, of course." He sets his wineglass down and I do the same, though I drain mine first. After kicking off his shoes, he lowers himself tentatively onto the pillows, opening his arms so that I can slide between them, press myself into his chest, and feel the beating of his heart, so regular and assured. Half-soothed already, I raise my face and cover his lips with my own, kissing him softly at first and then more deeply as I press against his hips and feel him hard through his jeans. I reach for his belt and he stops me.

"Vivian, I—"

I don't let him finish. "Please. It's what I want." There's cruelty in this. In shattering his idea of the woman he imagines me to be. Charlie is the first man I've met in ages who doesn't want the pert pose, he wants what's underneath. But of course there's nothing underneath. And Charlie is too much of a gentleman to refuse. So I unbuckle his belt and unzip his jeans. Then I slip out of my own. It's warm in the apartment—too warm—but I pull the duvet up over us, silencing him with another kiss as I take him in my hand and then guide him inside me.

It's this moment I love best, like that strange suspension when the houselights fall and the stagelights rise and I'm poised—for an instant—between one world and the next.

He hovers above me, supporting his weight on his knees and elbows so he won't crush me as he moves. But I want to feel him against me, forcing me into the mattress so fiercely that my lungs empty and I have to gasp for every breath. I wrap my arms around him to press him down.

"Vivian," he says, "look at me."

And I do, opening my eyes too wide, blurring the focus so that his face softens into a smudge. Then I let them drift closed again and go somewhere beyond thought until it's just skin and lips and his fingers working between my legs and then my whole body is shuddering and so is his.

As soon as my breathing slows, I slide away and slip into the bathroom, where I wet a cloth and clean myself, then tug a robe from its hook. Fastening the belt, I return to the room. Charlie reaches out to pull me back into bed.

The golden hair on his arms and chest glimmers even in the weak December light. Shaw said that as long as more people would pay to see a naked body than a naked brain, drama would languish. But even Shaw might have paid to see Charlie. There's material for a dozen plays in the arc of his shoulder, the muscle of his chest. But I resist it, perching at the edge of the mattress, my ankles primly crossed.

"Charlie," I say, "I know this is miserable timing, absolutely the worst, but I'm behind on an article—ridiculously behind—and I need the rest of the afternoon to work."

"Oh," he says, "well, I've got some invoices in my bag that I can—"

I smile with all the sweetness I can feign, which isn't much. "No, I'm sorry, I don't work well if anyone else is here. The place is just too small."

"Sure," he says. He ducks his head and reaches for his jeans.

"But thank you for lunch and . . . well . . ." I shape my lips into a rueful smile. "I don't feel scared anymore."

"Well, that's good, I guess." He has his coat on now and he looks as though he would like to be angry with me, but he isn't sure why. Or how.

I stand on my tiptoes and I kiss him again. "It's very good." Then I direct him toward the door. "Okay," I say. "I'll see you soon."

"But I don't even have your number," he says from the threshold. "Your texts just come in as Anonymous."

"That's okay. I have yours. I'll call you. Or I'll text you mine. Definitely." With that I close the door against him, securing each of the locks with a triplicate clunk. As I turn back to the bed, my eye finds the red bag from the Mystery Box. I pick it up and remove the knife, then press it down on my hand, my knee, my throat, marveling how each time I'm left unbloodied, unscathed. I catch a glimpse of myself in the mirror hung on the closet door—hair tumbled, half-naked, clutching a knife. I look dangerous.

Maybe I am.

Because I remember what Chekhov said. That if you introduce a weapon in an early act, you'll have to use it in the final one.

8

UNSPOOLED

In the city, everyone performs. Excepting the very rich and the very crazy, a person can't just walk Manhattan's grid as some gaping maw of need and id. Urban life demands a veneer, a pose. Esteban's—a swirl of hypercompetence, flair, and poise—is more practiced than most. Interns worship him. Assistant editors fear him. At last year's Christmas party, he seemed to have the whole of the sales division in his thrall. He's protective of me (I spoil him with the occasional eye shadow palette), which means that he passes along only the messages that he assumes are crucial. Or funny. Or from eligible men.

So when he phones late on a Wednesday afternoon, two weeks before Christmas, I answer.

"Some lady is here looking for you, gorgeous," he says in a shrill stage whisper. "And she's starting to freak my shit out, so get here quick."

"What lady?" I ask him.

"Doesn't want to give a name. Says she has something for you. I show her the basket for packages—nice, like I do—but she says she has to put it into your actual pretty hands. Are they pretty, bebita? You go to that manicure place like I told you? You start to practice some basic self-care?"

"Sure," I say. "I had them put your picture on both middle fingers. But Esteban, she's probably just dropping off some production swag. Which you're welcome to, by the way. Can't you get rid of her?"

"Think I didn't try? You know how hard I work to keep this reception area sexy. I gave her bitch face number six. El ultimo. No reaction. And building security won't make her go just because bad style hurts my eyes, so get your flat ass into the office now. Okay, my love?"

"Fine. I will. Give me fifteen minutes," I say.

"Buy this sad, parched thing a kombucha on your way?"

"Twenty minutes."

When I arrive with Esteban's drink, I find him alone.

"Where is she?" I ask.

He takes the kombucha from me and negotiates a straw with long, turquoise nails. "The ladies'. Maybe giving herself another dose." He leans toward me. "She's got pupils smaller than my ex's dick, and that was a thing invisible to the naked eye, bebita."

I remember Esteban's ex, a bouncer at a club in the meatpacking district with a shoulder span rivaling the average biplane. But just as I'm readying myself to murmur something consoling, a young white woman steps through the door to reception, her hair a mat of greasy blond, her face the mismatched angles of some cubist cartoon. The down-filled folds of a black puffer coat swallow her frame, but her neck and ankles suggest a build that would make a swizzle stick feel chubby. And as Esteban suggested, her pupils have shrunk to pinpricks on which not many angels could dance.

"Are you, like, Vivian?" she asks. When she says my name, her voice breaks like a mirror already wrecking your luck.

"I am. And you are?"

She has to think about it for a while. "Polly," she replies. "I'm Polly."

I try to steer her toward the sofa in reception, but behind her back Esteban makes a series of increasingly obscene gestures warding me away. It's going to take some luxury foot treatment before I'm back in his good books.

So I motion Polly forward. "Come through," I say, punching in the security code. We enter the office proper, navigating the warren of desks until we reach one of the oppressively neutral conference rooms that HR uses to hand you a tissue and discuss your severance package. I sit at one side of a table topped in dull white laminate. She jackknifes her body into a chair opposite and busies herself with a hangnail on her right thumb. Finally, she pulls it free with her teeth and I can see a drop of blood beading from the torn skin. Before she can mutilate herself any further, I begin.

"I understand you were asking for me, Polly? I should tell you that if it's about a show, email is best. And really it's much better to send the press release to my editor. He's the one who does all the assigning. Do you have his address?"

"No," she says. She looks at me fuzzily, as if there's a wall of cotton wool stretched between her and the rest of the room. Then, at last, some faraway synapse fires. "Wait. A show?"

I nod helpfully.

"You mean, like, a movie or a play or something? Oh. Right. You do theater?"

"Yes," I say. "I 'do' theater. Isn't that why you're here?"

"No," she says, swiveling back and forth in her chair. "Not at all. Didn't that guy out front explain? It's because I have your thing. I found it just before Thanksgiving. And like, I know I should have got it back to you sooner, but I had to, like, go home for a while." She darts her eyes toward the door, then increases her swiveling. "I had some problems."

The kinds of problems that come in glassine bags.

"But I'm starting college again. Like, I just had a meeting with the dean. And as long as I was here, I thought I should find you, but I didn't know how exactly? And then this friend of mine was like, try online, and I was like, online's so big. But I entered your name and I found you super easy, so I came over."

Her swiveling has made me motion sick. "You did. And thank you. But what do you mean, 'my thing'? I haven't lost anything." Not counting my emotional life, an integrated self, the ability to sleep through the night without a pill. But those aren't the sorts of things a girl drops on the platform of the Second Avenue subway.

In some hazy, remote way, this seems to upset her. "You have, though. I mean, it's yours. It has to be. It has, like, your name on it."

I've never gone in for hand-sewn labels or monograms. "Polly," I say, nearly snapping my fingers. "Focus. Just what is it that I'm supposed to have lost, please?"

She reaches into a frayed army surplus bag and pulls out a black rectangle that looks like a garage door opener. I have never owned a garage door opener. Or a garage.

"I'm sorry," I say. "But whatever this is, it isn't mine."

And I'm right. But then again so is she. Because she turns it over. And I see that it's a minicassette recorder, the kind that no one uses anymore. No one except David Adler. It's his, of course. His material artifact. Polly clicks a button and the tiny tape pops up. "See, the tape has your name on it," she says. "Like, right there."

In small script, ornate and almost feminine, I can just make out my name and the date of our interview. Polly and the tape and the room suddenly feel very far away. She's still speaking, but her cracked voice has begun to sound distant, echoing.

I reach for the recorder. The outstretched hand feels like someone else's, but it closes around the plastic all the same. "Thank you. It isn't mine. Not exactly. But I know whose it is. Where did you find it?" I ask.

"By the dorm on Third Ave. The one near the falafel place? There's this thing in the street, separating the lanes, like, this triangle, with grass? I just saw it there. And I took it, because, like, don't be mad, but I thought maybe I could sell it. Then I checked online and it's, like, not even worth anything. But I was thinking you'd be really glad to have it back. Like maybe you'd give me a reward?"

"Yes, of course. Thanks for dropping it by. I'll see that it's returned." I let fall the recorder into my bag. And then, to speed her on her way, I take out my wallet and liberate a $20, which flutters like some wounded bird toward Polly's side of the table. "That should buy you some school supplies," I say.

"Do you even know what school supplies cost?" She crumples the $20 into a yawning pocket of her coat.

"Excuse me a moment," I say. I turn away from Polly and take out my phone, then search the call log for the approximate day, just after

Thanksgiving, that I phoned Irina. I find an unrecognized number—hers, I believe—with the one that must be Levitz's following just behind.

I slide the bar to message her and peck out a text: Have David's recorder. The one he used in the interview. A student found it with my name on the tape. Can I return it to you?

Having hit send, I exhale and then spin back toward Polly. "Okay," I say, "all set. Let me walk you out."

I make to stand, but Polly stays seated, a pallid deer in headlights.

"There's one more thi-ing," she says, stretching out that last word into two keening syllables. "Something you should know. I listened to it and, I'm like, so, so sorry."

Maybe I ought to apologize, too. No undergraduate should have to hear my opinions on the avant-garde. But she doesn't sound bored or embarrassed. She sounds frightened. So I make my voice just as stern and dean-of-students as I can. "Polly," I say, "what do you mean? You listened to the tape of my interview, fine. What is it you think you heard?"

"No," she says. "I can't. It's like—No. You should really just listen to it." All the cotton wool has blown away and Polly looks at me unclouded, nakedly afraid. Then she stumbles from the room like an arrow loosed from some wobbling bow. I see her take a wrong turn near the production department, then she course-corrects and has sped through the edit cubicles and out the glass door before I can rouse myself to catch her.

I look at the recorder in my hand. Dull, inert. I try to tell myself that Polly must be suffering from some drug-induced paranoia or an undergraduate's tendency to overdramatize. But I'm not sure I believe it.

I sit back down in the chair. I hit play.

The sound quality is wretched, a breaking wave, a windstorm. But I can just make out the clinking of silverware and the placid crash of cups against saucers. The noise of the patisserie. Then I hear David Adler's quavering voice—grainy, worlds away—ask, "First up, how did you become a critic?" I let the tape spool forward for a few minutes more, cringing when I hear my voice—too quick, too high—and my shatterproof laugh. I don't understand why the tape scared Polly so badly. Or scared her at all.

I rewind and play the opening minutes again and then again, studying it the way I used to study scripts for acting classes, parsing each syllable and word and phrase. None of them sound upsetting. But what if there's something else on the tape, around and behind the words, something that wasn't meant to be recorded? I listen again. But the poor sound quality—no to mention the likely effects of too many jukebox musicals—means that I can't hear anything beneath our dialogue. I stop the tape.

Smoothing my hair and spackling a friendly expression to my face, I leave the conference room and turn down the hall. I drift past the dingy kitchenette, where a frozen dinner rotates glumly in the microwave, then through production and into editorial. I check Roger's cubicle, but he must have gone for an early lunch. So I recalculate and head for the narrow office that holds Jesse, the music editor. I find him sprawled in a desk chair. His feet, shod in Japanese-import sneakers, are astride his keyboard, his head leans back against a signed poster of an eighties hair metal band. His headphones are on, his eyes closed, his face empty, dreaming.

Jesse took dreadful advantage of me under a drafting table at the Christmas party two years ago. Or maybe I took advantage of him. They had very strong punch that year.

I clear my throat, and when that fails I walk around the desk and sock him in the arm in a way I hope he finds playful. "Oh, hey," he says, swinging his feet to the floor and sitting up straight. He is trying to look casual and he is plainly failing. "Haven't seen you in a while, Viv."

"I know," I say, thinning my lips toward sympathy. "It's been just ages. Hey, can I ask you a favor?"

"What kind of a favor?" Maybe I imagine the anxiety in his voice. Maybe not.

"Can I borrow your headphones?" I hold up the recorder. "I'm trying to listen back to an interview and the built-in speaker makes everything sound like it's coming through ten layers of Styrofoam peanuts and asbestos."

"Yeah, of course, you bet," he says. "They're Bluetooth, but I have a cable somewhere." He rummages in a drawer and then hands everything to me as quickly as he can. The succubus Jesse believes me to be might have come for his body or his soul. He doesn't mind if I walk away with his audio equipment.

Back in the conference room, I plug the headphones into the recorder and play the tape again. This time much of the buzzing falls away and behind David's voice, behind my own, I can just pick out the conversation at a neighboring table. Something about a dress on sale. At Bendel's? At Bloomingdale's? I can also hear the chime of the old-fashioned register and someone's ringtone. Nothing clandestine. Nothing dangerous.

I'm listening so intently that I let the tape run farther than before, startling when I hear a violent noise like a record scratched by a dentist's drill.

And then I don't hear the café anymore.

Traffic noise suggests a street or a sidewalk. I hear a girl's shrieking laugh and a plume of reggae from a shop doorway. Then a man's voice, thick and harsh, like a barbed-wire milkshake, says, "Come on, Davey. We know you got it."

And then another voice, David Adler's, but piccolo now, more fretful than I'd heard it in life, says, "I don't know what you're talking about."

"Don't go playing games with me, Davey."

"I'm not. I don't—Look, just leave me alone."

"Can't do that, Davey. But hey, I'm a nice guy, so I'm gonna give you a choice here. We can do this the easy way or we can do it hard. You ask me, Davey, I think you're gonna like the easy way. That's the one I like, too. The hard way just makes me tired." And then there's a noise like someone savaging a roll of bubble packing. Or maybe a man's knuckles cracking.

"I don't know what you mean," says David Adler.

"Yeah you do, Davey. Just give us what you got. Nice and easy. If you don't got it on you, just show us how to get to it and okay, all done, you never have to see my great-lookin' face again."

"But I can't give it to you. There isn't anything to give. I didn't do anything! I don't even know what you—No, come on. Oh my God. Oh my Christ. Please don't. Please!"

He's screaming then. I hear one dull thud and another, like dough being punched down in the back room of some grimy pizzeria. Then David Adler's voice snuffs out, replaced by the greasy purr of traffic and a reggae singer insisting, beyond all evidence to the contrary, that every little thing is going to be all right.

I listen for ten minutes more, my hands clutching the lip of the table so tight my nail beds turn white, then red. But there are no more words to hear. Finally, with dead and fumbling fingers, I turn the tape over and hit play again. The other side is virgin, silent. And still I let it play while I think the recording through. The man on the tape must be one of the thugs hired by Luck Be a Lady. Jake mentioned some heavies who searched David Adler's desk and roughed him up. Seems like one of them decided to get a little rougher. Maybe the same one who would later walk into my building and slide a note beneath my door.

Was the man looking for the program David Adler wrote that skimmed money from the site? Had he stored it on some kind of an external drive? Did he turn that drive over after this presumed beating? Did he refuse? And if he did refuse, what became of him then? My mind can't help flitting toward the cement plants along the Gowanus, the crumbling piers off the West Side Highway, the burned-out buildings of the South Bronx. Even in a city as crowded as New York, there are so very many places to hide a body if you don't want that body found.

Without a body, without answers, I am left with this tape. I now understand that I can't risk giving it to Irina. She might turn it over to her father, and the tape suggests what her father does to people who have things they shouldn't have, who know things they shouldn't know. It is problem enough that I have texted her, unthinking. Could the man who assaulted David Adler have known that he was being recorded? Could he have told Irina's father? What will these men do to me if they discover that I have this recording?

So Irina can't have the tape. The same goes for Jake. But I can't destroy it. Not yet. I owe David Adler that much. And I owe myself something, too. Having heard my voice on the tape, having found that note beneath my door, I understand that I have some further part to play in this. And some awful, needful part of me wants to play it. For now, though, I keep the role quite small.

I call the police.

"Hello," says the receptionist. "Is this an emergency?"

"More like a tragicomedy," I tell her. "Or just possibly a farce."

Receptionists, it turns out, don't really care about genre. After a brief précis of the situation, she tells me to just come to the station, and with a rushed farewell to Esteban, I hurry out of the building and into the bright day, the recorder clutched in both my hands, walking fast enough that I won't have to think about where my feet are taking me and why.

9

CRIMINAL CODE

I like rituals. I like routines. The man at the corner Chinese place knows my order. A few bartenders will mix my vodka gimlet before both my feet are through the door. So it's a wintry kind of comfort to find myself back at the same police station, in that same scarred interview room, staring across the table at Paul Destine, who looks more hawklike than ever. This time he's joined by a partner, who introduces herself with a finger-crushing handshake as Detective Lutzky. She's a foot shorter than Destine, with dyed blond hair pulled back into a low ponytail and broad shoulders straining against a purple sweater. She wears foundation a shade lighter than the umber skin of her neck; a slash of pink lipstick gores her mouth. I have seen brick outhouses with more obviously feminine attributes.

"Nice to see you back again so soon, Ms. Parry," Destine says.

"The decor, the ambience, I couldn't stay away."

"Paul brought me up to speed," says Lutzky. "You're the girl who found the overdose in Tompkins Square. This about that?"

"No," I say. "This is something else entirely. I have evidence." I place the recorder on the table with a small plastic clatter. "I believe it relates to a missing persons case. The one I asked you about the other week," I say to Destine. "Rhetorically."

"Rhetorically," he echoes. "How could I forget." He looks down at the recorder. "What's this evidence, Ms. Parry? What's all of this about?"

"I'm hoping you'll tell me," I say.

I take a deep breath, letting the air in through my nose and then out through my mouth, just as I used to do, circled up at the start of every scene study class. I force my shoulders down from their perch somewhere near the ceiling. Then I begin.

"I'm a journalist," I say, "a theater critic. A month or so ago a grad student named David Adler asked to interview me for a paper that he was writing. I agreed. We met. A couple of weeks later, a woman claiming to be his fiancée called and told me that he had disappeared and that I may have been the last person to have seen him. She had me speak to a private investigator and the P.I. informed me that David Adler also worked for an internet gambling site and that his boss had fired him earlier on that same day that he met with me, because the boss thought that he'd written a program to skim money from the site. That was the last I'd heard of him until earlier today, when a girl brought me the recorder he'd used during our interview. The label on the tape still inside had my name on it. I played the tape. I think you should hear it."

I see Lutzky flash Destine a crabby look that says she didn't go into public service to deal with uppity cranks like me. Destine's lips pull back from his teeth as he says, "You want us to listen to your interview?"

"It's more than just my interview. There's something else on the tape. An assault, I believe, or maybe worse." As I speak, I can feel that my jaw has clenched, hear my teeth clacking against one another like stacks of dominoes. "Will you please just listen?"

Lutzky sighs, shaking her head. But Destine nods. I turn the tape over and press play. The sound of my own voice, tinny as it issues from the cheap speakers, makes me hit fast-forward until I hear that violent shredding. I press stop, then play. Lutzky's brow furrows as the tape unspools; Destine sits up straighter in his chair. When only the traffic and reggae remain, I stop the tape.

"It goes on like that until the end," I say. "Just music and street noise. And there's nothing on the other side. I played it through."

Lutzky pulls a small spiral notebook from her pocket, a double of my own reporter's pad, and says, "What did you say the guy's name was? The one who interviewed you?"

"David Adler."

"And what did you say his age was?"

"I'm not sure. About mine, I think. Anywhere from late twenties to mid-thirties."

"Did he have any identifying characteristics?"

"You mean like a pronounced limp or six fingers on his right hand or scarring from a knife attack in childhood?"

She nods expectantly.

I shake my head. "Brown hair. Caucasian. Medium height. Medium build. Medium everything. Dark eyes. Glasses."

Lutzky pushes away her chair and hefts her bulk upward as if she's looking to stow it in some overhead bin. "I'll check the system," she tells Destine, smacking the door open as though it just made a crack about her sweater.

"So, Ms. Parry," Destine says when we're alone. "A dead man and a missing one. You seem to attract a lot of trouble."

"Guess I have a type," I say. "What's your partner doing?"

"Plugging the name and the description into our database. Seeing what turns up. You said this guy was fired from some online company?"

"Luck Be a Lady, I think it's called. From what the P.I. told me, the fiancée, the one who first contacted me, she also happens to be the boss's daughter, so—"

"So could be he did write this program or could be Daddy decided to change the wedding plans?"

"It occurred to me, yes. He's the one paying for the P.I. But the P.I. seemed like the kind of guy you hire when maybe you don't want a missing person found."

"You're a smart girl when you want to be, aren't you?" he says, his smile narrow, his eyes hooded.

"I've been called worse."

Lutzky bustles back into the room. "I checked the computer," she says. "There's nothing on this guy."

"What do you mean, 'nothing'?" I ask.

"He's got no record, no priors. There's a David Adler in the system with a pair of convictions for bad checks. But unless this one"—she gestures toward the recorder—"looks real good for fifty-eight, he's not our guy. All I get when I run what you gave me is a lot of blank screen."

"I never said he was a criminal. I said he's missing. Or maybe worse, depending on what 'the hard way' means. Shouldn't you be trying to find him? Or find whoever wanted to hurt him?"

"We can't find him if he isn't lost," she says, plopping back down with a grimace. "And he isn't. Not according to the system."

"But how is that possible?" Then I remember that first conversation with Irina. How she told me that the police turned her away before she could file a report. "No, that's right," I say. "His fiancée said that she tried to register his disappearance and that the duty cop told her that she couldn't, that she wasn't family, and that when a man that age goes missing it's on purpose and that probably he didn't want to marry her. She was still crying about it days later. What else do you people do for fun around here? Shove old ladies into traffic? Stone treed cats?"

"Maybe he doesn't get a decoration for sensitivity," Destine says, splaying his fingers on the table, each tendon a whetted edge, "but the officer told her the truth. It's like I said before. Men that age don't just vanish. Either they disappear on purpose—"

"Or they're dead," I say flatly. "A possibility this tape allows. Shouldn't you explore that?"

"There's no case here and there's no missing person, not officially," Lutzky says. "There's bupkis to explore."

I'm tempted to remind her that my tax dollars pay her salary. But I'm a junior critic. My tax dollars barely keep her in powdered creamer.

"And if he's dead," she continues, "there's not a whole heck of a lot we can do until some lucky so-and-so finds a body. But don't worry," she says, smiling in a way that shows the smear of pink lipstick on her front teeth, "bodies have a way of turning back up. And when they do, we'll find out who's responsible. Until then, this Daniel Adler guy isn't our problem."

"David," I say needlessly. "It's David." I gesture to the recorder on the table. "What should I do about this?"

"Whatever you want," Lutzky says, flipping her notebook closed. "Keep it, toss it, use it as a goddamn bottle opener. There's no crime. This isn't evidence. We're done here." With that she pushes out of the room. The door slams behind her like a rifle report.

I'm left alone with Destine. "Courtesy, professionalism, and respect?" I ask.

"She's good at her job," he says, rising from his chair. "Not so good at public relations. Long as you're here, why don't I grab the statement on Mendoza. You can sign it and be on your way. You want to call that friend of yours to come and pick you up?"

Of course he remembers Justine. Almost any man would. "I don't plan on fainting today," I say. "So I can see myself home. Besides, she's at a callback."

"An actress, huh? You're one, too, you know."

"Not for years."

"Not how I call it. You give me a straight response maybe one time in ten. Probably my partner didn't notice, but I did. You're faking it."

"I never fake it," I say, arms folded. "It gives men a false sense of expertise."

"You're good, you're funny, but you just keep making jokes so that no one will see what's going on underneath."

"And what's that?" I ask.

"That you're just some lost little girl," he says, smiling that same raptor smile. "Scared, too."

"Scared of what?" I say. But without conviction.

"That's what I'd like to find out," he says. He's looming over me now, enfolding me in his shadow.

I arrange my features into something like hauteur and shove the recorder back into my bag. "Like your partner said, we're done here." But before I've stood fully, Destine has his hand on my arm, easing me out of my chair.

"Take it easy, Ms. Parry. You said you weren't supposed to stand up too fast."

Grudgingly, I let him pull me upright.

"I'm not sure I like you going home alone," he says.

"I live close. I'm pretty sure I can make it. Even if I have to stop to swoon."

"My shift's up in just a minute. If you don't want an escort, how about a drink?"

"Isn't there something about that in the handbook? Fraternizing with witnesses?"

"You heard what my partner said. No case. No crime." He eyes me in that avian way, the blue of his irises so startling against his skin. "No witnesses."

I don't like that look. Or maybe I like it too much.

"Fine," I say, "but somewhere close. And only if you're buying."

He brings me by his desk, where I quickly ink my witness statement, then takes me to the bar around the corner, a moldy, moody place lit by the jukebox and a set of Christmas lights flickering above the bar. I order a shot of bourbon. Destine asks for the same and we take the drinks to a small table with wobbling legs. In the interview room I had noticed a gold wedding band on his left hand. His fingers are bare now.

I down the drink. "Another?" he says. Without waiting for my answer, he heads back to the bar. And when he slides the glass toward me, I don't say no.

"How long have you been a detective?" I ask.

"A few years. I was in vice for a while and before that, uniform."

"Did the ladies love a man in it?"

"That was more vice. And I don't know that I would call them ladies. Now how does a nice girl like you find herself in all this trouble?"

"Nice?" I say, holding his gaze. "That's sweet. And everyone needs a hobby. Macramé never did a lot for me. But let's talk about my non-case and this non-disappearance. If David Adler didn't disappear, if he isn't missing, then what do you think happened to him?"

"Sweetheart, can't you just forget about all that?"

"No," I say. I haven't told him about the note beneath the door. The threat that it implies. A threat that the tape has made more real. Because if I were to admit to frailty or peril, I wouldn't admit it to Paul Destine. "Let's say I can't. Rhetorically."

"Well, let's see. Maybe he did get tired of his fiancée."

"And maybe Christopher Marlowe wrote all of Shakespeare's plays, some of them posthumously. You heard the tape. What do you really think?"

He shrugs. "Maybe his boss had someone take him out. More likely he got real afraid of what his boss's someone might do and took the first Metro-North out of town. But I can't say for sure. Not enough to go on."

"What would you do next? If this were a real case. If you were really assigned to it."

"Go to his work and talk to his boss. Talk to his friends who aren't the fiancée. See if I can get a warrant for his cell phone, bank account, access to the computers he used."

I remember what Irina said about his personal computer. "But what if he cleared his search history?"

"Our techs can usually handle that. Nothing's ever really gone."

Some things are. Some people.

"But I'm just spitballing here," he says. "Understand, Ms. Parry? Leave the investigating to guys like me. You're a nice girl or yeah, okay, maybe you aren't so nice. Either way you don't want to get yourself involved with anything like this."

Then I have that strange sensation, that prickling at the back of my neck as through someone is watching me from far away. I duck my eyes and lean into Destine, inhaling his particular musk—whiskey, sandalwood, rain on pavement. "What should I get involved with?" I say.

Under the table he grabs my wrist and he holds it, hard enough to bruise. He jerks his head toward my drink. "You want one more?"

"No," I say.

He helps me out of my chair and escorts me from the bar, a hand on the small of my back. We walk quickly and in silence. If we spoke now, I might think better of it. I might tell him to go. But I don't want to think.

As he continues down Avenue A, skirting the park, I realize that he hasn't asked for an address or directions. He already knows the way. He's leading me home. I pull away from him. "How do you know where I live?"

"You told me. That initial interview."

"And you remembered it all this time?"

"Don't sell yourself short, sweetheart."

I unlock the outer door and he marches me up the stairs, so fast I think I might fall. As we near the third floor, one of the Slavic women opens her door a crack, but she shuts it abruptly as we pass and I can hear the sound of bolts and chains.

He's on me before we even reach the bed.

And when he leaves an hour later, with bruises on my breasts and the taste of him all through me, I'm drained and raw and perfectly numb. Shrouded in the top sheet, I see him to the door and turn the locks after him. Then I take the recorder from my bag, hit rewind, then play, then record, pushing the button down, down, down, until the tape clicks off, the side exhausted and now entirely blank. I'll pretend that I found it this way. That I heard nothing. That there was nothing to hear.

But maybe it's too late for that. In the morning, as I'm setting out for the corner store, I find the next note, slipped beneath the door. STOP LISTENING, it says.

10

ROLL OF THE DICE

Irina texts me later that same morning and we agree to meet, in an hour, at a temple on Fourteenth Street. After downing my second coffee, I walk over, under a slate sky that trades day for night, looking behind me at every Don't Walk signal. Because all of those times that I thought I felt eyes on me, maybe I really did. Someone must have been following me, close enough to know that I had found the recorder. That same someone could be following me even now.

The temple crouches near First Avenue, its sooty stone camouflaged against the gray. I find Irina at the back of the sanctuary, hunkered into a red-cushioned pew, chin sunk toward her chest, hair jammed beneath that same ridiculous beret. Her eyes are dry now, dual hollows above her cheekbones.

I sit beside her, both of us faced forward, and then press the recorder into her hands, careful not to touch my skin to hers. "A girl brought this into the magazine," I say. "A college student. She found it just before Thanksgiving. It's his."

Her fingers close over it. "Thank you," she says, the words sounding parched. "This is most kind. To hear his voice, his talk—"

She goes to press play, but I shake my head. "No," I say. "I tried to listen to it yesterday, but either the recording didn't take or the tape has been erased. I should have told you."

"Really," she says. "Erased? You are sure?"

I nod.

"No," she says. "I must try." She hits play and fast-forward, play and fast-forward, until the tape finally clicks off.

She bows her head then. "I am sorry," she says, her voice taut as she fights off tears. "So sorry. I do not mean for you to see me in this way. Already you have done so much. For me. For this man you do not know."

I turn to her. "I haven't done much at all," I say. "So you haven't heard from him? Jake hasn't found out anything about where he might have gone?"

"You have this meeting with Jake," she says with an icicle smile. "Is he a man who is solving these many cases, do you think?"

"Probably not," I say, steadying myself on the pew in front as I stand. "I wish there were something more that I could do."

But there is. And I will. That second note confirms it. If I want to extricate myself from all of this, to return to my blank days and rapt nights, to safeguard against any future threat, then I need to find out what happened to David Adler. I need to take action. To act. To learn what I can. Which means finding a way to contact David Adler's former colleagues at Luck Be a Lady and making a wager of my own. I know this now. And there's a strange pleasure coursing through me, a fork in the socket, every hair bristling sensation as I steal out of that cavern of a room. With a last glance I see Irina pressing play again, again, again, her swimming eyes fixed on the altar, her ears busy with the buzz of blank tape.

I hurry into a deli and then back home, tucking into bed with my laptop and a buttered roll. As I take a bite, one hand types "Luck Be a Lady" into the search bar and I then scroll through pages of song lyrics and chord tabulations until I think to add "online casino," which then offers up new results, one of which seems to be a gambling site. I click the link. The screen glows a muddy green, like a field the week after some outdoor festival has finished, and then shifts to an animated sequence. Chips plummet onto pixilated baize. Cards spiral. Finally, the legend "Luck Be a Lady" appears and then, below it, buttons for blackjack, poker, roulette, craps, and slots. There's no menu tab, no link to a staff directory. But as

I'm about to click on roulette, the program David Adler supposedly corrupted, my eye snags on a yellow banner at the screen's bottom, reading, "Now Hiring! Contact Us!"

That pleasure returns. Stronger now. Flushing my cheeks. I wanted a chance to participate, to meet David Adler's coworkers. Here it is. But how can I convince an outfit like Luck Be a Lady to bring me on? My programming know-how began and ended with a long-ago Tumblr page, so I can't sell myself as a coder. Could the site possibly need other kinds of help? Customer service? Administration? If Esteban, who has the timbre of a psychotic parakeet, can land a receptionist job, surely I can work the site's phones. Besides, the goal is to get a job, not to keep it, to spend a few days, a week at the outside, meeting some of David Adler's coworkers and trying to learn who he was, why someone wanted to hurt him, if that someone will try to hurt me.

I can't apply under my own name, of course. Sirko and the others have probably already gleaned my name from my mail slot. Irina knows it already. And I shouldn't risk anything being traced back to me. Since I don't know how to anonymize myself in the privacy of my own overheated home—a date tried to explain VPNs to me once, I finished my drink and ended the date—I rewrap myself in coat and scarf and set out, at a pace that's practically a jog, outrunning any reckoning with the choices I am making. I haven't moved this fast in years, not toward any lover, any curtain. In just minutes I find myself panting in front of a relic of the 1990s, the Village's last remaining internet café, which squats in the basement of a building on St. Mark's. It has long since rebranded as a down-market coworking space—one I use in times of emergency and construction noise—but at the back are two dusty PCs, one attached to a laser printer, the other available for rent by the hour. Unlike the computers at the public library, which are typically mobbed, I have never actually seen them used. Lurching into a low-ceilinged room with flickering fluorescents and a mushroom smell, I'm greeted, gruffly, by an elderly Asian man wearing a furry trapper's hat and bags beneath his eyes that could hold a week's wardrobe. I take out a $20 and hand it to him. He offers a chit stamped with a password code, also a religious pamphlet.

"One hour!" he barks at me. "No porn!"

None of the creatives toiling at the plastic trestle tables even raise their eyes.

I settle in front of the aged PC, enter the code, and navigate to a free email site. Time now to decide on an alias, a stage name. Something more plausible than my college chat room pseudonym, LadyM. My mind flits to the actresses whose portraits I used to tack to my dorm walls, like Sarah Siddons, the famed tragedienne; or Elizabeth Robins, the woman who introduced Ibsen to English-speaking audiences; or Ellen Terry, beloved of the Pre-Raphaelites. Fanny Kemble. Sarah Bernhardt. Nell Gwyn. In the end, I choose Eleonora Duse: introverted, intense, able to dissolve into her characters so entirely that it looked like witchcraft. Her motto: "To save the theatre, the theatre must be destroyed, the actors and actresses must all die of the plague." My kind of woman.

Armed with the handle Nora L. Duse (the truncated first name and the middle initial should protect from any offhand searches), I open an email account. Then I push back from the keyboard, close my eyes, and begin to imagine the woman Nora is. It's work I haven't done since college—inventing a backstory, building a character fact by imagined fact until the words on the page take form and heft and breath. Will I really do this? Assume this moral hazard for a man I knew for just an hour, a man I maybe didn't know at all? But this isn't about David Adler. Or even about the man who left the notes beneath my door. They are the proxies, the patsies, the excuse I give myself so that I can speed toward the one pursuit—besides criticism, better than criticism—that has ever made me feel whole. I haven't dared this in so long. But as gamblers say, you can't win if you don't play. What they don't say: You will probably lose anyway.

Necessity demands that Nora share my height, my build, my features, give or take. She has to have grown up near me. (I'm terrible at accents.) But she requires her own history, habits, tastes. I'm guessing she has more wholesome attitudes toward men and pharmaceuticals. Almost any woman would. Slowly her picture emerges. The skirts just above the knee. The shiny water bottle. The paperback books with *Girl* in the title. I bet she wears makeup. I bet she packs her own lunch. I bet she eats lunch.

Why is Nora seeking employment at an online gambling firm? Let's say she's younger than me, just out of college, half-desperate for work, and applying to everything shy of the sleazier masseuse ads. Perhaps she has a passion she'll work any survival job to fund: small-batch distilling, stop-motion animation, an epic novel in verse?

Or something much closer to home.

Nora's an actress, I decide. And just to fit a sliver of daylight between us, I give her a particular enthusiasm for musical comedies. An out-of-town gig just fell through, and to pay the rent on the sublet she's hanging on to, she needs a job fast. An uncle with a close personal relationship to the Atlantic City slots saw the Luck Be a Lady ad and emailed the link to her. As life stories go, it is slim, yes, but it's enough.

I reenter the Luck Be a Lady portal and click on the application form. A pull-down menu suggests several hiring areas and I click administrative as the likeliest, then invent a brief work history, mostly summer internships and work-study gigs. In the space for further comments, I mention that I'm resourceful, self-motivated, eager to immerse myself in the fast-growing world of online entertainment, and a lyric soprano. I hit send, my head half in Nora's world and half in my own, a dangerous excitement binding us together.

With the first hour up, I pay for another. Which is ridiculous. I can't expect an immediate response. It might take days for my application to be processed. Weeks. Still, I click refresh so often that my clicking finger cramps, then distract myself with the crankier theater chat boards, searching for my own name, for the bitter comments it invokes. When even this palls, I read the hellfire pamphlet, which threatens "Sin Will Find You!" (No surprise. We have mutual friends.) As the minutes tick away, that floating feeling returns and the room recedes until it resembles a maquette for a stage set, just cardboard and toothpicks and cotton fluff. Then the computer gives a soft and welcome ping.

To: Nora L. Duse <LaDuse@gmail.com>
From: Raj Patel <rPatel@lbal.com>
Subject: Employment Inquiry

Dear Ms. Duse,

Thank you for your interest in Luck Be a Lady, LLC. We're in the process of expanding our business and after some recent staff turnover, we do have an opening for a receptionist/executive assistant. So if you've got the skills to pay the bills—or to file the invoices that will get those bills paid—go ahead and email your résumé. I'll look through it the first chance I get.

Sincerely,
Raj Patel
COO, Luck Be a Lady, LLC

The better the gambler, the worse the man. ~Publius Syrus
You got to know when to hold 'em. ~Kenny Rogers

My breath comes fast now, my blood hums. Having pulled up a word processing program, I rough out the résumé, writing Nora's name and the magazine's address at the top of the page, giving her a BFA from a sizable school upstate. If Luck Be a Lady checks the reference, I'll tell them I've since adopted a stage name as per Actors' Equity guidelines, a dark mirror of my own history. To shorten the résumé, I make her graduation date many years more recent than my own. Yes, I throw my body around like so many party streamers, but I stay out of the sun. I can pass as twenty-five if needed. Elaborating on her previous employment, I place her data entry job at a firm that recently imploded and give her a cocktailing stint at a closed bar. To account for the rest, I call Justine, who sounds like she's just woken from a barbiturate coma. Which she has.

"Whayawan?" she asks, slurring the question into a single word.

"I need the name of that temp agency," I say softly, a hand cupped around my mouth. "The one you used before you tried to bring that sex harassment suit."

"Guy at the law firm was totally looking at my ass," she says, slurring the *s*.

"Your skirt was see-through."

"Consignment store Gucci. Very fucking classy. Fuckface agency that dropped me was called Elite Prestige."

"From now on it's called Prestige Elite, and if anyone calls and asks," I say, darting my eyes around the room, "you head it. Also, you have an employee on the books named Nora Duse. That's me. With a fake name. Don't ask."

"Why would I fucking ask? 'S too early to fucking ask."

"Just say Nora's hardworking and punctual and whatever else good temps are."

"Pathetic?" she says with a yawn. "Depressed?"

"Just tell them she can type."

"I will remember literally none of this. Send a fucking text."

I end the call and add the name of the temp agency. After proofreading the document, I save it to the desktop, then attach it in the reply to Raj Patel. I have a book in my bag, a collection of plays by Hrotsvitha, a medieval nun who wrote tragedies and comedies of martyrs and whores, one of which I am set to review tonight. From what I have read so far, the good girls get tortured and mutilated, the bad ones die peacefully or not at all. It's reassuring to see one's life choices affirmed. I ought to finish the collection, but instead I read and reread the same few lines until the machine pings again and another message from Raj Patel appears. In my stomach I feel that same eager dread that I remember from college, standing near the Theater Department doors, waiting for a director to post a new cast sheet. That same roiling hope and hollow anxiety. I open the email.

To: Nora L. Duse <LaDuse@gmail.com>
From: Raj Patel <rPatel@lbal.com>
Subject: Re: Re: Employment Inquiry

Yeah, that résumé looks super. It's so great that you have phone experience. And we probably won't need you to serve any cocktails, but it's a fun office, so you never know! Kidding! But no, it is pretty fun. Why don't you come by Monday for an interview? How's 9:30 in the AM? We're very shorthanded right now—that's how it is with start-ups, lots of action, lots of turnover—so if it all works out you can start right away. The office is at 632 West 39th, suite 516.

Sincerely,
Raj Patel
COO, Luck Be a Lady LLC

The better the gambler, the worse the man. ~Publius Syrus
You got to know when to hold 'em. ~Kenny Rogers

I send a quick email to Raj, allowing Nora to confirm the interview time. Then I leave the café, though not before the owner hands me one more pamphlet, this one decrying makeup and tight clothing, which reminds me that I ought to give some thought to Nora's appearance. (The pamphlet I save for Justine.) On Third Avenue, I turn in to a pharmacy devoted to drag queens, the women who love them, and any lost soul in search of nipple glitter. Excepting the Orthodox Jewish neighborhoods, it has the best wig selection in town. Nora could use a new hairdo.

The back of the store houses the wigs, each one set atop a Styrofoam head balanced on an improbably long neck. There are pink wigs here and green ones, an Afro nearly as tall as I am, a blue pixie, an auburn shag. I pinch a tiny nylon cap from a plastic bowl and stretch it over and across my scalp, back to front. In the mirror, I look alien, denuded, and I can see how thin my face has become, cheekbones standing out like paired razors, a pale smear of purple under each eye.

I test a mess of cheerful blond ringlets and snatch it off before I am forced to self-harm. A short, curling chestnut wig looks all right, but uncomfortably like Irina's mane, so that goes back on its eyeless head, too. Then I find a wig several shades lighter, easing from a pale mouse into a honeyed blond in a length that brushes the tops of my shoulders. Even before I look in the mirror I can tell it suits me. The woman I see looks blandly pleasant, pretty even. She might go to yoga classes. She might drink smoothies. She might very well work as an occasional receptionist.

I bring the wig to the register and watch as a Latinx woman—a trans woman, maybe—with perfect brows, immaculate baby hairs, and lipstick the plum yellow of a contusion enters the amount into the register. On impulse I add a tinted lip gloss and a bottle of nail polish the pale pink of ballet shoes and raw chicken breasts. Nora seems like the kind of girl who does home manicures.

On the street I phone Esteban. "Are you ready for a shock?"

"Does the pope wear foundation garments?"

"Worse. I just bought new makeup."

He makes sniffling sounds into the phone. "So proud, bebita. I'd cry, but I don't want my very expensive mascara to run."

"Hey, also, I was wondering. Your cousin, the computer genius who makes the fake IDs, is he still in business?"

"Diego? Yeah, he does IDs. You need one, bebita? And all this time I thought you were old enough to drink," he says, cackling.

"I am, but I have a girlish dream of matching my blood alcohol level to my age. It involves shaving off a few years. Or switching to ethanol. Is he around?"

"Lemme check. Call you back."

While I wait, I watch my breath condense in the winter air and finger the paper bag with my wig in it. Is it really this easy to walk out of my own life and into another? Is that what David Adler did? The L train rattles below, and as I imagine myself sinking down, down, down, falling through the grate and into some other world, my phone rings.

"Diego says he can do your ID. Meet me after work and I'll bring you by."

"Does he work fast? I've got a show in Chelsea at eight. I have to see some virgin martyrs get their tits cut off."

"Bebita, your job is very fucked up."

I don't argue.

"Yeah, Diego can do his thing quick," Esteban continues. "He says to stop at one of those passport photo places and get a couple of pictures taken. His fee is a hundred eighty. Bring a few Chunky bars if you want him to treat you nice."

"A man who enjoys the finer things in life," I say, hefting the bag and turning toward home.

"A man who is morbidly obese and maybe still a virgin."

"Tell him to watch his tits."

Back in the apartment, I eat a few bites of the club sandwich I've collected, then change into a silk blouse. I shake the wig out and pull it on, back to the front, pausing in the mirror to apply lip gloss. Vivian enters the apartment, but it's Nora who leaves, with a bounce in her walk and the opening number of *Into the Woods* on her lips. It takes Nora four bodegas and a supermarket reeking of wilted greens before she finds Chunky bars. (Justine has had less trouble locating cocaine on a wet Wednesday.) Then she stops into a copy store and a man with blackheads all across his nose takes her photo as she flashes bicuspids. She collects the pictures with gratitude and cheer. As the shop door slams, I remove the wig. Enough Nora for now.

By five thirty, I'm waiting under the office awning for Esteban, who emerges swathed in a black satin bomber jacket and olive harem pants, a white leather satchel strapped across his chest.

"Now are you gonna tell me why you really want this ID?" he says, stroking my face like an appraiser about to lower the minimum bid. I have trained myself not to startle at his touch.

"Let's just say I thought I'd try being someone else for a while," I say.

He fixes me with the look he reserves for chubby white women in crop tops. But then his expression softens, his own performance on pause. "You serious? 'Cause that's some dangerous shit, bebita. You go away from yourself too long, can be hard to come back."

"You speak from experience?"

And just like that the mask is back. "You don't remember my Lurex year?"

"This plan involves a minimum of man-made fabrics. Promise."

He leads us toward Union Square, to a tenement building above a ramen shop. Buzzed in, we climb the stairs and Esteban beats a syncopated tattoo on a third-floor door. Behind it, I hear a sound like an emphysema patient in the middle of an aerobics workout and then Diego is there, wearing a sweat-spotted T-shirt and a scraggly beard that half conceals several chins.

"She bring the stuff?" he says to Esteban.

"Ask her yourself, cabronito," he replies. "She's not a blow-up doll." Then he turns to me. "Excuse my cousin. He doesn't meet many ladies with mouths made for speaking."

"Charmed," I say. "And if by 'stuff' you mean the cash, the passport photos, and several chocolate bars, then I have it all right here, yes. I also have a curtain at eight."

We follow Diego into a living room piled high with stacks of comic books and a model of a Death Star that looks at least half scale. Against a wall there's a bank of drives and monitors that would force my own sad laptop to crash from overwhelming inadequacy if I ever brought it near.

I put the fee on the desk and Esteban leans over to examine the Nora photos.

"Oh, bebita," he says with that same disconcerting softness.

"Is it the wig? Do you hate the color? Am I really more of an autumn?"

"No, gorgeous," he says. "I always said you should go lighter. It's just that I don't think I've ever seen you smile that way. Or at all."

Diego shuffles between us and sits in the reinforced desk chair as he unwraps a Chunky. "She just needs the standard license?"

"What else do you have?" I ask.

"Nondriver ID, motorcycle class A, student travel. That gets her a discount on Eurail and shit. There's other stuff"—he gestures to the discarded wrapper—"but it costs a lot more."

"A regular driver's license should work fine," I say.

Although he directs all questions to Esteban, I communicate my chosen name, as well as height and eye color. When he requests a home address, I give him the magazine's.

"You can hold any mail that comes in under this name, right, Esteban?" I ask.

"Will you use that Korean snail sheet mask I gave you?"

"I will," I say.

"And you'll send pictures? Beautiful mask pictures that will live on the internet forever if you defy me?"

"Agreed."

I sign Nora's name using an electronic pen and watch it appear on the screen in swooping script. Diego scans the photo and prints it onto heavy card stock, then reinserts the card and prints the reverse side. He runs the completed ID through a laminator.

"Hologram's not perfect, but it should pass. What does she want it for?"

"For a job," I say, turning then to Esteban and offering the story I have readied. "It's a reporting assignment. Undercover, if that doesn't sound too grandiose. But anyway I don't want anyone to know my real name."

"Should be fine," Diego says, reaching for another bar. "Unless it's a government thing. Does she know she's going to need a Social Security card? If she wants to get her salary and shit?"

"Is that harder to fake?" I ask.

"Not a lot. Though you should probably quit before tax time comes around. It'll cost an extra hundred."

By the time I return from the ATM, Diego has completed both cards. He hands them to Esteban, who hands them to me. I slide them into the back of my wallet, then toss one more candy bar into Diego's lap. "Think of it as a tip," I tell him.

That night, hours after the show, I take the last but one of the little green pills and this time I have a dream that I mostly remember, a familiar one for actors. At first, it's so beautiful I nearly wake myself with weeping. Because I'm onstage again, warm in the lights, turning my head this way and that so that the gels spin my hair into gold. But then I recognize the set from the Hrotsvitha play and I find that I'm dressed as the actresses were, in an ivory-colored chiton and a pair of gladiator sandals. The lights get brighter and I stare into them, half-blinded. That's when I realize: I don't know my lines. I don't know the scene. I can't see the audience, but I can hear them growing impatient, shuffling feet, rustling programs.

My mouth is a desert, my stomach a sailor's knot. I look to either side, hoping a colleague will cue me. But no one steps out from the wings, and when I try to call for a line, the words turn to ash in my throat. I go to move offstage, but my legs lock. Looking down at them, I see blood, a crimson spatter across the front of my costume. It's just an effect, of course, a burst blood pack hidden under my clothes, but the red keeps spreading, covering every pleat. No blood pack could ever hold so much.

That's when the screaming starts. I startle myself awake, still screaming and then screaming more as I notice the red drops flecking the sheet. I've bitten my tongue. I stagger to the sink and fill my mouth with water from the tap, rinsing and spitting as the water swirls red, then pink, then clear down the drain. I try to sleep again, but when I close my eyes, all I can see, all I can taste, is blood. I take the last pill.

11

PRIVACY

Further dreams hound me toward morning, and even though I can't recall them in any detail, they leave me edgy and bleary in a way that even a heroic coffee can't soothe. I shake out an Ativan and score it with my thumbnail, downing the larger half. Some people have a cocaine pinky. Give me a benzo thumb any day.

Chemically quieted, I compose my five hundred words on the Hrotsvitha play, starting with the meat of the review and then working outward toward the introduction and the kicker. I email the file, along with a proposed headline, "Breast Intentions," which I know will play well online. As I hit send, I remember Roger's occasional nudge that I develop a stronger social media presence—join Instagram, reserve my quips for Twitter. I've resisted it so far. But Nora, I realize, seems much less obstinate. If Luck Be a Lady searches for her, won't they expect a reasonable size-eight online footprint?

I am not a social creature, online or off it, and mostly ignorant of what it takes to create a credible profile. Justine, unsurprisingly, excels at social media. She has nearly a hundred thousand followers on Instagram and had monetized a quiet corner of YouTube until some killjoy reported her tongue-twister videos as obscene. In fairness, they absolutely were. But I can't ask Justine for help. Even the alibi I've prepared—this sham piece of embedded journalism about the life of a working actor—would make her wary. She knows what happens when I act as anyone other than myself.

So understanding that this is what I shouldn't do and enjoying that sharp, sickly feeling of doing it anyway, I dial Charlie's number. I gave him mine, as promised, but in the week since we slept together, I've responded to his texts with the minimum character count. When he hears my voice, he speaks with puppyish eagerness. I'm grateful he can't lick me through the phone.

"Hey!" he says. "If it isn't my old pal Number Withheld."

"It's a cheap way to retain my aura of mystery," I say, leaning back against a pillow. "How's the indoor weather?"

"Not bad. Corinne's been testing a hail effect. I don't think we'll ever get clearance. One of the chips hit Darren in the eye and sort of half blinded him, so he's wearing a patch and making a lot of pirate jokes. But it's all good. How are you? Has the season slowed down for you yet?"

"Actually, I'm free tonight—"

"Great! Do you want to get dinner? Or maybe see a band. I have a friend who's playing a show in Red Hook—"

"Dinner's possible," I say, smiling to gentle my voice. "But I could use a favor first. You said that you manage Jack Frost's Insta?"

"Yeah. Sure. What do you need?"

"Nothing too tricky. Social media mostly. I'll explain later. What time do you finish work?"

"Around five. Why don't you come by the warehouse then? And maybe—"

"Sure, Charlie. Absolutely," I say, already hovering a finger above disconnect. "See you tonight."

I check my email. Roger has replied, dotting my draft with a few requests for clarification and his usual remarks about adverbs. He has also deleted most of my more egregious wordplay, but as I write those puns just for him, I don't mind.

As I revise the article, I think through the coming week. I had hoped to maintain a truncated theater schedule, but if Luck Be a Lady hires Nora, a receptionist's duties won't leave much time for edits and photo memos, even assuming a generous lunch hour. So I had better arrange to take some vacation. Which ought to be fine. I have plenty saved. A kick line in perfect unison? That is my usual idea of a holiday.

Really, I couldn't choose a better time to step away. By mid-December, nearly every significant show has already opened. Only seasonal fare remains, which rarely offers anything like catharsis. So while I'd rather eat my old character shoes than give Caleb any further column inches, he can handle the Christmas cabarets. Besides, when I finally told Roger how David Adler had lied about the panel, it didn't faze him. And he hasn't mentioned the chief critic position except under duress. Maybe my brief absence will make his heart grow fonder, if his clogged arteries allow it. Or maybe I should acknowledge that nothing I have done, no rave, no slam, no coruscating turn of phrase, has brought me any closer to the job.

Once I've submitted my revisions, I dial Roger's desk. I can hear him chewing as he greets me.

"Roger, you know that vacation I never ever take?"

"Sure," he says, with the sound of what might be a napkin or possibly a lavash roll swiping against the speaker. "You've got a few months of it squirreled away somewhere. Personal days, too."

"Well, I'd like to use some. Just a week. Next week, if you can spare me."

"Sure I can. And good for you, Viv. Somewhere nice?"

Quickly, I invent a destination. "Not especially. And before you ask, there are no bikinis involved. My maiden aunt feels neglected, so I'm bound for New Hampshire for hardscrabble cheer and surprisingly stiff eggnog. I leave Monday and I'm back late Friday, so I can still cover the elf installation if you need it. Will that work?" I'd never told Roger that my aunt had died, never mentioned it to Justine either. It is funny—almost—that she will provide in death what she never could in life: help, support, a presumed place of refuge.

"Of course. But are you sure you only want the week? Wouldn't you rather stay on for Christmas?"

"If you'd met the woman, you'd know she isn't moved by the holiday spirit," I say, straightening a few *Playbills* as we chat. "Her idea of a madcap revelry involves turning on the central heating. I'll be back in New York long before Santa slides down any heating vents."

"So we'll see you at ours? Cheryl would love it. Come all ye faithless and so on."

"I'll tell Father Christmas to route my gifts to the Upper West."

I spend the afternoon tinkering with Nora's backstory and soon I'm running for the bus that speeds me along First Avenue and then west on Fourteenth. Out the scratched windows, I see the city swathed in a gray haze the Christmas lights can't penetrate. The sky and the buildings and the pavement all blend together into the same listless shade, relieved only by overbright banners advertising new dollar stores and slice joints. Then I'm off the bus and into the mist and I can feel myself growing hazier, grayer, too—not Nora, not myself, not anyone.

It's fully dark by the time I reach the warehouse, but there's light inside and a sultry warmth as Charlie pries the door open. He smiles at me and I reflect that smile back, holding up the bottle of Shiraz I've bought on the way.

"I thought it would be a good color on you," I say.

"Hey," he says. "Thanks." He moves to kiss me on the cheek, the bottle lodged awkwardly between us, a disapproving chaperone. "Come in and tell me what you need."

Charlie seats us at one of the worktables and flicks open his laptop while I recite the story I've prepared. "I'm doing a piece about the life of a working actor. Participatory journalism. The plan is to arm myself with a fake name, fake headshot, fake résumé, and see if I can book work. Then I'll write about the experience, whether it's dehumanizing, if casting couches are actually pretty comfortable, that kind of thing." I wait for his answering smile. It doesn't come. I continue. "I need to build up a basic online presence. Just in case some producer or director decides to look me up."

"But aren't you worried that someone who knows you as a critic might recognize you?"

"Not really. I spend my nights on the wrong side of the footlights. Besides, it's amazing what a little change of costume can do. All the

Shakespeare comedies say so." From my Drama Book Shop tote, I furnish the wig and wave it at Charlie. "Meet Nora L. Duse. My ingenue alter ego. I figured I'd slip this on and take an arm's-length cleavage shot that you can upload for the profile pic. And then maybe a few more."

"Sounds good," he says. "Do you have an email address for her? Background info?"

"Yeah, LaDuse at Gmail. Capital L. Capital D. All one word. I emailed you the password. And I sent you a few files before I left, some Nora stuff I worked up—résumé, past credits, things like that. I have it that she graduated from a SUNY school a couple of years ago and since moving to the city, she's temped and waitressed and shot some student films, maybe there's a way to include that?"

"Can do," Charlie says, fingers already flying.

As he hunches over the screen, I flounce toward the bathroom in the light-footed Nora walk I'm developing. Inside, I fix the wig, fluffing the ends, and apply gloss until my mouth looks raw, flayed. I hardly recognize myself in the mirror, which is of course the goal, but the mirror and the lights and the face staring back at me feel increasingly far away. I grip the sides of the sink, forcing my knuckles white. *These are your fingers*, I tell myself. *This is your hand, your palm.* And it works, to a point. But when I walk back out the door, the fingers feel as much like Nora's as my own.

On my return, Charlie glances up from his computer. "Wow, you look—"

"Younger? Dumber? Like I have more fun?"

"You look great."

Holding the phone as far away as my right arm will reach, I lean against a cinder-block wall and contort my pinked lips into a series of smirks, pouts, and puckers, looking up through my lashes. After changing shirts and styling the wig into a topknot, I repeat the exercise. I email the photos to Charlie and he uploads them, his fingers flicking and skipping across the keyboard, choreography in miniature.

"So here's the basic template," he says, turning the laptop to me and showing me an Instagram page. "We don't have to fill in much as long as we select the maximum privacy settings. That way if any casting director checks up on you, it'll show your name and your face and the city, but no one will see how many followers you have or that we've left most of the info boxes blank. You want all the privacy settings, right?"

To say that I value my privacy is like suggesting that Strindberg had occasional girl trouble. I doubt this holds as true for Nora, but it simplifies the task. "Sure," I say. "Give me the works. If anyone asks, I'll just look extremely meek and mumble something about a bad boyfriend and stalking behaviors."

"Meek? Really? That I'd like to see."

"No, you wouldn't," I say, risking a Nora pout.

"No." Charlie laughs. "You're right. I wouldn't. Okay. Instagram's done. Now I'll make sure she shows up on some other sites. LinkedIn, Facebook, a few others. Give me half an hour."

Left alone, I remove the wig and then amble around the studio, running my hands over the tangle of wires and tubes, wondering how materials so solid, so ordinary, can create anything as transitory as fog or snow or mist. I wonder how my own wiring, this particular assemblage of blood and bones and nerves, will double for Nora's, how my eyes will become her eyes, my voice her voice, my busy head and too-small heart her own. I apologize preemptively for our shared liver and poor circulation.

In the kitchenette, I wash my hands and collect a corkscrew and a couple of coffee mugs. I half fill one mug and swallow it medicinally, letting the tannins roll past my teeth and down my throat, its bitterness centering me. Then I pour wine into each and head back toward Charlie, careful not to spill.

"Almost done," he says. "Just putting Nora's name into the cast of an undergrad *Oklahoma!* and adding her to the list of Fringe Festival participants. I've tagged her in a couple of photos, but only large group shots. Want to check it out?"

He opens a new window and types Nora's full name into a search box. At the top is a link to my new Facebook page, and a few inches lower is a notice for a student film that screened last September.

"She's famous."

"And she already has two friend requests." He clicks open Facebook. "For everything, the username is her email. The password is the one you gave me: 'NoraNoraNora111.' Watch this." He clicks on the tab for images and there's Nora's honey hair and sugarless smile, in black and white and then in muted color, followed by the group shots he mentioned.

"Really, Charlie, sterling work, platinum, palladium." I hand him the mug that reads "World's Best Grandma" and click my *Rent* one against it.

"To life," Charlie says.

"To other lives."

Maybe I'm anxious, maybe I'm bored, maybe I'm starved for the salt, citric taste of his skin, but I want Charlie again. Before I give myself over to Nora, I want, just once, to play someone else: the girl he sees in his pretty green eyes, the girl I might have been. I stand up from the table and walk toward the demonstration space, lingering beneath the metal box. Over my shoulder I call, "What does a person have to do for a white Christmas around here?" Charlie hits some buttons on the console and then joins me, his chest pressed into my back, his arms around my shoulders, as the snow starts to fly around us. A few flakes spiral dangerously near my wine. "Better drink up," I say. "I don't think soap improves the flavor profile."

"I'm good," he says.

"I'm not," I say. "Not at all." The snow swirls around the tips of my boots and lands in my hair. Ducking his arms and sloshing only the merest drop of wine, I slide to the floor in a gesture that's very nearly elegant. I pull Charlie down to me. "Want to make snow angels?" I say sweetly. "Or something just a little messier?"

He leans away slightly. "Are you sure you don't want to get some dinner? Or there's that show later. . . ."

"I'm not hungry at all and I don't go out to Brooklyn unless the magazine is paying." I reach up to kiss him, but he leans away.

"Vivian," he says, "I really like you."

"Well, I like you, too," I say. "And sometimes, when a boy and a girl like each other very much—"

"No," he says. "I don't want to do this. I mean, I do. Of course. But not like this. I want to get to know you."

"Charlie, we've had lunch, we've had drinks, we've had sex, and let's not forget I've fainted in your arms. Lesbian couples have moved in together on thinner pretexts. You know me as well as anybody." Which is very nearly correct and at least a little depressing. "If it will make you feel better, you can even take me to dinner afterward. Or I'll take you. What do you say?"

I offer a smile that isn't mine, because I understand now that who I am, who I will allow myself to be, isn't what Charlie wants. This smile is sweeter, gummier, girlier, Nora's. It works.

But just as we start to kiss, my phone chimes.

"I'm sorry," I say, pulling away. "One sec. I promised the copy desk I'd be available for any final queries."

Charlie shrugs, looking away and toward the floor as I open my phone. It isn't the copy desk. The message is from Destine. "I need to see you," it says, which does something to me, to my stomach and lower.

And I could go to him. But Nora wouldn't. So I won't either.

"It's nothing," I tell Charlie. "It's no one." I tilt my face upward and let the false snow melt into my skin, cloaking me, veiling me.

"Kiss me," I say. I say it soft-voiced and honeyed. Just as Nora would.

12

HUMAN RESOURCES

Among my triumphs: becoming an adult without ever having had to dress like one. No one cares what journalists wear. My tryout for the fact-checking spot all those years ago? I showed up in jeans, fourteen-hole combat boots, and a cardigan that the moths had been at. I got the job anyway. In consequence, I have little to wear to my Luck Be a Lady interview, which I acknowledge early Monday morning as I survey the contents of my wardrobe layered across my duvet like drooping geological strata. The one viable garment? The black dress I wore to my mother's funeral. I pair it with black tights, black boots, and the same gray blazer I had on when I met David Adler. The outfit is too grim for Nora as I've conceived her, but I neglected to budget for costume, so here we are. I take the wig from atop a vodka bottle and center it on my scalp, pulling the strands back into an approximation of a chignon, secured with a fistful of bobby pins, then I polish my nails and finish with a smear of tinted gloss and a spray of Je Reviens. Having emptied my wallet of anything with my own picture and name and subbed in Nora's meager ID instead, I add that to my purse alongside her other accoutrements—a copy of her résumé, pens, a legal pad, recent issues of *Backstage* and *Vogue*, the burner phone I bought from the kiosk on St. Mark's. In the zippered pocket, I cache my own phone, too.

As I maneuver for a seat on the train, I diagram the upcoming scene just as my acting teachers used to advise. My motivation is to win gainful employment as a receptionist. My action is to attend the interview and answer questions with warmth and professionalism. Learning more about David Adler's past and the company that once cut his paychecks?

That's what we call subtext. And while I know the risks inherent, I can't pretend I'm not enjoying this. I have that feathery feeling in my stomach that I used to get just before I'd step onstage and feel the heat and glare and embrace of lights more flattering than the train's.

"I'm Nora," I whisper to myself as the train slows and stops. "I'm Nora. I had a breakfast bar and a half-caf and now I'm taking the train to my job interview. I can't be late on rent again, so I really hope I get this one."

At Port Authority, I navigate the bus gates and magazine shops until I emerge on Forty-first, continuing west and slightly south until the neon and bustle wane. For a moment I think I see the man in the red cap, but red caps, caps of all colors, really, are plentiful in city life. And that is Vivian's problem, not Nora's. No one would think to follow me when I look like this. Before I know it, Nora is standing in the shadow of the address Raj Patel gave, a towering beige edifice not far from the West Side Highway, built on brutalist lines that only an architect who experienced a loveless childhood could design. I sign in with a security guard who's watching a soap opera on his phone and barely glances at my fake ID. A short elevator ride, a shorter walk down a slender hallway, and I've arrived at the tan door of suite 516. A shiny placard, red on white, announces "Luck Be a Lady, LLC," David Adler's last known place of employment. I look down at my pale pink nails, ready my Nora smile, breathe deeply—in through the nose, out through the mouth—then try the door, which swings open more swiftly than I'd predicted and delivers me stumbling into the office.

To call it nondescript would be to give the decorator too much credit. It looks barely inhabited. In the main room, I see a pair of mismatched file cabinets and a desk that even a flat-pack store might regard as flimsy, with a push-button phone atop it. The carpet is colorless—beige or gray or greige—save for worrying stains. The fluorescent panels in the ceiling emit the feeble buzz of a depressed beehive. Near the window there's another rickety table with the sort of plastic percolator that gives coffee a name so bad it should sue for libel.

Just then, an inner door opens and a South Asian man with luxuriant black hair, the beginnings of a double chin, and a paisley tie so loud I want to cover my ears comes through it. "Hey, are you Nora? Great, great. Raj Patel. Welcome. We were just finishing up the morning meeting." He gestures to a pink cardboard box under his arm. "Danish?"

"Oh my gosh," I say, my voice star bright. "Thank you, but I just can't. I'm trying this no-gluten plan my voice teacher suggested. It's the worst!"

"Wow," he says. "Rough. Anyway, great you made it. Really great. As you can probably already tell, most of our engineers and programmers work remotely, but this right here is the heart of the operation. At least that's what the tax documents say! Come into my office."

He takes me through a different door and sits down at a somewhat more substantial desk, beckoning me into the chair opposite and shoving the bakery box into a too-small garbage can. "Let me pull up your résumé," he says, keying a few commands into an outmoded desktop. Actually, nothing in the office looks especially fresh—not the fixtures, not the furnishings, not the dusty venetian blinds. Certainly not Raj.

Along the walls are a couple of unframed posters, one an old Rat Pack shot, the other an ad for a 2015 celebrity poker tournament. Near the computer, Raj has arranged a replica roulette wheel and some picture frames, all angled away from me. The virtual pit bosses of Luck Be a Lady don't seem to spend much on overhead. I have been in real casinos before—once in Atlantic City, once more on a reservation in Connecticut—and had recognized in each a kind of immersive theater, a theme park environment eager to unburden its guests of the outside world and to absorb them into a new one with its particular rituals, rules, and oxygen content. This office, in contrast, has the feel of one of those off-off-Broadway plays that can't afford a proper set designer and makes do with whatever Goodwill has on sale during tech week.

Finally, Raj turns from the screen and I rearrange my face into a smile. "So about this job," he says. "We've lost several associates lately. That's why we're hiring in such a hurry. We'll take anyone. Kidding! But you said you've had phone experience?"

"Yes," I say. "Oodles!"

"Great, great. Honestly there's not a ton of traffic for a receptionist to handle right now. Most of our communication happens online. But if you're manning the phones—wait, am I still allowed to say 'manning' or is someone gonna cut my balls off for that? Kidding. But I think 'manning' is still okay. Anyway, if you're on calls then the rest of us can get on with our own highly important jobs. The last receptionist we had left us to squeeze out a kid. If she wants to come back, we have to let her. Frickin' equal employment opportunity, am I right? But probably she won't, which means this could be the beginning of a rewarding Luck Be a Lady career for you. Let me tell you a bit about the company and introduce you around and then we'll get this trial going. Sound okay?"

"Sounds better than okay!" My voice is staging a pep rally for an audience of two.

"Great," he says. "Great. First the spiel. Then the tour. Luck Be a Lady—I call it LBAL—is a vanguard internet company."

"Wow," I say. "I use the internet all the time."

"We offer the online consumer the excitement and visceral thrill of an upmarket casino experience, all in the privacy of their office or home. Without the free drinks or the smokin' cocktail waitresses, but we're working on that! Joke. Do you gamble?"

Only with my health and well-being. "Gosh, well, I buy lottery tickets sometimes."

"It's like that, but a lot more high-class. We're not one of the leading gambling sites, not yet, but we have a reputation for fine service and competitive payouts, and our user numbers are growing even faster than in our initial projections. Frickin' gangbusters. Soon we'll launch a publicity campaign that should push those numbers higher. It's gonna be great, really great." His fingers stalk the keyboard and he swivels the monitor toward me. "Check it out," he said.

On the screen, I see a cartoon of a woman leaning over a craps table, wearing a dress so low-cut her breasts threaten to spill onto the baize.

In her generous cleavage a pair of red-and-white dice nestle. The legend reads, "Get Lucky!" The Luck Be a Lady URL is splayed below.

I have known beer commercials more high-toned and circumspect.

"It catches the eye," I chirp. Like a sharp stick.

"Yeah, it's going to make those numbers blow up. Like, boom!" He follows with various sound effects, then clears his throat. "So the site itself is housed offshore. And like I said, most of our programmers work remotely. We've got a couple of designers in Guam. Frickin' Guam! But let me show you around what I call the command center." He takes me back to the main office and then escorts me through the door from which he first emerged. At twinned desks are a grim-faced white man, bald and blond goateed, with shoulders that suggest a powerlifting practice, and an Asian woman with broad cheekbones and a small pointed chin, her hair pulled into a severe ponytail. Their heads are bent over matching laptops, their skin gray in the reflected light.

Raj gestures toward the male half of the duo. "This is Jay. He heads up the technical end, debugger extraordinaire. I call him Pest Control. Get it?" Jay flicks his eyes toward me, then returns them to the screen. "So if you get calls from the programmers, route them over to him."

"What's his extension?" I ask, scooping a pen and the legal pad from my purse, enjoying the feel of the props in my hands. Nora's hands.

Raj looks momentarily confused.

"It's eleven," mumbles Jay.

"That's right, eleven. Yo-leven. That's how you say it in craps. And this is Lana, our CFO, the money honey. She handles budget, billing, and payroll. If any of the credit card companies call about fraud or whatever, send them to her. Extension eight. Right, Lana?"

Lana mutters something resembling an assent.

"Although usually there's no problem. Customers just don't realize how much they've spent, so then they go whining to mommy and daddy multinational bank about it. But hey, you've got to bet big to win big. Am I right?"

Jay and Lana fail to respond, so I improvise a chipper, "You know it!"

"Great," Raj says. "Lana will work the phones during your lunch hour, so give her a heads-up before you head out. Annnnnd," he says as he leads me back into the main office and gestures toward the wobbly desk, "this is where you'll sit. Your extension is three. To transfer someone just press the star key and then the number. I'm—" He pauses for a moment and calls behind him, "Hey, what's my extension?"

"Seven," Jay and Lana chorus. Then one of them slams the door.

"That's right," Raj says without embarrassment. "Lucky number seven. Easy to remember. I'm COO, as you know. I also handle media requests and advertising. We're in the process of finding a new customer service contractor. So if you get customers who want to complain about the quality of the games or that they're being deep dicked by the algorithm, just direct them back to the website and tell them that all complaints need to be made in writing. And if my wife calls, don't put her through. Kidding! I don't have a wife, so if you want to get a drink sometime . . ."

"Oh, wow, thanks, but I'm not drinking." This ranks with the more profound lies I've ever told.

"Are you religious or something?"

"Only about my vocal cords!" I say. "I trained as an actor and protecting the voice is paramount."

"Well, as long as you can act like a receptionist, this should work out great," he says, gesturing with open palms. "So now that you know your way around . . ."

Which means I have seen the whole of the office. There are no other doors leading away from the main room, no space for Irina's father and his pet thugs. Is this really where David Adler worked? Could I have clicked on the wrong Luck Be a Lady site? With less insouciance than I would like, I gesture around the space, asking Raj, "So who's the owner here? Is it you? Is all of this really yours?"

"Well, I definitely run the office," he says, scissoring his tie with his thumb and index finger. "But LBAL's actually owned by this big-dog investor. He doesn't come by much. We're one of like thirty companies he has. Bankrolls start-ups as a frickin' hobby or whatever. Like it was either this or ships in bottles."

I'd like to ask if this big-dog investor happens to be named Boris Sirko and if a couple of his heavies had anything to do with the disappearance of one David Adler, but I can't think of a way to phrase all of this while staying even vaguely in character. So I trill, "Then I guess you're the one I have to impress!"

"You got that right," he says. "So get on those phones! Well, phone."

"Will do," I say. But as soon as I've sat down at the desk I realize he hasn't had me fill out any sort of employment form, hasn't requested my ID or asked for my Social Security card. Considering what I paid Diego, this seems like a waste. Also, I imagine Nora would be curious about her salary. I am.

Raj Patel has closed his door, but I tap a placid beat and then lean into the room.

"Mr. Patel?"

"Please. Call me boss. Or sir. Or Your Excellency. Kidding! Call me Raj."

"Okay . . . Raj. I don't want to bother you or anything, and I'm so grateful for this tryout, but I just wondered if you needed me to fill out any employment forms or anything?" Nora's uptalk frays my voice like a worked-over knot.

"Well, let's see if the job pans out before we get the taxman involved. Am I right?"

This doesn't seem exactly aboveboard, but Luck Be a Lady can't be the only internet gambling concern to take a carefree approach to accountancy. "Sure," I say. "I never understand all those deductions anyway! And when we were talking earlier, I think I forgot to ask you about salary?"

"Oh. Right. Well, let's start you out at fourteen an hour. And if it works out, I might definitely consider a raise. For Christmas."

Barely above minimum wage and assuming a thirty-five-hour workweek, just under half of what I make at the magazine. Raj Patel's generosity overwhelms me. "Wow. Sounds great," I say. "And I think I forgot to give you my phone number. I was in the middle of changing plans so I left it off my résumé." He wrestles his phone from his pocket and I recite the digits of the burner. "One last thing," I hazard. "Where's the ladies' room?"

"It's down the hall to the right. Or no. The left. Look for the stick figure in the skirt. You don't need a key or anything."

"Super!" I say. Bereft of further conversation starters, I'm about to lean back out when I realize that from my perch in the doorway I can see the framed photos on his desk, and in the one nearest me, I spot Raj wearing a silver party hat and holding a drink, standing between two men. He has an arm draped over the shoulder of one of them. That man is David Adler. So it looks as though I've gotten lucky after all. But then I notice the other man. I've seen him before. On a cold day in a trash-strewn park, crumpled beneath a tree. It's Vinnie Mendoza. Which means I've gotten even luckier. So lucky I might throw up.

"I'll just pop into the ladies' now, if it's okay," I say, my jaw forced into a tooth-cracking smile.

"Powdering your nose on my dime? Kidding! Go ahead."

In the otherwise empty restroom I lock myself in a stall, drop to the seat, and lean over, head between my knees, until the nausea passes. David Adler worked here. He entered through that beige door. He drank coffee from that wretched machine. He sat behind Jay's desk or Lana's or one wedged in between. And he knew the man I found dead in Tompkins Square Park. Destine attributed Vinnie Mendoza's death to an overdose, but now I can't be sure. Was Vinnie part of David Adler's alleged embezzlement? Were the threats I heard on the tape not really about embezzlement at all? Could David Adler have seen or known or done something else? Something more?

These are mysteries I am unlikely to solve astride a toilet. So I raise myself slowly from the seat and approach the sink, where I splash cold water on my face and reapply gloss. Time for Nora's next scene. *I am personable,* I tell the face in the mirror, *I am proficient. I am perhaps just the slightest bit dim. I am ready to begin an exciting career as a receptionist while also trying not to get disappeared by a Russian gangster and his hired heavies.*

But as it happens, the first phone I answer is my own, buzzing in my purse as I return to the office. I see it's Destine calling. Jay and Lana's door is closed. So is Raj's. I tap to connect.

"Hello," I say, low voiced.

"Vivian? I can hardly hear you. Speak up."

"Can't," I murmur. "Performing Arts Library."

"You didn't return my text. What's the matter, Ms. Parry? I come on too strong?"

I think of the bruises on my breasts, on my arms. "Was there a reason you phoned?"

"I checked up on that guy for you. Your disappearing act."

"And what did you find?"

"It's my day off. Why don't I tell you in person?"

"Why don't you tell me now? I've got a stack of performance videos to watch before closing."

"All right, Ms. Parry. Have it your way. We have three David Adlers who have resided or are residing in the major metropolitan area. None of them are late twenties, but maybe you got the age wrong. There's the one writing bad checks that Lutzky found, but nothing on the other two. Not even a parking ticket. So there's no way to get approval to run a trace. You got a middle name for him, a Social Security number?"

"Does a cell phone help?"

"Not much. I'd need a warrant for the records."

"Give me a day or two. I'll find out what I can."

"You sure that's a good idea, sweetheart?"

Good ideas have never been a specialty. "I'll be careful, discreet. If I can learn anything, I'll get in touch."

"Not sure I feel like waiting, Ms. Parry. Call me when you're out of the library. But you're not in the library at all, are you?" And then he laughs, in that cheerless way I can feel all through me.

13

WHITE OUT

During my first day as a receptionist, Luck Be a Lady, LLC, receives exactly four calls. One is a wrong number. One confirms the delivery of Jay's lunch. And one is almost certainly Raj attempting a Long Island accent and testing my phone manner. When an actual bank representative calls regarding a contested transaction, I transfer him to Lana and I feel like singing. Unfortunately, Nora has to rely on my indifferent knowledge of the American songbook: "If I were a bell, I'd go ding dong . . . something."

Seemingly, I have no other duties. No supplies to order. No meetings to schedule. So here is an office koan: If there aren't any calls to receive, is our heroine still a receptionist? The shadiness of Luck Be a Lady, it rivals a solar eclipse. I know even less about business fraud than I know about Frank Loesser's back catalog. Nevertheless, I have suspicions. If someone wanted to launder money or commit some other financial crime, a dubious gambling site might come in handy. Could that be what David Adler discovered? What Sirko had to protect?

I deliberate this as I sit in my squeaking chair, waiting on a battered phone that won't ring, trying to answer questions I can't ask and don't properly understand. I would say that I never imagined that something so dangerous could feel this boring. Then again, I've had unprotected sex with lighting designers. Still, it's not entirely boring. Or no, it absolutely is. Underneath that, though, there's a perceptible third-rail thrill, an adamantine satisfaction. Because I have made all of these people believe that I really am Nora. I have played the part—I am playing the part—to something like perfection, hiding myself in plain sight. This is what I have always wanted. To disappear, with everyone watching. But while the doors stay closed, no one is there to notice.

By the end of that first day, Nora has read *Vogue* from cover to cover, including the beauty articles, and paged through every listing in *Backstage*, circling all the ones that seem to apply, even those that say, "Some nudity required." She has actually considered attending a non-Equity casting call—a phenomenon Justine compares to mass rape with headshots in hand—just to get out of the office for a few hours.

Raj dismisses me shortly after five, whereupon I trudge to the subway, shedding my wig and shaking out my hair, though not without some small, sharp pang of regret as I turn back to myself. Off the train I head along Avenue A to the Jigger, the place that Vinnie Mendoza used to work, a speakeasy hidden behind an old botanica. I have put away Nora for now, but I am not quite off the clock. Not yet. Having seen the picture on Raj's desk, I have another performance to give, a small encore.

Through the botanica and past the steel-reinforced door, I take a seat at the bar. A Black woman with hair marcelled into 1920s kiss curls, dressed in the regulation bow tie and apron, slides a menu and a bowl of wasabi-coated nuts in front of me. She meets my eyes briefly. She doesn't like what she sees. Single girls don't tend to tip well. I fashion my face into another mask, less callow than the one I wear for Nora but more approachable than my usual expression.

"Vodka martini, please," I say. "Shake it. Stir it. Do you."

If she registers the pleasantry, she doesn't show it, stirring the martini for a regulation thirty seconds, before setting it down noiselessly atop the coaster.

I take a tingly sip—"Perfection," I say—and slip a twenty, a significant portion of Nora's day rate, across the bar. "No change. And hey, friend of mine works here. I haven't seen him around in a while. His name is Vinnie. Do you know him? Is he working tonight?"

Her hauteur liquefies and she looks at me with real alarm. "Oh my God," she says. "Vinnie, you mean, like, Vinnie Mendoza?"

I nod expectantly.

"Oh my God. I'm so sorry. But he, um, yeah. He died."

"He what?" I fabricate the kick of sudden shock.

"You knew he had a drug problem, right?" she says, scrubbing at the bar where no stain exists. "I mean, I only started here at the end of summer. But we did some shifts together and it was pretty obvious he had a habit."

"Yeah, for sure. I guess I didn't think it was that bad."

"Turns out it was. He overdosed just after Thanksgiving. They found him in the park." She jerks her chin easterly. "In Tompkins Square. One of the other bartenders told me the rats had already—Forget it. How did you say you knew him?"

"From when he was a stagehand," I say, swallowing another mouthful. "I'm an actress. Or I used to be. We lost touch for a while, but I heard he was working here, and like also for some online start-up? Did he mention that?"

"A start-up?" she says. "Could be. Everyone who works here has like a million hustles. But you know Vinnie, not a talker."

"Right? I just don't even know what to say. He always seemed so—" Knowing nothing of Vinnie Mendoza, I struggle to finish the sentence. "Alive. So alive. Is there anyone here he was close to, who would have known what was going on with him?"

"Not really," she says. "He pretty much kept to himself. Chipped the ice. Brought out the glasses. I didn't know him super well. I don't think anyone here did. There wasn't even a funeral. Turns out most of his family still lives in the Philippines."

"And none of his friends are planning any kind of . . ." I make a spinny gesture with my wrist that mirrors the lemon twist. "A memorial or something?"

"Not that I know of. But if I hear of anything I'll let you know. Want to give me your number?"

I give her Nora's and she writes it on her order pad. Then she pushes the $20 back toward me and tells me the drink is on the house. I sink it before she can change her mind. I may have hit a wall in my attempts to connect Vinnie Mendoza to David Adler, but who says I have to hit it sober? And yet, even after the vodka has overrun my bloodstream, my heart thuds like a boxer's heavy bag. So on the way home, I call Destine. Just after I've changed out of the rest of my Nora drag, he clambers up that final flight and into my apartment.

He pushes me down onto the bed. I let myself fall.

I sleep alone and poorly, and in the morning there's a knocking in my head like a melodrama landlord demanding the rent. As I stagger from the bed, my foot finds the whiskey bottle that Destine and I emptied last night, so there at least is one mystery solved. Coffee and a half of a long-hoarded Vicodin kill the pain, but the opiate leaves my skin itchy and too tight. Slipping into Nora's outfit, a lightly altered version of yesterday's ensemble, comes as a kind of relief. No unsuitable men visit Nora's apartment too late. No one has ever slid even a single threat underneath her door. So there is a lightsome enjoyment in approaching the office with her gait, her emptier head. That sensation of eyes raking over me? Yes, I feel it. But those eyes are admiring Nora's swiveled walk, her honey-blond bounce.

At Luck Be a Lady, I find the door unlocked and the main room deserted. The winter sunlight, trickling in from the smeared windows, spotlights every dust mote and carpet stain. Gradually, Nora's coworkers arrive. Jay first, then Raj, who enters his office and slams the door almost before I can greet him. If anyone notices that Nora has worn the same dress, with somewhat different accessories, they are too polite to say so. The phone stays silent. No one comes out to make coffee, meaning that my opportunities to ask leading questions about the firm's financials are few. What's worse: I'm deprived of an audience. The collision of actor and spectator is what makes theater. Performing Nora in this vacuum of an office suite feels like no performance at all. No consummation. No thrill. The itching starts again, worse now.

Around eleven thirty, when I have seriously contemplated huffing copy toner just to break up the day and just as seriously contemplated whether we even have a copier, I recommit to my role and knock on Raj's door, entering unprompted. He pivots the monitor away from me, but not before I can catch a few frames of what looks like a faux medieval video game and a character holding what might be a trebuchet. Today's tie stars a pattern of red pheasants on a blue background.

"Hey!" I say, baring most of my teeth in a reasonable imitation of a smile. "I was just wondering if there was anything I could do to contribute. The phones just don't seem to be ringing today!" This morning's tally runs to one robocall and Lana saying she wouldn't be in until after lunch. "I hate to think of you paying me just to read my magazines. So I thought I could help with your correspondence. Or maybe do some filing? Employee records, that kind of thing?"

"No," he says too quickly. "No filing. No way. Those file cabinets are private. Vital materials there." I wait for him to add his typical "Kidding!" But it doesn't come. There's firmness in his voice and something spikier behind it.

"Are you sure? There must be something I can do."

He stands up from his seat as if someone had just stuck several thumbtacks through it. "You will not touch those cabinets! Is that understood?"

Were he taller than five feet six and not wearing a shirt in a consoling shade of rose, I would likely feel more intimidated. As I don't, I fake it. "Oh, wow," I say, taking on the expression of a kitten recently kicked. "Sorry. I was just trying to be helpful."

Raj settles back down. "Yes," he says, "of course. And that's great. Just the kind of initiative LBAL wants to reward. But those cabinets have very sensitive information. Like credit card statements. And security codes. They must remain locked."

"Okay," I concede. "You're the boss!" That pacifies him, so I move a step closer to his desk, toward the photograph I noticed yesterday. "That's such a great picture of you," I say, pointing. "You're so photogenic. Is that at a party?"

"New Year's," he says. "Total frickin' rager. Went to a club in the meatpacking district and must have spilled like frickin' five thousand on Cristal and—" Then he clears his throat and attempts to deepen his voice, stumbling into a lower register. "Well, yes, quite a night. And it never would have happened without LBAL. You could have an amazing future here, see?"

Somehow, I don't imagine my hourly $14 will keep the Cristal flowing. "Do you think so?" I say. "Because that would be so amazing." I point again to the picture, to David Adler. "Is that, like, a friend of yours? Boyfriend?"

"Hey! No way! I'm as straight as a die. Wait, is that the expression? Because dice are cubes, right? But I'm straight. So straight. That's just my man Dave."

He turns his eyes back toward the photo. I do the same. Raj in the party hat, smiling drunkenly, David leaning into his shoulder, streamers in his hair and in his hand a small object that he has lifted toward the camera's lens, a scale model of the Chrysler Building that looks somehow familiar. He's smiling, too—glassy, overbright—as though a bottle's worth of champagne bubbles has hit his bloodstream all at once. Vinnie, eyes hooded, looks down toward the floor.

I press Raj further. "That Dave guy, I feel like maybe I've seen him around? Like maybe at an audition? Does he do theater?"

Raj makes a face as though he has just swallowed something bitter. The office coffee, maybe. "Theater? What? Ha. No way. Not really a creative type, Dave. Had more of a nutty professor thing going. He worked here, you know. Did Jay's job. Supervised the code monkeys."

"Really? Why did he leave?"

Now Raj looks even less comfortable. "Vanguard internet company. Lots of responsibility, lots of challenges. Some people just can't handle it. Dave was one of those. At least, that's what I figure."

I curl a lock of Nora's hair around my finger and assume an expression of doll-like innocence. "You figure?"

"I took some vacation days in November," he says. "Went down to

South Beach with some guys from my old fraternity. Great town. Awesome time. Got back and his frickin' desk was cleaned out and half his stuff was gone from the apartment."

"You shared an apartment?" I remember Irina mentioning a roommate.

The set of his lips tells me he hadn't meant to say that, but he pushes through. "Yeah, a two-bedroom in the Village. And actually it sucks because his bed and his dresser and all his frickin' books are still there and I don't know if I should throw them out or put them in storage or if he's going to just show up again next week. Meantime, I'm paying double rent." He breathes in, noisily, like an air conditioner beginning to fritz. "But it's fine. A job like this—" He gestures toward his mostly empty desk. "Cash flow's not a problem."

I'd like to ask him more, about Vinnie especially, but then, from the central office, I hear the phone begin to ring, and maintaining Nora's fiction does include fielding the occasional call. "Oh gosh, I should probably get that," I say.

"That's why we pay you the big bucks. Well, the competitive bucks," Raj says. He rises from his chair and walks toward me, forcing me out of the office and shutting the door before I've passed the threshold. A lock clicks behind me.

Having closed the distance to my desk, I pick up the phone. An automated voice asks me if I want to save money on my car insurance. "This is New York," I snap at the recording. "No one drives here."

I want to search the file cabinets immediately, to learn what Raj doesn't want me to see, but some faint spark of self-preservation tells me that I should wait until he leaves for lunch. Only he doesn't leave. Lana finally arrives at twelve thirty. A quarter hour after that, Jay has food delivered, Peruvian this time, which means I actually get to answer a call, if only from the lobby. Otherwise I'm forced to reread *Vogue* and paint stripes on my nails with correcting fluid.

Around two, Raj finally emerges, speaking in a low mumble on his phone, which has a case patterned with poker chips. He could take a full lunch hour or he could quickly return with a pizza box, as he did yesterday. Worse, he might only be headed to the men's room. But even that affords me at least a couple of minutes, so as soon as the hall door closes, I scuttle over to the files.

I begin with the cabinet on the left. Raj had said they were locked, but I try the first drawer anyway and it opens with a squeaking scrape of metal. The interior is dusty and only half-full. The papers in the folders seem to relate to licensing and corporation status. But the copy is so smudged and the legalese so opaque that I don't waste much time perusing them.

As I slide out the second drawer, it occurs to me that I have no idea what I'm expecting to find. A signed confession regarding David Adler's disappearance? Evidence of LBAL as a money-laundering front? Plans to deliver a hot shot to Vinnie? I'd settle for David Adler's résumé, the address of the apartment he shared with Raj, a Social Security number to help Destine's search. But this second drawer holds only take-out menus.

Hurriedly, I jerk open the third drawer and find a stack of the free dailies that hawkers in neon vests thrust into your hands as you enter the subway. Could someone have concealed sensitive documents there? Grabbing a few papers from the middle, I shake them out, disgorging only an offer for laser hair removal. Even a conspiracy theorist couldn't mistake the coupon for a clue, though examining it through Nora's eyes, it looks like a decent deal.

The other file cabinet—taller, slimmer, somehow even more beige—stands inviolate, and even though my phone tells me I've been attempting corporate espionage for four minutes longer than I'd allotted, I can't resist a tug at its top drawer. The drawer gives an inch, then grates against a sturdy lock. So maybe Raj wasn't lying after all. Maybe he was just too embarrassed to admit that the company doesn't have enough sensitive information to fill two cabinets. Maybe—

At that moment the office phone rings, startling me. It's a wrong number, they want someone named Colby, a name only a cheese enthusiast could love, but by the time I hang up, the window for malfeasance has closed. Ten minutes later, when Raj bustles back in rustling a grocery bag with a family-size pack of tortilla chips on top and a clinking underneath that might be a six-pack, I have returned to *Vogue* and my Wite-Out manicure. As he thwacks his office door shut, I decide I'm due my own break, so I tell Lana I'm taking lunch and promptly flee.

In a sunless bar, I kill what appetite I have with a vodka soda. It isn't what Nora would order, but I don't want to be Nora just now. Nora, alone onstage, is hopeless. Here she is, plunked at the palpitating center of business intrigue—of murder, most likely—and the best evidence she has uncovered? A drunken photo and the promise of smooth pubes. I wish Nora a lifetime of botched auditions. I wish her the stomach flu on press nights. I wish her years in summer stock in somewhere untouristed and chill.

But too soon I'm back in the lobby, sucking on a mouthful of mints, finding my way back into Nora's peppy heart and mind. My heels clack like scant applause as I totter toward the elevator.

Time was I had a fascination with stage directions—long, bullying Edwardian ones. There was a line from Shaw's *Man and Superman* about how the heroine wears *a trace of contempt for the whole male sex in the elegant carriage of her shoulders*. I used to practice that one in the mirror.

On the foggy morning of my third day at LBAL, waiting for the train, I'm forced to acknowledge that even Shaw wouldn't have found much to italicize. My heels pinch, my scalp prickles, my skin feels as if it shrank in the wash. I board the car and grope in my bag for something to read, having stocked up on replacement magazines. With little in the way of revelation and no one to admire my performance, the excitement of playing a role has palled. My sojourn as Nora has begun to feel like one more ruinous choice—the joke I shouldn't have made, the drink I shouldn't have taken, the no I didn't say or said too late.

Last night, when I returned to my apartment, nothing felt quite real, not even after I had removed the wig and the shoes and settled in with some hot and sour soup. It didn't feel like my dinner. It didn't feel like my life. So I had a drink and put myself to bed, hoping the morning might return me to myself. It did not. The world has gone wispier since I started this, more distant. And for what? But this I know: for the body, for the tape, for the notes shoved beneath my door, for that sweet, spiked thrill of performing again, for feeling alive—or nearly—in daylight. If only someone could see me.

What could rescue this enterprise from absolute farce? That second file cabinet. Raj wouldn't have warned Nora away if those drawers contained further take-out options, so they must hold something more significant. I don't know where Raj keeps the key, and I can't bear letting Nora sidle close enough to find out, but last night, while I waited for my soup to cool, I watched several lock-picking demonstrations on YouTube and they made the process look relatively simple. In preparation, I've lined my coat pocket with a tweezers and a couple of bobby pins bent into hook shapes.

A few hours later, re-ensconced on my wobbly perch, I've nearly finished another glossy—it has given Nora some cunning ideas about workplace separates. I startle when Raj's door thumps open and he bounds toward me with a smile so blinding that it outshines his iridescent tie.

"Hi there, Mr. Patel," I yelp.

"Call me Raj!" he says. "Or Daddy! No. Kidding. Don't tell HR I said that. Anyway, exciting day. Really exciting. Just great."

"Wow," I say. Does Luck Be a Lady even have HR? "What's going on?"

"We're getting a visit from the big dog himself," Raj says. "Boris Sirko. He's coming in for a conference about that new ad campaign I'm launching."

"Really?" I say, the syllables emerging high and tight.

"Yeah, he just called." I look at my silent telephone, and then so does Raj. "On my cell," he continues. "But you have no idea how great this is. He never comes into the office." Considering the overwhelming lack of bustle and consequence, this may not be the shocker Raj imagines.

"You might want to clean up a little," he says, nodding toward the magazines on my desk. "Make sure we look professional, best feet forward. And maybe put on some lipstick. Kidding! But seriously. It would help."

While Raj delights Jay and Lana with the news, I take myself to the ladies' and dutifully gloss my lips until they glisten like sushi-grade salmon. Then I fluff Nora's wig and consider how to work this visit to my advantage. Introducing my disguised self to a man like Boris Sirko isn't the least precarious choice I might make. But if I value my sanity (an open question), I'm not sure how many more days either Nora or I can last at LBAL. Better to offer this command performance now. So I smile into the mirror—placidly, warmly—immersed once again in my role.

Boris Sirko must have told his chauffeur to take the scenic route, because it's a good hour before he arrives. He's a large man. Extra-large. With a chest that would intimidate most barrels. He looks as though someone set out to make a cement truck and then grudgingly altered the specs to accommodate a middle-aged man instead. Girded against the cold in a coat clearly made from the skins of clubbed seals, he accessorizes with sunglasses, gloves, and a Sinatraesque trilby. A splotch of blood hunkers on his chin. Likely it's a shaving cut. Or the remains of the rival he ate for breakfast.

Then I notice something genuinely terrifying, something that freezes the demure smile to my face as though I've laced my gloss with liquid nitrogen: Boris Sirko hasn't come alone, and he hasn't brought whichever thug menaced David Adler. He's brought someone so much worse. Someone who has met me out of my Nora guise.

His daughter.

Irina stands behind her father, dressed in a black coat. She has left the beret at home this time, and her tears have dried since the synagogue. She seems flintier somehow, more resolute.

I can't have her recognize me, but I also can't exactly dive roll underneath my desk. Without reasonable hope of flight or concealment, I have to trust that wig, makeup, and unfamiliar context will protect me. I'm trusting so hard that my palms have turned subtropical. Raj immediately brings dad and daughter to me.

"Nora," Raj says, "this is Boris Sirko, the CEO of Luck Be a Lady, and his terrific daughter, Irina."

"Oh my gosh. So charmed," I say, eyes lowered deferentially. Behind those lids, I am thinking, with fevered intensity, about Nora—her character, her backstory, how she needs this job, how she will want to make a good impression on her boss's boss even though she likely feels uncomfortable around people in power. These circumstances inform the tone of my voice, the angle of my head, the placement of my hand on the desk's edge.

"And this is Nora. Our great new receptionist," Raj says. The frickin', I suppose, is silent.

"I love phones," I say softly, keeping my eyes on a careful perusal of my shoes. "All kinds of phones. Love them."

"Yes," booms Sirko. I'm glad he's wearing sunglasses, because I don't think I'd like the way he looks at me. "This is the way of you American girls. Always on these phones. Irina, she is the same. Always her phone is doing this la la la, la la la." He emits a series of notes that could fright birds from the sky. "How do you say it?"

"Ringtone, Papa," Irina murmurs.

"Yes. Ringtone. Nora, this is a good American name, yes? And you are from New York, yes?"

"No, Mr. Sirko," I improvise. "New Jersey."

"Ah, New Jersey, the state of the gardens. The girls of New Jersey, do they have this beautiful hair like yours? This, how do you say it?"

"Blond?" I chirp, like a sparrow that has just wandered into a box trap.

"Blond. Yes. To Irina I say, you are this American girl now. You must have this blond hair. But she says to me no." Sirko utters a sound that in a smaller man might have passed for a sigh. In him, a minor hurricane. "Is very beautiful," he says. One meaty hand reaches out to the other, removing a leather glove, and then yellowed fingers reach out to touch

Nora's hair. Or to put it another way, my wig. There is no way that Sirko's hand, an extremity like a cudgel, will leave that wig in place. I'm frozen, a stalagmite in three-inch pumps. But a moment before contact, Irina, who has apparently completed at least one online sexual harassment seminar, diverts his hand. "Papa, puzhalsta!"

Sirko shoves the offending ham hock back into his pocket. "Forgive me," he says. "Your beauty, it makes me this most bad man." He turns to Raj. "Okay. Come. Show to me this new campaign." He charges his way into Raj's office, a tank in a trilby, and to Nora's unspeakable relief—and mine—Irina follows, though before she disappears inside, she gives me a careful, pursed-lip glance. It might be an apology for her father's boorishness. It might be something else.

The door shuts. And for the first time in several minutes, I breathe. I'm not Nora anymore. But I don't feel like myself either. When I look down at my Wite-Out-painted fingers, they look sculptural, alien. I don't trust them to hold those bobby pins without shaking, so I can't attempt that second file cabinet now. Besides, Irina could emerge from the room at any moment and it's best if I'm not here when she does.

I do the only thing I can. I take an early lunch.

In a few minutes, I'm bellied up to yesterday's bar and I've downed a double vodka. Soon I feel far away, cocooned in a high-proof cloud. Not the dingy fog outside, but something brighter, whiter, softer, that wafts me away from Irina's parting glance, Sirko's yellowed fingers. As I feel myself drifting, I place my hands firmly on the bar and begin my litany. *These are your fingers*, I tell myself. Then I stop. I'd rather drift.

My phone pings. Not my phone. Nora's. It's a text from Raj, asking where I am and inviting me to lunch with Sirko and the team. I text back that I took lunch early, which I accessorize with the appropriate emojis—sad eyes, white praying hands—and that I've eaten already. Then I have one more drink and ready myself to return.

In the bathroom, which smells of urine, wet cement, and sage, I reapply lip gloss. The face in the mirror doesn't look like me, it doesn't look like anyone, it hardly looks like a face. But I need to wear it, for a few more hours at the least, so I pull myself back into the role. Should Sirko and Irina return to the office after lunch, I need to ensure it's Nora that they see.

I'm Nora, I whisper. *I'm Nora. I spent my lunch hour browsing the self-help racks at the bookstore and then I ate a candy bar for lunch and that's really awful because I'm trying to cut way back on sugar, but I just love candy bars! Now I'm going to go and spend the rest of the afternoon being the best gosh-darn receptionist I can be in an office where the gosh-darn phones just never seem to ring. Okay?*

I reach up toward the mirror and caress Nora's cheek, smudging the glass. And then, in my own voice—lower, harder—I say, "You betcha, you gosh-darn imperiled bitch."

14

WALK ALONE

When I enter, I find the office deserted. Relief transmutes into nausea and I barely make it to the ladies' room before I puke into the toilet, a bitter stream of vodka and bile. I ought to know better than to drink on an empty stomach. I also ought to know better than to infiltrate a mob-owned shell corporation in a midrange wig. I rinse my mouth, raw from the vomit burn, crunch a few more mints, and return to my desk.

I have no guarantee of when my colleagues will return. But after an hour of silent phones and Raj's continued absence, restlessness trumps anxiety. Draping myself across the second cabinet, I assail the lock with my homemade picks. But either I've bent my bobby pin incorrectly or the residual vodka in my system has wrecked my coordination or that YouTube guy was an absolute fraud. The lock's as unyielding as a Greek tragedy.

Raj returns after four and hovers near my desk, his body at a vertiginous lean. "Hey," he says. "Did I miss any calls? Long lunch with the boss. Great. Really great. Too bad you took off. Mr. Sirko really liked you. He wanted you to come along."

"Oh, wow, really? I'm so sorry I missed it. But I had to go early. I have this hypoglycemia thing and when my blood sugar gets low I have to eat right away or I just get really woozy, you know?"

"Well, don't worry. I'm sure he'll be back in the office soon."

Which is precisely what I'd feared. Despite the temptation of that second file cabinet and the desire to wring more David Adler information—any

David Adler information—from Raj, I can't risk Irina recognizing me. Then there's the floating feeling I had at the bar, that desire to drift away. Despite the choking boredom of these three days, I have let myself fall further into a role than I have in years. Now it is time—fingernails torn, knuckles bleeding—to scrabble my way back out. Nora has to give her notice.

"Mr. Patel," I say.

"Come on, call me Raj already!"

"Okay. Raj. I'm so sorry and oh gosh, please don't be mad at me, but it's just that I don't think I can work here anymore." I search for an excuse to give and I remember how Raj spoke about David Adler. "An internet company like this, there's just so much responsibility, so much pressure, and I don't think I can handle it."

"Really? But you're doing great here, Nora. And it's just your first week. You'll adjust to the pace. Even in those high heels. Kidding! But it does seem like they'd be hard to walk in, right?"

Adjusting to the LBAL pace would require multiple amputations. Then inspiration strikes. "I'm sorry," I say. "I didn't want to tell you this, but on my lunch break, my manager called. There's a part in a touring production of *Carousel* that just opened up and I can't quit on my dreams, Raj. I have to take it." I make my eyes go big, like gibbous moons. "It tours to Grand Rapids. Also Duluth. Just like I've always imagined. Rehearsals start tomorrow. I'm so sorry to spring it on you like this." I cast my eyes down toward the carpet—which doesn't reward closer inspection. "I know what an amazing job this is and how lucky I've been to have it. And I'm really grateful that you trusted me with this opportunity. But acting is my life, you know?"

Raj takes on an affronted tone. "If that's what you want." He circles his wrist in a gesture of annoyance that resembles a faulty sprinkler. "Step into my office," he says.

Behind his desk, he takes out his iPhone, swiping and tapping until a calculator app opens. "Let's see, you worked three days for seven hours at fourteen an hour, that's . . . two hundred ninety-four." From his desk he draws out a manila envelope and begins to count out a series of $20 bills. "Two twenty, two forty, two sixty. You have change for a twenty? No? Well, let's make it three hundred. A Christmas present." It's difficult to imagine Raj as Santa, though obviously soothing to picture him stuffed down a chimney somewhere. "Don't spend it all in one place!" he adds.

This barely covers dry cleaning. "Wow, I sure won't!" I trill. "I'll take it all on the tour bus."

"Which part did you say it was?"

I didn't. Mostly because midcentury musicals have never sent me. I can't recall a single character name, only a few songs such as "You'll Never Walk Alone" and "A Real Nice Clambake." So I say, "I'm playing the carousel. It's an experimental production. And a big part. All those horses."

"Well, let's drink to it, Nora. What do you say? Can your vocal cords manage an after-work round or two?"

Normally, I'd rather give a spirited defense of the female characters of Arthur Miller than clink glasses with Raj, but this marks my last chance to prod him for details about David Adler. If I play my cards right—as any current or former employee of LBAL ought to—I might even compel him to take me home. Yes, that will entail sexual contact and the legitimate risk that I may never feel truly clean again. Still, if I can get inside David Adler's room, maybe I can discover some scrap of information, some overlooked clue, anything to make the shambles of these last several days worthwhile.

"What the heck!" I say. "Maybe just the one." Which seems to surprise us both.

Raj leads me to a greasy sports bar in the bowels of Penn Station. It's the sort of place that makes you long for a time before the smoking ban. Cigarettes would mask the scent of body spray and aged fryer oil. Nora doesn't rate Cristal, apparently. Instead, Raj orders me a Nora-appropriate cosmopolitan, which I sip delicately, trying not to gag. "I can't believe I'm drinking this," I say with some truth. Even so, it takes real effort to pace myself with Raj, who crunches each individual piece of ice, then strafes the bottom of the glass for the last drops of whiskey and ginger ale.

While he's absorbed in the baseball game that occupies several screens, I order one more round from the bartender, whose sweaty scalp glistens beneath his comb-over. Pointing to Raj's, I murmur, "Make his a triple. And don't be stingy, baby."

When I return with the drinks, I say, "My treat. I just want to thank you for being such an amazing boss and all. And here's to me for being such a great employee. So cheers to us!"

I clink my glass against his, but then something on the TV seizes his attention and he yells, "Go, go, go!"

Regretting every choice that has brought me to this pass, I loose a button on my cardigan and scoot my stool closer to his. "Maybe it's the drinks, but gosh, I'm feeling wild," I whisper to him. "Like crazy, you know? Let's go somewhere else."

He turns back to me, genuinely puzzled. "Where?"

Fighting down revulsion, I press my lips to his and then mash them around there awhile. "Well, we can't go back to mine," I say. "My roommate. She's such a snoop. So take me home. Your home."

"Oh," he says. "Okay. Well, that's great. Yeah, really great. We can do that. Definitely. But hang on. I have to take a piss."

Another man unstrung by my charms.

He returns, wiping his hands on his pants, and says, "Hey, can we get something to eat first? 'Cause you're super hot and everything, but I'm frickin' starving."

Having accepted this evening could well end with this man's exposed penis in some proximity to my person doesn't mean I want to spend more time with him than necessary. "Are you sure we can't just go? Because you're just so darn cute and everything. And didn't you have that long lunch with Mr. Sirko?"

"What can I say? Fast life. Fast metabolism. I'm just gonna get a burger, if it's cool with you. You know, for stamina."

This begins such a horrific chain of associations that I am rendered briefly speechless.

"You want anything?" Raj asks, signaling for some menus.

I clench my teeth into something like a smile. "Oh, wow, okay. A salad, I guess?"

Raj gives the order. And while we wait, I press him, gently.

"You really do live alone, though, right? You had just that one roommate? That other guy in the picture on your desk, he never lived with you?"

"Oh, you mean Vinnie?"

"I guess?"

"Nah, he's just a work friend. Great guy. Really great. Helps Mr. Sirko out with special projects. Import stuff or something. Haven't seen him in a while. Too bad. Vinnie really knows how to throw down."

Then his attention returns to the game and remains there until a gray burger and a less than verdant salad clatter to the space between us. As he chews, one eye on the game, I pick out bits of bacon and consider what he's told me. That Vinnie used to do part-time work for Boris Sirko. In importing. Which almost certainly means drugs. It makes sense. A barback's salary wouldn't have supported a habit like his. A stagehand's? Please. It confirms my hunch that LBAL is a front for a different kind of gamble.

It's thirty minutes and a triple play before Raj swallows his last limp fry and settles the bill. Outside, in the drizzle, he apps up a car, a CR-V with plastic across the seats, and slides in after me, close enough that I can smell the house bourbon on his breath. Once the car is moving, I kiss him again, just long enough to maintain the fiction, then I lean back in my seat at a diagonal, placing my knees between Raj's hands and the more tender parts of my anatomy, though those hands don't seem as inclined to wander as I'd feared. He does make a grab at the nearest breast. He lets it go quickly. Honestly, there's not much to grab. Dissociating from the inevitable, I review Nora's given circumstances and my own discrete motivation: find something more about David Adler—a driver's license number, a Social Security number, a middle name.

"You're sure no one will be home?" I say. "Your old roommate, he never comes by?"

"Why are you so interested in my roommate?" Raj asks.

I giggle. "Because of what you said, silly! About how one day he just disappeared. That's, like, so random!"

"Yeah, well, it's less frickin' random when you can't rent the room because all his stuff's still in it. Though I did finally box up most of it."

"But did you ever find out why he left? Do you ever hear from him?"

Raj sweeps his eyes around the car, as though assuring himself that no one is listening in. With the driver muttering into his Bluetooth in what might be Arabic, eavesdropping seems unlikely.

"I guess I can tell you this," he says. "Seeing as you're no longer an employee. Which also means you can't sue me for sexually harassing you. Kidding! But seriously. I don't think you can. Anyway, it's like this. I got Dave the job at LBAL like nine months after I started working there. The website was ready to go live and we needed someone to ride herd on the programmers—tally bugs, track fixes, shit like that. Dave had been my roommate for a while, and he was a smart guy for sure, but not exactly a STEM god or anything. Wanted to be a frickin' communications professor. Still, I mentioned the job one night and he said he'd taken a ton of comp sci in undergrad and he would be super into it. Which was mostly bullshit. He'd taken, like, an intro course. Two maybe. But I didn't know that then. The job paid a lot better than tutoring, so I guess he just said what he had to say.

"I hooked him up with an interview and yeah, he was chill, said the right shit, so Mr. Sirko was like, sure, okay, whatever,. And mostly Dave did fine, because programmers don't really need that much supervising. You just tell them what to get done and threaten to take away their energy drinks if they don't do it very frickin' fast. And Dave, credit where it's due or whatever, dude knew how to outsource. Basically, he figured out who the smartest code monkeys were and let them tell him what needed fixing and who should do it and how. So at work, he mostly just fucked around, doing his reading or whatever, but the updates got updated, bugs got unbugged. All good, right?

"That was in the spring. But then, in the fall, the boss or his accountant or someone very frickin' high up ran the numbers on the site one month and according to Mr. Sirko they didn't check out. Like, there's this standard advantage that the house has, right? It's different from game to game and it's not even that huge, but when enough people play, it guarantees a sweet profit. And at LBAL, the house was still winning, still making money, but not as much as the algorithm predicted. Especially on roulette. Some people were winning more often than they should have. And when the accountant dude looks into it, he finds out they're winning with some frickin' high bets.

"And, yeah," Raj continues, his fingers flicking the lock on his door back and forth, "so clearly that's an issue, but I don't really deal with the tech side of things or even the money part all that much and it was probably just some bug. And like, I had this Florida thing planned and like, what? I'm going to bail on my boys just 'cause some coder who's never been laid in his whole frickin' life put in a one when he should have typed a zero? Hell no. 'Cause if this screwup's been going on for months, it can stay screwed up for one more frickin' week, right? But the day before I fly out, Mr. Sirko comes into the office and says he thinks that Dave has written some, like, crazy frickin' embezzlement program. And I don't want to tell Mr. Sirko that Dave barely knows where the power button is, so I just say that he's a loyal employee and that we need to look elsewhere. That it's just some fuckup further down the chain.

"And that's frickin' that. But on Tuesday, when I get back from my break—and oh man, South Beach, crazy town, right?—he's not at the apartment and that's fine. Like, maybe he's staying with Irina. The boss's daughter? You met her today. Nice kid. Smart, too. She was actually the original programmer on the site. She and Dave had a thing going. Like they were gonna get married. So I just assume Dave's with her. But maybe I never really knew Dave at all, because I get to work the next day—"

At that moment the car pulls up in front of Raj's building and Raj stops talking. What happened to the good old days, before apps, when a driver would take you from midtown to the East Village by way of Staten Island and give the nice man in the back seat time to complete his monologue?

Raj lives in a building near mine, though infinitely more upmarket, a new construction on St. Mark's Place with a lobby bedecked in gleaming black tile and outsize pendant lamps, each of which likely costs more than my annual salary. Certainly more than Nora's. He ushers me into the elevator and then paws at me, like an unusually clumsy cat. I think of Destine, how he'd have me shoved against the back wall, both of my wrists pinned above my head. And for a moment I think of Charlie, too, how he might slip an arm around my waist and press my head against his shoulder. But here I am, prey to Raj's slurping. It's a fast elevator, mirrored to give Versailles pause, and I can see the graceless shape of our bodies replicated infinitely. The eleventh floor can't come soon enough.

Then it does. Raj's apartment is just to the left. He opens the door with his key and I feel a jab of dêjá vu. Another man, another night, another apartment. Though this apartment is nicer than most. The living room holds a dark gray sofa and a sleek glass coffee table. On the wall hangs a framed color field print in rich, riparian blues. I had expected postfrat ambience—beer helmets, the higher class of swimsuit calendar. Instead, the place is very nearly classy. And yet, something about this situation—this room, my place within it—sounds a warning note. But I'm just tipsy enough that as I step out of my high heels and onto the deep-pile carpet, I can't pinpoint what's wrong.

Besides, I'm supposed to be Nora. After tonight I won't ever be Nora again. But in the minutes that remain to her, Nora does not pinpoint. She is too busy being friendly and nice and a little bit dumb. So I giggle in a manner that I hope is flirtatious, unshouldering my purse and tossing my coat in the general direction of a bentwood chair.

Arranging myself on the sofa, a tipsy odalisque, I again catch my reflection, this time in the coffee table—the lip gloss, smeared from kissing, the swirl of blond hair. And finally, my brain, muddled from triple sec, makes a late deduction. That my hair, the same hair that Boris Sirko nearly manhandled, is going to be a problem. As soon as Raj runs his fingers through it, it will likely come away in his hand. So I had better learn what I can at speed and then see if that elevator goes any faster on its way down.

"Which bedroom is yours?" I ask.

He points down the short hallway to the door on the right.

"Wait for me there," I say, "I just have to pee."

He points farther down the hall and I totter there, exaggerating the drunkenness in my walk. Running a trickle of water in the sink, which should simulate the sound of urination, I wait a few seconds after I hear the door to Raj's room open. Then I slip out of the bathroom and tiptoe to the second bedroom, which must have belonged to David Adler. The lights are off and I don't dare turn them on, but the glow from the street illuminates, barely, a stripped bed and a dresser, its drawers yawning, the contents likely dumped into the large cardboard box I bark my shin against, which nests with several others beside the bed.

On top of the desk, where a computer might have sat, I find a crumpled tissue and a pen with a chewed cap. I remember what Irina said about David Adler keeping his passwords taped to the desk's underside. Even though I don't know precisely what I'm looking for, I run my hand underneath. It comes away empty. I feel up and down each of the wooden legs, too. Nothing. Noiselessly, knowing that I don't have much longer, I slide open the desk's single drawer. Bare. I shut it. Or I try to.

It won't close all the way.

Working to keep my hands steady, my breath hushed, I lift the drawer out and turn it around. Taped to the back is a small object, hard and spiky. A model of the Chrysler Building. The one David Adler brandishes in the picture on Raj's desk. I realize where I've seen it before. In the gifts and oddments store on Avenue A, in a window display: the Chrysler Building, the Empire State, the Statue of Liberty. They aren't models—or rather, they aren't only models. They're also portable flash drives.

If David Adler bothered to hide this drive before coming into work that Tuesday morning, then likely it contains something important. A program designed to beat a casino at its own crooked games, say. Or evidence of something else. Something worse. Like a money-laundering operation masquerading as a chintzy internet site, like proof that he and Vinnie were working together on something more lucrative than a roulette hack. The kind of lucrative that gets Vinnie a hot shot. The kind of lucrative that disappears David Adler from the Manhattan grid.

Before Raj can wonder where I am, I nestle the drive inside my bra and return to the bathroom, where I flush the toilet and run hot water over my hands, scrubbing them with a juniper-scented soap that doesn't make me feel any cleaner.

I find Raj in his bed, tucked beneath the duvet, still in his button-down, tapping at his phone.

"Oh, my gosh," I say, the words scattering like beads from a broken chain. "I'm so sorry. This is, like, the most embarrassing thing ever. But I think I just got my period. And also I maybe just threw up. Don't worry, I tidied up in there and I like you so much and this has really been the most amazing night, but I think maybe I should just go, right? But don't hate me, okay?"

A look that might be relief passes over Raj's face. "Yeah," he says. "Okay. That sounds pretty bad. I guess you should. Do you need me to get you a car?"

I suppose he never looked at my résumé. The address I gave, the address of the magazine, is just a few avenues over. My actual apartment is even closer. "No," I trill. "I've got that amazing Christmas bonus you gave me. Thanks for everything and wish me luck with *Carousel*." I issue one last artificially sweetened giggle, then grab my purse and coat, pinch back into my heels, and dash for the elevator, away from Raj and into the night.

Outside, in the sprinkling rain, I snatch the wig from my hair and deposit it in the nearest trash can. The sidewalk seems to ripple beneath my feet, concrete like a waterbed, and I stumble more than once. I'm fuddled, foggy, in a kind of mourning, grieving the loss that comes with taking off a role, reckoning with what that role required of me. In the last seventy-two hours, I have committed theft, attempted corporate espionage, and overstayed my lunch breaks. I have been forced to use a professional phone voice and have kissed, with tongue, a man who almost certainly majored in economics. And yet the sharpness of the drive wedged into my bra reminds me that these humiliations weren't entirely without reward.

When I open my phone, I see that Destine has texted. I delete the text. All I want is a bath as hot as I can bear and half an Ativan to tuck me in after. But as I approach my building, there is Charlie, hunched on the stoop like a gargoyle that just wants to cuddle. I am too tired to pretend for him now.

He favors me with a misty smile, made mistier by the rain. "Figured you had to come home sometime," he says, "to shower, to sleep."

"Who has time for hobbies?" I say. I know he wants reassurance, comfort, for me to make my eyes go large like some nocturnal animal as I tell him he's the only man for me and that my absence has some entirely plausible explanation. But I can't summon the necessary energy.

"Were you just in the neighborhood?" I ask. "Or is there something you need?"

"I live a few streets over, so I'm in the neighborhood a lot. But Vivian, I was worried. I left you a couple of voice messages and you didn't respond."

"Sorry. I play voice mail like once a decade."

"I sent you some emails, too."

"I've been working on that article I told you about. Going undercover. I haven't braved my inbox in days."

"I just wondered if you were okay or if I did something wrong last time, if there was some reason—Wait, Vivian, have you been crying?"

"No, Charlie," I say, with something less than perfect confidence. "It's the rain. And Charlie, you are lovely. Really. Much, much too good to be true. But I'm wet through and tired to the bone and maybe we could do this couples counseling session another time. Or at least indoors?"

I push past him with my keys and heave the door to the building open. He hangs back, uncertain.

"Just come in already," I tell him. He follows me up, flight after flight, and waits, a scolded puppy, as I struggle against the locks and stumble in. My small kitchen holds few drawers and fewer cabinets, but I search through most of them until I find a bottle of sugarcane rum in the compartment below the oven. I lift it to my lips, not measuring, not monitoring, letting it run down my throat, fierce and sweet. Because I want to feel nothing now. I offer the bottle to Charlie. He shakes his head.

In the bathroom, I switch my clothes for my robe, hiding the drive behind the aspirin in the medicine cabinet. Then I slink underneath the blankets, which feel wonderfully heavy and warm. Charlie looks at me, eyes sad, smile tight. "Maybe I can just hold you?" he says.

I let him. And for once—without benefit of pill or concussion—I'm instantly asleep. But then, at some thin and fearful hour of the morning, I'm awake again, breathing sharply and too fast. I've had my usual nightmare or one even worse. I see that I have woken Charlie, too.

"Shhh," he says, stroking my hair, my real hair, and in his eyes, glittering down at me in the dark, I know myself again. Or not myself, exactly—someone kinder, less brittle, more human.

"I'm sorry," I say. "I had a dream. A nightmare."

"I know. I could tell. You were thrashing around."

"In the dream I couldn't find my way," I say. "I was so alone."

"That's terrible," he says. He rings me with his arms, murmuring into my hair. "But you're not alone, Vivian," he says. "I'm here. I won't leave. Go back to sleep."

I shut my eyes. I fold my body into his. But sleep won't take me. Until it will. And in the morning, when he does leave, whispering a kiss to my forehead, I stumble from bed to bathroom to find that my period really has come, early, and that I have bled through my underwear and onto the robe. It's only after I have cleaned myself and put some water on for tea that I see, on the floor, another note, red to match the blood.

VIVIAN, it reads, WE WARNED YOU.

Does the note mean that Sirko and his men know about my time as Nora? That they saw through my performance from the start? I have hazarded so much. Cracked the frangible stability I have built this life around. Gambled and very likely lost. I'm on the floor then, curled into a crooked ball, and from somewhere far away I can hear someone—me, maybe—crying as the kettle screams away.

15

LONG WINTER'S NAP

I lose the days before Christmas to collected works, deli sandwiches ordered through a delivery app, and a marked increase in my alcohol ration, so that I won't think or feel anything more than necessary. After an abortive attempt to download the flash drive's contents onto my computer—and a text from Esteban informing me that Diego is out of town for a few days—I place the tiny Chrysler Building back in the medicine cabinet. Roger writes to confirm that I'll be joining them on Christmas Day. But when I ask about the January schedule, he doesn't respond. I worry that this means that I will never have the job, that the distractions of this last month have wrenched it from my grasp. Or that I never held it at all. I pour another drink.

On Christmas Eve, I order lobster lo mein and corkscrew open a Malbec before starting *The Man Who Came to Dinner*, a comedy about a pitiless drama critic, Sheridan Whiteside, who invades a nice midwestern home. I consider him a personal hero. I chase it with *All About Eve*, mouthing along to Addison DeWitt's every line: "We're a breed apart from the rest of humanity, we theater folk; we are the original displaced personalities." Then I chase sleep—catching it, letting it go—toward a cheerless dawn.

In the morning, with no stocking to unpack or presents to open or even another note to unfold, I leave my apartment for the first time in days (because no one can follow you when you never go anywhere) and brave a lonely, nauseated subway ride to the Upper West Side. Though my eyes scan back and forth across the cars, they find no one watching me. Maybe my pursuers took Christmas off. It had snowed in the early hours, but by the time I emerge from the station, the drifts have already turned sludgy and brown tipped. My galoshes slosh through freezing grit, spotted with salt and dirt, dog mess and beer caps. As I wait for the streetlight to change, I can just glimpse the skeletal trees of Riverside Park, peering out from between the buildings. Beyond them, the Hudson sprawls, unmoving, the water a tourniquet tightened around the city.

Roger's lobby has marble floors, brass details, and heaps of molding that look as though a wedding cake collided with the plasterwork. He and Cheryl have lived here ever since he graduated from Columbia, and rent stabilization means they probably pay as much for their classic six as I do for my cramped studio. In the narrow elevator, a golden grate slides in front of me as I'm conveyed squeakily to the fifth floor.

Roger is Catholic, his wife is Jewish, and they take an ecumenical approach to holiday decorations. I dodge some mistletoe as Roger greets me, then knock into a side table that holds a menorah. The Christmas tree, agleam with blue and white tinsel, stands just inside the foyer and I'm counting the points on the star atop when Roger speeds me into the kitchen, redolent of yeast and meat drippings.

Cheryl enfolds me in an embrace of frizzy hair and floury palms as I try not to squirm. She heads early childhood education at some upscale West Side private school and tends toward the terrifyingly maternal.

"Vivian!" she says when she lets me go. "I'm so glad you could join us. I'll have the goose cooked—oh, isn't that funny, like, my goose is cooked! Like, the jig is up! Anyway, I'll have it done in just a few minutes. And how are you? Are you well? You're looking so thin. Roger, isn't she looking thin? Roger, get her something. There's pâté left over and water crackers in the cabinet. Or the fruitcake your aunt sent. Vivian, do you like fruitcake? It's very rich."

"Sweetheart, I think Vivian would rather have a drink."

It's the truest thing he's ever said. I turn to him before Cheryl can discuss the virtues of taking my gummy multivitamins and wearing a hat when I go out to play. "Nothing would please me more," I tell him. "And speaking of drinks . . ." From my bag I extract a bottle of Jameson twelve-year, tied with a jaunty bow.

"Wonderful!" he says. "How can I ever thank you?"

"Assign me fewer O'Neill revivals."

"I'll consider it."

"And Roger, about the job—"

"Shhh. No job talk. We're celebrating the birth of some guy. Jesus, his name is. Should have been on Broadway. There's a man who can hold a crowd. Now what would you like? Vodka martini? With a twist?"

My face falls to some lower floor and I turn away, busying myself with a can of chestnuts so he won't see. "A drink with a surprise ending?" I say. "My favorite."

Roger goes in search of a shaker and tells me to stow his present under the tree, where I cram it among the litter of fallen tinsel and pine needles. For Cheryl, I've bought some ritzy loose-leaf teas. I hadn't really known what to bring their children—Mark, a sophomore in college, and Cass, a senior in high school. What would I have wanted at that age? Better drugs? More privacy? Failing that, I've brought chocolate.

Roger places the cocktail in my hands, hits play on a klezmer CD, and goes to summon the children: Mark walks in clutching his iPhone, which squawks at irregular intervals. Cass, all in black save for striped stockings, refuses to lift her dyed-pink head from a book of Simone de Beauvoir essays.

"Vivian," he says, "ask Cass about school."

With the drink's help, I oblige. "How's school?"

Cass rolls her heavily mascaraed eyes. "Um, it's fine? I have all my college applications in so I can basically just coast."

"She's going to Columbia!" Roger says.

"I am not. Dad made me apply early. But I'm not going unless I don't get accepted anywhere decent and very far away. And I crushed the SATs, so I totally will."

"Well," says Roger, "we'll see if I totally pay for it."

"Dad, can we not do this? Like again? Like in front of guests? Mark's at Cornell and you're paying for that obviously."

"Vivian is not a guest. She's my prized employee. And Mark is not my daughter. He can range farther."

"So true," says Mark. His phone shrieks in agreement.

People wonder why I have tubal ligation FAQs bookmarked on my browser.

Before domestic bliss devours me, Cheryl announces that lunch is served and we make our way to the table. Roger pours me a glass of something classy and red, and by the time I finish it I'm no longer so blazingly aware of my voice, my every gesture, of the profound effort it takes to behave like a sane and pleasant person. The goose—dense, unctuous—I can't stomach, but I force down some green beans, some bread, half of a yam. I've found that as long as I make some headway with my plate and nod when appropriate, Roger's family will eventually forget about me, busying themselves with old grievances and older sympathies. If I blur my eyes, I can even pretend I'm safe in the theater's dark, watching another dysfunctional family drama—though this one has real food and better than average bonhomie.

After toying with a serving of plum tart and letting Roger delight me with one more glass of burgundy, we retire to the sofa. I'm wobbly now, but I brazen it out as a shuffling kind of dance. Cheryl switches out the klezmer music for a recording of the *Messiah*, which makes the living room feel a lot more crowded. On creaking knees, Roger lowers himself to the floor and pulls out several presents from beneath the tree.

"We opened most of ours this morning," he says apologetically. "I may now have enough dress socks to last out the century. But we do have a couple of things for you."

"Roger, please, I don't—"

"Come on, kid. Of course you do. Everyone should get to open a present on Christmas or Hanukkah. But not on Kwanzaa. That's a fake holiday."

"Dad!" says Cass. "That is so racist!"

He lifts up the bottle of Jameson. "Children, look what Vivian has brought. A present—and one not intended for my feet. Vivian, you're too good to me."

I don't think I've ever been too good to anyone.

"If you don't want socks," Cheryl says, emerging from the kitchen with a plate of gingerbread men, "you shouldn't always ask for them. Here, Vivian, please, you hardly ate, have a cookie."

I pluck one from the tray and eat the head first. Roger hands around the rest of the gifts I've brought. Cheryl coos over the tea, while Mark swallows the artisanal chocolate bar seemingly whole, just as a snake might gulp down a single-origin mouse. Cass passes her chocolate off to her brother.

"Chocolate is, like, one of the most exploitative industries in the world," she says.

"That one's fair trade," I tell her.

"Well, it makes me break out," she says.

"Here," says Cheryl, thrusting a package at me. "Your turn, Vivian. Open mine."

I rend the paper, open the box clumsily, and pull out a lumpy blue scarf that makes my hands itch on contact.

"Do you like it? I made it. I've been learning to knit. It's meditation for my hands."

"We all received one," Roger says, raising an eyebrow. "Isn't that splendid?"

I knot the scarf around my neck. "Mmmm. Warm." The scratchiness of the wool threatens to obstruct my breathing. "Really warm. I'll have to wait to put it on until I go back outside."

"And this is from me," Roger says.

The wrapping reveals a hefty tome. I recognize it as Kenneth Tynan's *Curtains*, one of the great collections of theater criticism by one of theater criticism's many terrible men.

"Do you know the motto he used to have above his desk?" Roger asks.

I do. But I shake my head. I let him say it.

"'Rouse tempers, goad and lacerate, raise whirlwinds.'"

"'S wonderful," I tell Roger, making the most of my slight slur. "'S marvelous. Thank you."

"Look up his review of Vivien Leigh in *Caesar and Cleopatra*."

"The one where he calls her 'pert, sly and spankable'?" I'm slurring more, but he doesn't seem to notice.

"Genius, isn't it?" He arches an eyebrow. "Always reminds me of you."

"Dad!" says Cass.

"Now who would like another cookie?" Cheryl asks.

I slip away as soon as I reasonably can, retreating from enforced cheer into the sleet and bus fumes. As I near the subway, a buzz alerts me that Destine has texted again. He's on duty today, but his shift ends early and he wants to see me. I wonder how he'll explain this to his wife. In a gesture of goodwill toward men, I tell him to come by.

I'm home again, flipping through *Curtains*, when the buzzer rings. And then Destine is at my door, scented with cold and whiskey. I pull the vodka from the freezer and retrieve a couple of glasses from above the sink. He joins me on the bed, and when he slides a hand up my thigh his fingers are like ice. I shiver. He smiles.

"How was your holiday, Ms. Parry?" he asks.

"A small crippled boy taught me the true meaning of Christmas. So pretty nice, all told. Yours?"

"Slow. A few domestics and reports of some guy dressed as an elf flashing kids near East River Park, but those are jobs for uniform, so mostly I sat around. Some transit cops came over with eggnog."

"No visits from the ghosts of Complaint Review Boards past?" I've stood to slide off my tights.

He catches my wrist in his hand and squeezes it, pinching the joint until my eyes find his. I see that it isn't sex he has come for. Or not only sex. "You've got a smart mouth, little girl," he says, but it's nearly a growl now. "You know that?"

"It does well on most standardized tests," I say.

He smiles at me in a way that isn't a smile at all. "Don't you ever shut up?"

I hear the hardness in his voice and lazily, without thought, I meet it. "Make me."

He hits me with the back of his hand. He does it casually, mechanically, the way another fussier man might brush lint from a shirt cuff. The blow isn't so hard that it sends me sprawling, but it's hard enough. I can feel my cheek reddening, the corner of my bottom lip beginning to swell. And through the pain, I notice how the sensation shrinks my world, concentrates it. Christmas dinner, David Adler, Charlie with his wounded eyes, these all fall away. Every nerve centers on the heat and sting of my cheek, and I've never felt so quiet, so calm, so easy in this body. Not since I walked offstage all those years ago, away from the light.

I take another sip of vodka, filtering the liquid through my clenched teeth. Then I set the glass on the floor. "Again," I say.

He obliges. Harder this time.

"Again," I say.

"No," he says. "You like it too much. Get undressed."

I do what he says—stripping off my blouse, my skirt, my underwear, as briskly as I can, without flirtation or delay.

"Lie down," he says. "On your stomach."

I do. With an efficient motion he pulls my arms over my head and pushes my face into the blankets. "Stay like that," he says. "Don't move."

I can hear the soft rustle as his coat slides to the floor, the chime of his belt buckle as it unfastens, the thud of one shoe hitting the floor and then another. My body is rigid, tensed. But then I feel his hand on me, parting my legs, pushing his fingers roughly inside, and I want to tell him not yet, that I'm not ready, but he places his other hand on the back of my neck and I realize it won't matter what I say.

He forces himself into me and there's pain, of course, and something else, too, like when you tilt your face toward the sky on a clear day and aim your closed eyes directly at the sun. It's black in front of my eyes, but there's color also, lightless but intense, reds and purples that pulse in front of me like flowers opening and opening and opening.

The next day and the days after are spent eating less than I should and drinking more. In this great city, even the liquor stores deliver.

I check the listings in search of some distraction, some useful labor. But between Christmas and New Year's there are no new shows to see. Nothing to pitch. I'm scared to leave the apartment anyway. I'm uncertain of who might follow me if I do and what he might want. And so I stay beneath the blankets, trying to repair my broken sleep. But several times each night, I startle myself awake, half convinced that someone's in the room with me, watching me. Asleep, I dream. The dreams are feverish and formless and dark.

Nora has gone the way of her wig, but my own skin won't slide back on, no matter how hard I dig my nails into my palms or finger the bruise below my right eye, a souvenir from Destine. My body feels like a dress bought on clearance, one that never really fit. I could parade it around for those few hours on Christmas Day, but not since. I don't know how to hold my head anymore or what to do with my hands. With the sleeping pills gone and the Ativan already low and no openings until early January, I'm left with my vodka and my thoughts.

Justine phones the day before New Year's Eve and demands that I join her the next night. I don't demur for long. I don't bother. If Justine ever gives up acting, she could have a marvelous second career as a detention camp interrogator.

"We're going to a lovely party," she says with the tenderness of a thumbscrew. "It's hosted by some internet zillionaire the doctor knows from Princeton and we're promised champagne that's actually from Champagne and an assortment of pills arrayed like so much caviar. Also actual caviar."

"I hate caviar."

"So put downers on your toast points. Come on, Vivian," she says, stretching out my name into a whine. "Parties without you are boring. I hate being bored. And, look, I wanted to keep this a surprise, but I scored you more sleeping pills."

"Did you? Well, twist my arm," I say, looking down at my real arm, its wrist still bruised.

"Yeah," Justine says with an exhalation I might mistake for a sigh. "I thought that might do it. I'll come and pick you up around nine. Just so you know, the party's in Brooklyn. Don't even, babe. It's just over the bridge. It's fine. We'll take a car and—Hey, what the actual fuck! My brunch table just opened up and some bitch is angling for it. Have to run. Oh, meant to say, it's a costume party. So dress up or I'll literally murder you—and yes, fuck you very much, I know what literally means—and then bring you to the party anyway. Okay. Love you. Bye."

I don't sleep much that night and the next day, in the bath, my eyes close and I wake again, panicked, spluttering. I pour the first drink early. Sometime in the afternoon, willing to brave the outside if only to clear my head, I venture in search of a sandwich, but as I'm turning back onto my block, I see a dead rat in the gutter, its stomach bloated and pale. I throw the sandwich away.

A costume party. A costume. My first thought: cut eyeholes in a black sheet and come as a shadow of myself. But I don't have a black sheet. I may not even have scissors. And then it comes to me.

From between the hangers, I pull out a long-sleeved knit dress that stretches nearly to the floor, in a shade of red so venous it's nearly purple, another relic of my mother's. Then I enlist my meager collection of makeup, recalling those long-ago tutorials opposite lit mirrors in cramped dressing rooms. I powder and powder until my complexion gleams palely, then apply a kohl eyeliner, using a finger to smudge it. I take a small container of blush I can't remember buying and recruit it as eye shadow, swirling it all around the socket. Careful not to mar the makeup, I slip the dress on over my head, where it clings to my small breasts and outlines each jutting hipbone. I find a hammered silver choker—also once my mother's—and pin it to my hair like a diadem. Then I step into the high black boots that Justine talked me into and which I wear only when I want to look intimidating during Critics' Circle meetings. I check the wardrobe mirror. I don't look intimidating. I look thin, haunted. I slip the trick knife into my purse.

When the bell rings, I make Justine climb the stairs. "Just finishing dressing," I shout, even though I finished half an hour ago. "Come up for a drink."

Eventually, she does, sheathed in a swirl of white feathers. "How can you live this high up?" she says, collapsing onto the bed and massaging her ankles. "I'd need, like, fucking supplemental oxygen."

"Justine, you live on the tenth floor."

"Of an elevator building. Like a civilized person. What are you dressed as?"

"Lady Macbeth," I say. "Driven half-mad with guilt and troubled sleep. Very into hand hygiene." I take Justine in—her false eyelashes, her orange lips and heels, the abundant plumage. "And you are?"

"I'm a seagull," she says. "No, wait, that's not it. I'm an actress. Didn't you yell something about a drink, babe?"

I hand her the vodka bottle. She opens it and tips it back, smudging the rim with lipstick and taking a long swallow that makes all her feathers tremble. I take one last slug myself, feeling it speed down my throat and then out to every limb, softening me, readying me for friendly conversation.

"How are rehearsals?" I ask.

"We start previews in three days, so, you know, *dire*. But the sheep-shearing scene is pegged to a level of idiocy so profound that I think it might actually be amazing. Did I tell you about the phalluses?"

"You did not," I say as I pass the bottle back.

"Well," she says after she takes a second swallow, "they are legion and papier-mâché and truly fucking horrifying. But my act three speech is tremendous, obviously. And I'm getting really good at standing still." She strikes a melancholy pose. Not a single feather ruffles. "So yay, me. On the other hand, Leontes still isn't off book and the bad doctor's starting to complain about all the time I spend at rehearsal. Wait, I forget, have you actually even met him?"

"Just that time you brought him to the bar on Fourth and he sulked because they didn't have bottle service."

"He gets bored if he can't throw money around."

"At least he can throw samples around?"

"Wow. Subtle. Relax, Lady M. You'll get yours. After midnight. New

Year. New drugs. Fucking festive, right? Now get your coat on. And try not to knife any partygoers."

Downstairs, Justine goes to swipe for a car, her feathers a snowy blur, but a gypsy cab stops in the meantime and after haggling with the driver in a boob-forward way, she shoves me inside and soon we're swooping through the Village and then across the bridge. Below is the East River, black and chill. I turn my head around and look back at Manhattan—at all the headlights and stoplights and streetlights and skyscraper tips glowing together, like some great stilled firework.

We arrive in DUMBO, a treeless neighborhood of old warehouses and new money. The cab stops before an imposing building with wide, arched windows, a center of manufacturing long since converted to luxury lofts. Justine flounces out and says a few words to a doorman in honest-to-God epaulets, who gestures toward the elevator. Without the push of any button, it levitates us toward the penthouse. The doors split and the party surrounds us. I take in the range of costumes. There's a Lady Liberty who might actually be a man and a Supreme Court justice in a shorty robe. Several of the men have opted for rubber masks of former presidents—three Reagans cluster around a bottle of what looks like excellent Scotch—and many of the women have clothed themselves in lubricious versions of blue-collar uniforms: sexy firefighter, sexy police officer. I see a sexy mail carrier, swiftly completing her appointed rounds in hot pants.

Justine has gone to find the bad doctor, but she returns instead with a pair of champagne flutes. What I pour down my throat tastes like gently carbonated gold, only possibly more expensive.

"Come on," Justine says. "You should mingle. Maybe you'll meet someone rich."

Between Charlie, Destine, and my narrow escape from Raj, I need more men in my life like *Timon of Athens* needs a sixth act.

Justine notes my aversion and sticks her tongue out at me. "Ugh. You are massively no fun. I was counting on you for vicarious sluttery, babe."

She reaches into the folds of her feathers and liberates a pill case, handing me a capsule a cart horse might have difficulty swallowing.

"Go on," she says. "If you're not planning on fucking tonight, you might as well take it. The doctor says it's the Cadillac of downers."

"You mean passé, oversized, and with terrible mileage?"

"I mean smooth, stately, and an American fucking classic. Here"—she fishes out her own pill—"I'll join you. Chin-chin or whatever." We go in search of more champagne.

Twenty minutes later, as I'm swirling the bubbly dregs, I begin to feel it working. It's slow but sleek, as though someone has gradually drawn a silken drape across the room. The music sounds more subdued, the colors softer. I float along, my legs steady—even graceful—in the heeled boots. Out on the balcony, under some heat lamps, I lean out and look down again at the river, which now reflects the moon, hazy behind a circlet of clouds. Another president, one of the Bushes, I think, reaches out for me, but I whirl away and glide back into the penthouse.

The main room, large even at first glance, seems to have expanded. Everyone, everything, feels farther away. The people look like stage pictures, arranged prettily into clumps and clusters. I see two girls in stewardess outfits grouped near the kitchen, George Washington arguing with Jimmy Carter at the breakfast bar. Justine perches in the hall that leads to the bedroom, back arched and gesturing in a way that makes all her feathers flutter. She's fifteen feet away at most, but she feels infinitely distant, as though separated from me by that unbridgeable gulf that divides the lip of the stage from the first row of seats.

Lolling against a fawn sectional, I watch the scene—the music, the dark lights, the bodies passing before me. *It's just a play*, I tell myself. My peripheral vision catches my own arm, crimson gowned, but it doesn't feel like mine. I bring my gaze down to my breasts, my belly, my lap, my legs. They all seem separate from me, parts of a character's costume. I take the knife from my purse and I press it into a thigh, a biceps, a hip. I feel nothing. I could feel this way forever. Then a light catches my eye as the bathroom door opens and a man emerges, tugging a Nixon mask back over his face. There's something familiar about the line of his jaw, the glint of a sideburn before it disappears beneath the latex. And with a feeling as though someone has just emptied antifreeze down my throat, I recognize this man. It's David Adler.

I'm unused to running in heels, or maybe the downer has affected my coordination, because as I race after him I stumble against the edge of a rug and have to grab on to the glass coffee table so that I don't somersault. By the time I'm upright again, he's vanished, gone. I plunge into the master bedroom first, disturbing a naughty nurse and her patient entwined on a pile of coats, and stagger into the second bedroom, which appears deserted, though I do check under the bed and in the closet. I head back to the patio, lurching through the knots of party guests. But he isn't standing beneath a heat lamp or perched on any of the lounge chairs surrounding the disused grill.

And then, just at the edge of the balcony, I see him, his masked face turned toward the river, where I've sometimes wondered if his body was submerged. I start toward him, but a fat man in a Teddy Roosevelt mask blocks my path, laying outsize hands on each of my shoulders.

"What's the hurry, sweetheart?" he says. "You some sort of a witch? You gotta spell you wanna do?"

Twisting away, I light out for the patio's edge. David Adler has disappeared. But where could he have gone? I'm sure he didn't slip past me. I hoist myself onto the ledge, leaning out as the metal railing bites into my palms, knifing my body so that I can lean farther, scanning the balcony and beyond, then faltering, overcorrecting, and tumbling back onto the slate, where I am suddenly, copiously sick, acid foaming from my stomach and splashing onto my dress and the paving below. I stand back up, walking my hands up my thighs, shaking the dark spots away, then stumble back into the apartment and into the waiting elevator, hitting Doors Close over and over until I think my thumb will sprain. Delivered to the ground floor, I skitter into the lobby and out onto the sidewalk.

"David!" I call. "David Adler." But the rattling of the subway over the bridge steals my voice away. No one answers. Which means that David Adler is one fast runner or that I saw someone entirely else, just as I had superimposed his living face over Vinnie Mendoza's dead one as it lay beneath that tree. It means that the thrill and the strain and the vast stupidity of pretending to be Nora, combined with that downer and too much champagne, have left me with a shaky grasp of perceptual reality. I think of my costume, of poor Lady M, of how Macbeth describes her: "a mind diseased."

Retching takes me again and I stoop toward the pavement, heaving dryly. When I had the stomach flu as a girl, my mother would bring me compresses moistened with a drop of her jasmine scent, because she knew I loved it, wiping my face clean and kissing away each tear. But there is no one to care for me now. And I feel other tears, stinging my eyes, splattering the sidewalk. A spider's thread of saliva hangs from my mouth to the grit below and I can feel myself start to spiral down toward it, but then there are fierce, slender arms encircling me, hauling me upright.

"What the actual fuck," Justine says. She thrusts my coat at me. As I put it on, I realize just how cold I am.

"I'm sorry," I say, scrabbling in the pockets for something to wipe my mouth. "I thought—"

"Babe: I don't fucking care what you thought," she says. "That was, like, supremely embarrassing. You were sick all over the patio and it's not even midnight. When did you become such a fucking lightweight? Craig's going to kill me for leaving early."

"Craig?"

"The bad doctor, okay? Nicknames are so fucking juvenile."

"Justine, I'm fine. Go back inside. I had too much to drink and that pill you gave me messed with my head and it was all, as you put it, supremely embarrassing. I am supremely embarrassed. But I'm fine now. I'll get myself home." I take a step along the sidewalk, but my knees nearly give way and I have to grab a parking meter.

Justine doesn't say anything, but when she inhales I can hear the air hissing snakelike through her teeth. She grabs me under one arm and hauls me toward Front Street, standing in the road, feathers ablaze in the headlights, demanding the attention of a passing cab. She bundles me in and gives the driver the address of her building.

"Are you going to a party?" the cabbie asks, favoring her with a grin. "You are perhaps dressed as Mother Goose?"

"No. I'm a seagull," Justine snaps. "And apparently a fucking nursemaid, too."

"I'm sorry," I repeat. I don't dare tell her what I saw. What I'm half convinced I only hallucinated. "I didn't really eat today—"

"Fuck that. You're a big girl now. Old enough to know how much you can handle. If you puke again, I am so not holding your hair."

"You must vomit?" the driver says. "There is no vomiting in my taxi. I will stop the car. You must leave."

"Oh shut the fuck up," Justine says. "That's fucking illegal."

We drive on, and through the closed windows I can hear a collective roar building and then fireworks begin to explode, tinting the windows gold and red and fiery white.

"It's New Year's," I say.

"There's that critical fucking acumen you're so famous for."

The fireworks—the noise and the color—overwhelm me. I shut my eyes, wishing I could sleep, and lean my head back against the window. "It's midnight," I say, without opening them. "You promised me those pills?"

"Seriously? Five minutes ago I was figuring out whether you needed to have your stomach pumped. And now you want pills? For the primordial goddess's fucking sake, Viv! That drink all the drinks, snort all the lines, down all the pills bullshit? Maybe it looked cute in our twenties. Probably not even then. Definitely not now. So honestly, grow the fuck up. Because I'm very fucking sorry that your mom died, that you couldn't act anymore, that you went a little crazy for a while, and that none of the absolute deadbeats at University Health could make any of that all better, so instead you got stuck with me and an endless scroll of shitty coping mechanisms. That all sucks. But surprise, babe! It's adulthood now. Everything fucking sucks. You get on with it. You make the best of it. So yeah, no more fucking pharmaceuticals for you. Overdose on your own goddamn scrip."

"I have tried to get on with it," I say. "I am trying. Right now I just want to sleep."

"Yeah? For how fucking long?"

"Just through the night, okay?" I open my eyes and angle my face toward Justine's. "And since when are you a public service campaign for healthy fucking living? Or are you just conveniently forgetting the razor scars, that one STD scare and then the other STD scare and—"

Another firework bursts, and in its momentary flash I see a tear, bright as pearl, slip Justine's perfect cheek and splash her quivering feathers.

"Oh, Justine," I say. "I'm sorry. I'm so sorry." And I am. For her. For me. For all the motherless girls who never grew up, who never knew how.

But she's turned away from me and toward the window, each firework coloring her face like a fresh wound.

16

CANDID

I spend a fitful night on Justine's tufted couch, upholstered in labial pink, and most of the next day there as well, vomiting politely into the footbath she uses for pedicures. Justine leaves in the early afternoon, tossing a spare key ring among the various crystals on the coffee table and reminding me to lock up if I can, as she puts it, "play the starring role of someone with baseline fucking survival skills." An hour later, I obey, tidying the place and then slinking back to my apartment after a brief stop at the corner store. Inside, I force a milky tea and half of a buttered role down my bruised throat. Then I crawl into bed, covers pulled over my head, huddled in the dark, waiting for something like sleep.

I wake too early, immobile beneath the tangled blanket, my mind staging and restaging the events of New Year's Eve. Did I see David Adler at the party? Or did I only imagine him? Given the darkness, the costumes, the drink, the pill, I may never know. But I do have his flash drive. Which needs to be unlocked. I pull my phone from the charger and after an almost infinite number of rings, Esteban answers, blearily, though his tone hops an octave when he hears my voice.

"Hey, bebita. You make some resolutions?"

"I've promised to stop buying the bargain vodka," I rasp. "I'm better than that. Look, I need your cousin's help again. Is he back yet?"

"Diego? I think so."

"I've got a flash drive and I can't open it. But maybe he can?"

Five minutes later my phone begins to vibrate:

$120 and he says you're good to go, the first message reads.

Want me to bring you by?

I have a date but I can make him wait.

Dick pic he sent was: A string of disappointment emojis follows, with a single solitary eggplant in the middle.

The next message is an image. I drop the phone.

That's okay, I text when I have picked it up again. No chaperone needed. And Esteban, you deserve so much more.

We all do, putita.

Some hours later, I'm slumped on Diego's floor, an airplane bottle of Malibu sloshing in my stomach—hair of the tropical dog—watching as he runs another antivirus program. He hasn't let the flash drive anywhere near his multiscreen setup. Instead he's plugged it into a ravaged laptop that looks as though it has done battle with many other personal computers and lived, somehow, to fight on. He has been at this for an hour, more. It's unbearable. I would jump out of my skin if I could, if jumping didn't sound so exhausting, if my skin still fit in the first place.

"Clean now," Diego mutters. He still hasn't risked eye contact or direct address. "Gonna open this drive up."

"That's great," I say.

"Maybe yes. Maybe no. Shit came loaded with serious malware. Programs I ran were pretty harsh. Lots of scour power. Could be the data didn't survive."

I stand, slowly, and watch over his shoulder as he slots the drive into his desktop, then swigs from a bottle of orange soda as it loads. On the screen an icon appears. Diego clicks it and a small window opens. A cursor flashes inside a blank rectangle and below I can see a few words written in characters I don't recognize. Cyrillic, maybe.

"Is that Russian?" I ask.

Diego twitches a husky shoulder in what is probably a shrug.

If the flash drive is in Russian, then maybe it doesn't actually belong to David Adler at all. Maybe he stole it from Boris Sirko. Or Irina. Raj said that Irina was good with computers, that she was the original programmer on the site. Could she have written the code that implicated David Adler? Could she have set him up? I recall her red-rimmed eyes, the catch in her voice when she spoke. Was she frightened for him or for herself? Did she contact me to help her find David Adler? Or to make sure he stayed lost?

"Is there a translation program we can run?" I ask him.

"I know what it says," he mumbles without turning from the screen.

"You read Russian?"

He points to the cursor. "Don't have to. It's asking for a password."

"A password? Okay. Do you know how many characters? Or do you have a program that works through letter and number combinations?"

"That shit takes hours. And it only works if the password is short. Most people, they just use obvious shit—birth year, first dog, street they grew up on." For just a moment he meets my eyes. "Got a guess?"

"Not really."

"Then we're done," Diego says. He unwraps a candy bar and wrests half of it into his mouth, the caramel straggling from his teeth in oily strands.

"Wait," I say. "I know his girlfriend's name. Can we try that?" I hear my voice climbing toward a whine, a tire's screech on wet road. "I can type it, if you want."

"Fuck no," he says, shielding the keyboard. "Keep your hands in your goddamn lap, okay? Look, I can do like ten more minutes. Have to sign on to a game after. So if you have a guess, guess it fast."

"Fine. Great. Try Irina." I spell it for him.

The screen refreshes with new characters, colored red.

"Maybe we should try it in Cyrillic. Can you do that?"

He sighs and swallows down the last of the candy bar. With a few keystrokes he translates Irina and transfers it into the box. Red again.

"Okay," I say. "Try Luck Be a Lady. Try Luck. Try Lady. Try David. David Adler. Wait, you forgot to do that one in Cyrillic. Try Raj," I say, my voice growing hoarser. "Try Patel. Try Sirko. No, with an 'i.' Try it without the initial capital."

But it's red, red, every time red.

And then somehow, I know what to try. My body knows, too, my stomach clenching like a squeezed lemon, sharp, acidic. I remember those words written so neatly on the cassette Polly gave to me, on the latest note shoved below my door. "It's Vivian," I say, pronouncing each syllable carefully, cleaving the word into its component sounds, freeing it from its meaning. "Try Vivian. Or Vivian Parry. In English, then Cyrillic."

It works the first time.

The box disappears and a new screen flashes, a file directory with folder icons lined in neat rows like so many manila gravestones, all unlabeled.

"Pick one," I say, my voice gone lower now. "Dealer's choice."

He clicks, opening up a screen with various thumbnail images. He chooses the first and there I am, in a candid shot, slightly blurred, dressed in a turtleneck sweater and jeans. I'm exiting an off-Broadway theater, my lips set in a strained line like the zipper on a too-tight skirt.

"That you?"

I don't answer. Diego clicks on another photo. This picture's more recent and clearer. I'm wearing my winter coat and wild, bed-mussed hair, leaning against the door to my building as I hold a large coffee in one hand and grope for my keys with the other.

A third image: me in my blond wig, standing outside the Luck Be a Lady office, freshening my lip gloss before I enter, my mouth pursed in a pink grimace. And a fourth: in the liquor store, from the back, the two-liter bottle of vodka I've set before the register filling the shot. And on. And on. And on.

"Stop," I say. I say it as though I am a passenger in a speeding car, the gas pedal fixed to the floor, the driver gone away. "Enough."

"Madre de fucking Dios," Diego says as he stills his hand. "Did you know you had a stalker?"

Of course I did, those feelings of being watched that I couldn't shake, the sensation of eyes strafing me top to toe, those notes shoved beneath the door. But only in this moment does the range and thoroughness of this enterprise bear down on me. There are at least a dozen of those folders and that first picture predates my meeting with David Adler. Which means that all this time I have been looking for him and for months before, he and how many others have had me in the plainest sight. The irony doesn't elude me. I have spent my adult life sitting in the dark—incognito, I believed. Observing, not observed. Private and alone. And all this time I have been centered in the camera's lens, the watcher's eye, unknowing.

My own vision shrinks to pinpoints. Blood hurtles, breath comes hard. Am I being watched even here? I lurch away from Diego's desk, toward the living room's sole window, its curtains pulled mercifully tight. Flicking them aside, I stare down at the bodies passing back and forth below. I don't see anyone I recognize, which doesn't mean much. Because who is David Adler undisguised? And would I know him?

I remember my conversations with the conference organizer, the managing editor of *American Stage*. How they had never heard of David Adler. How Destine ran a check and couldn't find any age-appropriate David Adlers in the area. How I had searched for him before our meeting and never caught his trace. I had thought that David Adler was like me, a chitinous shell playing at being a person. But he was something far more common and familiar, another costumed actor performing a role.

And he was not the only one. If I was meant to find this drive, in Raj's apartment, taped to the back of a desk drawer, then Raj must have been an actor, too. And Boris Sirko. And Polly. And Irina. And probably Jake and everyone at LBAL. The Greeks have a word—anagnorisis—for the scene of recognition, the moment a character realizes just how wholly deluded they have been, how he's killed his father and bedded his mother, how the lion cub she's murdered is her own beloved son. And here, at the window in this filthy living room, the scene is mine. Because while I have worried my brain with problems of embezzlement and espionage and indifferently organized crime, a simpler explanation has been available:

that this has all been a piece of theater, with me in the dual role of its sole intended spectator and its spotlight-blinded star.

The room grows darker then and somehow larger, with Diego and his computer impossibly far away. As I step back from the window, my legs fail me and I'm falling then, with the darkness rushing up to enfold me, and I want that darkness, but not yet, not here. So I sit back on my knees, rocking softly, husbanding the strength to stand and go.

I hear the squeak of Diego's computer chair as he wheels toward me. For the first time, he addresses me directly. "You okay?"

I shake my head.

"You need something? Soda?"

"No," I say. "I need to find out what exactly is on that drive and who put it there. Files leave traces, right? Metadata? Can you tell when those pictures were uploaded and from what phone or camera or whatever?"

"Worth a try," he says.

Diego right clicks on one of the folders. Then another and another, scanning the code that emerges. "Looks like they were uploaded from a couple of phone cameras. I can give you the model numbers, but that won't tell you much. Earliest ones look like they're from October, but they go up through November and December. And it's not all pictures. There's an audio file here. Video and shit, too. Not from a phone. From something different. You wanna see it?"

I don't. But I do. "Go ahead," I say, dragging myself to a sitting position. Diego presses the play icon. It loads immediately. The screen is a grainy wash of gray that suggests poor lighting, and at first, I'm not sure what I see. Then I realize it's my apartment, my bed, my breasts, and Charlie's face, lips parted, eyes closed, as he moves above me.

"Stop it," I say. "Close it. Close the window."

"Hang on," Diego says. In the faint glow of the screen, I can see the pimples crowding his chin, the gleam of sweat that clings to his upper lip.

I stand, fighting off the darkness. "Stop it now."

His hand tightens on the mouse.

I grab the orange soda from his desk. "Diego! You want me to maybe accidentally pour this all over your hard drive? No? Then you will close the fucking window now."

The video disappears. I replace the bottle.

"Got no tits anyway," I hear him mutter.

"I'm going," I say. "Give me the flash drive."

His fingers zip over the keyboard.

"Do not even think of copying the files or I am going to come back here with a stack of magnets and a hammer ten times the size of your tiny, impotent dick. And if I ever find any of this uploaded to any website, then I will tell my very close friend on the police force about you and your pet laminator. Questions?"

Within moments I'm back on the street, the drive in my pocket, the sky clear and my mind a blizzard, so shaken I can barely see to walk. From my purse I pull out my emergency bottle and shake an Ativan into my hand, nearly dropping it into the slush. I crunch it between my teeth, gagging as the bitterness fills my mouth and trickles down my throat.

The video suggests that someone has been in my apartment, that someone has planted a camera there. I have enemies, I'm sure. Producers, actors, playwrights. Smiling Caleb is no fan. But none of them could have gained entry, even by strategy or stealth. When I moved in I had extra locks installed. The super lacks the requisite keys, and it would take a lot more than a YouTube tutorial to reckon with my dead bolt. I have yet to let a single deliveryman past the threshold, not even the good-looking one from the liquor store on First. The photos seem to date from a few months back. In that time only three people have entered my apartment: Justine, Destine, Charlie.

I don't really believe that Justine could have done this. But I don't know what to believe anymore. I call her first and it's only after several rings that I remember her show has its first preview tomorrow. She'll either be at the theater for a desperate late-night run-through or in bed with the phone off, eye mask on, a glaze of moisturizer across her face, the contents of a sleeping pill—what I would not give to sleep and sleep and sleep—drifting softly through her veins. Or she's blocking my calls. But she isn't. She answers on the fifth ring.

"Justine," I say. "Look, I know this will sound crazy—"

"Crazy. From you? What an exciting fucking surprise from a girl who has her picture on several pages of the latest DSM."

"I'm sorry. But listen. Someone's put a camera in my apartment. They've been recording me. They—"

"Oh. Wow. So fun. Are we seriously adding paranoid schizophrenia to the list?"

"I'm not paranoid, Justine," I say, sheltering under the awning of a shuttered discount store. "There are files. I can show you. Pictures. Video. Going back months. No one asked you to put anything in my apartment, right? Like maybe it didn't even look like a camera. Maybe it looked like a pen or—"

She's laughing. Only the laugh sounds strange. Gouged out. "No, Vivian," she says. "If someone had asked me to put a camera inside your apartment or even a fucking pen, I would have kicked that someone very definitely in the balls and then blown my bedazzled fucking rape whistle. So you can cross me off your list. I love you, you lunatic," she says. Her voice has gone lower now and soft. "I would never hurt you. Not on purpose. Not when you're already so good at hurting yourself."

"I know it," I say. "I just had to be sure."

"You should have been sure already. Look, babe. I'm fucking exhausted from dress and about as useful as a secondhand tampon. Let me make it through the first couple of previews and if you still think you're dealing with some Peeping Tom situation, we'll sort through it then. You're still coming tomorrow, right?"

"Right. Of course. But Justine, there's one more thing. Two days ago, at the party, I thought I saw David Adler, the man who disappeared. That was who I ran after. And I think now that David Adler isn't even his name. But has the bad doctor—sorry, Craig—have you ever seen him with a man with curly brown hair and glasses? Only maybe the glasses aren't even—"

She stops me. "Vi-vi-an," she says. She says my name slowly and precisely, an eternity between each syllable. "I extremely fucking can't right now. Go the fuck to sleep. I'll see you after the show tomorrow, when you bring me the biggest bouquet the corner bodega can legally fucking sell and we can talk about all of your exciting delusions then. Are we clear?"

"Venetian crystal," I say. But the call has already disconnected.

I had never really thought that Justine could be a part of this. And nothing in the call convinced me otherwise. Which leaves Destine and Charlie. Destine has the native cruelty and detachment for a job like this. And he must have trained in surveillance at some point. But I met him by accident. Because I went out for lunch, which I so rarely do, and found Vinnie Mendoza. That body, at least, was real. The crime blotter said so, as did the bartender at the Jigger. No one could have planted it or planned for me to find it, for Destine to be on shift at just that moment. Which leaves Destine out.

So when the music stops, it's Charlie. Lovely Charlie. A man who seemed freighted with no wiles, no agenda, no apparent game. I didn't dream up that feature on winter effects until weeks after I'd met David Adler. But Charlie works in the theater. We like the same experimental playwrights. Which means he could have found his way to me by several forking paths. And as I remember it, I pitched that feature only because Jack Frost sent me a press release announcing their new line of stage effects. Several press releases. So Charlie met me. And then, when I wouldn't take him to the play that night, he found me again at the flea market. He bet, correctly, that I would take him home, that he could leave a camera in my room, likely while I was in the bathroom washing him from my thighs. Charlie. The man who saw me, I believed, as something like the girl I used to be. I can recall so easily those first moments with him—his smile, the soft rumble of his voice, that scent of his, citrusy and sweet. And then what came later, what the camera saw: his cheek pressed against mine, our legs twined, his lips mouthing my name as he grasped the bedsheet in his fist.

He answers the phone on the first ring. Behind his greeting, I can hear the shriek of staticky electric guitars and loud conversation.

"Charlie," I say, still sequestered beneath the awning, amazed that my mouth can form words, "I need to see you."

"Hey! Amazing. And, yeah, listen, Happy New Year. I've got some of the guys from the studio over at my house—oh, come on, Corinne, I mean guys in the general, nongendered sense—and we just ordered pizza. You want to come by, hang with some of my friends?"

I wonder if any of these friends helped to set up the surveillance.

"Charlie. I need to talk to you. Alone. It's serious."

"Really? Okay. What's going on?"

"Meet me. Tompkins Square Park. Near the Temperance Fountain." I'm spiraling, yes, but still capable of irony. And he must hear the rime in my voice, because he doesn't protest.

"Yeah. Okay. Give me like ten."

My body walks, my feet barely skimming the sidewalk, first to the liquor store for another airplane bottle, and then suddenly, without knowing exactly how, I'm delivered to the corner of the park. Maybe I should be frightened. Here. At night. Alone. Knowing, for certain now, that someone really has been watching me. But I'm past fear. What I feel now is worse than fear, a wild panic that runs at me with such force that I think I might shatter. As I make for the fountain, on a route that avoids the tree where I found Vinnie Mendoza's body, I try to prepare a speech for Charlie. But my mouth no longer feels made for words. I want to turn wolf. To howl and howl and howl.

The fountain nestles beneath a neoclassical canopy, shouldered by four Doric columns. Each side represents a different virtue: Faith, Hope, Charity, Temperance. Worst girl group ever. As I round my back against a column, I see Charlie approaching with his long-legged lope, hands thrust into the pockets of his jeans, only a raveling sweater standing between him and the frost. He moves to kiss my cheek, but I twist away, scrabbling for the words I'll need, the rage.

"Hey, Viv," he says. "What's wrong? Are you . . . ? Is it . . . ? Viv, are you pregnant? Because I know we didn't always use protection and I figured you were on the pill. But that was stupid. I should have asked. And of course I'll support you. Whatever choice you make."

I have never seen a script that could switch from tragedy to comedy so fast. The shock propels me into speech. "No," I say. "I am not pregnant. And if I had your baby inside of me I would tear it out with the first rusty coat hanger I could find. So before I go to the police and report you for stalking and illegal recording and God knows what else, I have just a few questions, please." The pill has come on, finally, and though the words are harsh, the voice speaking them is blank, almost monotone, icier than the slush underfoot.

"But, Viv," he says, reaching out a hand toward me.

"If you lay one fucking finger on me, I will bite that finger off," I tell him. "Charlie, I found the drive. Just like you wanted. I figured out the password, too. So I know you put the camera in my apartment. Who else are you working with? Who is David Adler, really? And I would be so very grateful if you could explain how and why you decided to fuck with my life in just this way."

This time it's Charlie who retreats, eyes wide as though they've been clamped that way, hands splayed in front of him, a valley between each finger. "A drive? What do you mean a drive?" Confusion sounds in his voice, an edge of panic, too. "And what is this other stuff? Stalking, recording? Viv, are you okay? Because nothing that you're saying makes any sense. Are you high or something? Did you take something? Can you please just tell me what is going on?"

I see dozens of actors every week, some virtuosic, some less so. With all but the absolute best, there's a tell that lets you know they're playing a part—a catch in speech, a hitch in gait, some small denatured tic that levers open the gap between the person and the role. Charlie has none of these. So either he's a new Olivier or else he isn't lying. And for a comforting moment I let myself enjoy that possibility. That I have it all wrong. That he's real. Too good to be true and true all the same. Then the moment ends. Because there's no other way that camera could have been placed in my apartment.

"Charlie," I say. I say it slowly, as though I'm speaking to a dim and naughty toddler. "Someone has set up a camera in my apartment and hardly anyone else has been to my apartment except you. So I don't exactly need Occam's fucking razor to figure this one out. But okay, let's try it your way. Did someone ask you to bring something to my place and to leave it there?"

"Viv, I haven't brought you anything! I was going to get you flowers last time, but then I remembered how you said you hate them, that once they're cut, they're already dead."

In the yellowed haze of the streetlight, I study his features, his clenched posture. I haven't known Charlie long, but in that time, he has never concealed anything from me, not his gentleness, not his hurt, not his guilty desire. Even now he's wearing his distress on the tattered sleeve of his sweater. I don't know what to think. Slowly I step toward him, removing the flash drive from my coat and displaying it in my upturned palm. "I found this."

"This? What is it?"

"A computer flash drive. There are photos of me on it, going back a couple of months, taken around the neighborhood and at the theater. And there's video, too. It's of us. In my apartment. In bed. So someone must have put a camera there. And I haven't let anyone else inside." Except my best friend. Except Destine. "You know I have about a million locks, so a break-in is next to impossible. Not even the super has the keys to all of them. So it has to be you, Charlie. It has to."

"But, Vivian, I would never—"

"I want to believe you, Charlie. I do. But I don't understand how else it could have happened."

"Vivian, are you sure you haven't taken anything? Because what you're saying—photos, videos—it sounds sort of like a bad trip."

It is. Very bad. But the drugs I've taken don't have side effects like these. And I know, from some inner place that's beyond knowing, that I am in my right mind. I know what I saw on Diego's screen and I know that Diego saw it, too.

"It's real," I say. "Someone taped us and uploaded it to this drive. If you don't believe me you can watch it yourself."

"Okay. Wow. Are you sure? That is super freaking weird. And you have no idea who did this?"

I shake my head. "I thought it was you. I was sure of it." I'm still not entirely unsure.

"And you don't know where the camera was hidden?"

"I haven't been back to my apartment and I won't go back. Not while someone is watching me."

"Let me watch the video. Just long enough to sort out the angles and figure out where the camera is. Then I can go in and disable it. I'm really worried about you, Vivian. Let me help you. Can I help you?"

And because I don't know what else to do, I tell him that he can. I give in to him, lean into him, let him hold me, carry the slight weight of me until the shuddering—and up until this moment I hadn't even known I was shuddering—stops.

"Do you want to stop by my place? It's pretty crowded right now, but we can grab my laptop and take it to a coffee shop or something."

We're only two blocks from that café on St. Mark's. The one where I created Nora's CV. For the fake job at the false company with the horrific boss who was seemingly a day player. I straighten up, fighting against the dizziness. "I know a place close by," I say. "Come on."

We pay our money to the man in the trapper's hat and I drag an extra chair over to the terminal, placing it close to Charlie's. Then I hand him the drive. "It had some viruses on it, but it's clean now or it should be. The password is Vivian. Just right click on the files until you see the one formatted for video. I don't want to watch." I turn my head away and close my eyes, letting the Ativan soften the clanging of the radiator, the harsh whisper of car wheels against the street above, the click click click of the mouse in Charlie's hand.

"Okay," he says, "I have it. But it's really grainy."

"I know," I say, "we had the lights off. Can you tell where the camera is?"

"Well, it's to the side of the bed, you have a nightstand there, right? Or . . ."

Then his words bleed away. I turn back toward him, toward the screen. I can see myself there, naked, face crushed into the pillow, but the man looming over me, his fingers wrapped in my hair, isn't Charlie. It's Destine.

I take the mouse from him and click to close the window, feeling him flinch as my fingers brush his. He'd like me to plead or cry or insist that it's all been a terrible mistake. But I can't. "I'm sorry," I say, "I didn't know that was on there."

"Who is that?" he asks. "Is he an ex or something?"

I look at him. He has his lips clenched so tight it looks as if he's doing a ventriloquist act without a dummy. "He's a friend," I say.

"Yeah," he says, swallowing hard. "He looked pretty friendly. I saw the date stamp on that video. It's from after we started sleeping together. Were you ever going to tell me?"

"Charlie," I say, "I like you. But I don't wear your letter sweater. I'm not your girlfriend."

"Not his?"

I think of Destine's hand against my face. The cold heat it can still conjure between my legs. "No," I say. "Not his. Not anyone's."

He pushes back from the counter and stands. "Maybe he's the one who taped you."

"No, Charlie. He couldn't have. The timing's all wrong."

"Okay," he says. He is smiling now, but the warmth has leached away. "I'm done, Viv. I get that you're a little nutty and I thought that I could handle it. I mean, I'm in the arts, too. I know a lot of nutty people. But seeing that. What he was doing to you. How much you liked it. I'm tired of waiting for you to realize I'm actually a really good guy."

"I know you're good," I tell him. "Better than good. You could probably wear a halo if it didn't clash with your work boots. But Charlie, I don't want what's good for me. I never have."

"I know," he says. "I just thought that maybe you wanted me."

I did. I do. "I'm sorry, Charlie," I say.

But he's already gone.

I'm afraid to return to my apartment until I know where the camera is. So I force myself back to the files, clicking until I locate a video. It's the first one, the one Diego chanced on, and for a few moments all I can see is Charlie's face, how his hair seems to glow red and gold even in gray scale, how it looks like sunshine.

I close my eyes, and when I open them I home in on the angles. The camera's trained on the right side of the bed. But Charlie's wrong. There's no table there. The nightstand is opposite. I try to picture that part of the room, but there's nothing right there—just an old poster of a Middleton and Rowley revival. Nothing else except the radiator.

And the window.

The window. The window I keep open throughout the winter to counter the steam heat. The camera is in the window.

Then the man who runs the café is behind me, his face red, his ear-flaps shaking.

"No porn!" he screams. "What did I tell you? No porn!"

I could tell him it isn't pornography, that it's art, that it's theater, that it's material evidence and documentary proof that someone is trying to smash up my life better and faster and more thoroughly than I ever could have managed on my own. But it seems easier just to close the window and replace the drive in the pocket of my coat.

"You stay out," he says as I rise to leave. "You go away. You are a bad girl."

"I know it," I say.

Back on the street, I swerve into a dive bar—a haven for day drunks that deigns to open at night—and down a vodka as soon as I can wrap my fingers around the glass. I follow it with another, which I convey to a stool in the bar's darkest corner and sip more slowly. Dutch courage.

Russian bravado. Because even though I'm so numb from the Ativan that I'm at risk of frostbite, I don't want to go up to my apartment alone.

So I call Destine. And even after all the horror and catastrophe of the evening, there's something in his gruff, muffled greeting that makes my knees weak. Weaker.

"Hello, sweetheart. It's late. You tucked in tight like a good girl?"

"Paul, I need your help. I realize this sounds insane, but someone has been spying on me. Following me. Taking pictures and video of me. They've even installed a camera in my apartment. I need to remove it, but I don't want to go back up there by myself. Can you meet me?"

"How much have you had to drink?"

"Nothing. I haven't drunk anything."

"You're at a bar, Ms. Parry. I can hear the jukebox."

"Fine. I've had a drink. Two. But Paul, these videos are real. They're connected to that recording I played for you. That man I was trying to find, David Adler? He's been following me, photographing me. I still don't know who he is or why he did this. But I have evidence. I promise I do. A flash drive full of files. Files he created. Do you understand?"

"I understand," he says. And relief floods in, because really that makes one of us. But then he goes on. "I understand that I was on the early shift today. And that I'm home now. And that I'm tired. I'm not hauling ass over the bridge because some little girl hit the bottle too hard. If some big bad wolf's still taking pictures of you in the morning, give me a call at the station then."

"Fuck you, Paul," I say. "This isn't a fairy tale. It's happening. To you, too. The camera's been recording the apartment for months and it's trained on the bed. So congratulations. You've made your very own sex tape." I pause to take another sip. "I bet your wife wouldn't like it if that video turned up online somewhere."

"My wife?" he says. "My wife? You take those words right out of your whore's mouth. I don't know what you're trying to pull, but don't pull it on me. I'm a guy with a shield, sweetheart, and you're a mouthy little bitch. So whatever story you've spun for yourself, stop spinning. Let me put it to you plainly, in language you can understand, however many whiskeys in: you post anything about me online—video, photo, funny little joke—and you will wish you had never been born."

I wish it already. I wish it all the time. And still, this call has taught me something. I had already reasoned that he couldn't have put the camera there, couldn't have engineered the surveillance. His threats, the fear behind them, they confirm it.

"Goodbye, Paul," I say.

As I end the call, the vodka glass falls from my hand, spilling onto my thigh and shattering on the floor. Judging by the look on the bartender's face, I won't get served again. I slide down from the stool, angling my legs away from the shards and steadying myself against the bar. Then I press my way through the bodies and back out into the night. It's after eleven. The liquor stores are closed, their thin metal grates wrenched down toward the street. I slip into the first bodega I pass, my eyes seared by the fluorescent lights. I grab the six-pack nearest to my hand and drop it on the counter, next to stacks of plastic-wrapped fig bars. I can't remember the last time I ate. I can't remember the last time I wanted to.

The beers weigh me down as I make my way up the flights of stairs. I work the locks—one, two, three—and then, inside the apartment, I don't move to turn on the lights. Instead, I make my way to the window. Even in the dark it doesn't take me long to grope for the camera, a small rectangle, only slightly larger than my forefinger, nestled just below the sill and attached to a silver cord that reaches upward toward the roof, an expanse of brittle tar paper littered with pigeon droppings and the odd cigarette butt. No one in the building really uses it, but it's easy enough to reach, via a rusted ladder that sags just outside my door. I remember the night that I woke to the thuds of people moving up above me. That must have been when the man I knew as David Adler, or one of his associates, climbed those rungs and set the camera in place. Does the camera send its data automatically or has he had to return to off-load the memory card? How often has he or some confederate paused outside my door with only that plane of wood separating us, as close as breath?

In the kitchen, I find my only decent knife. A real knife. I heft the window open wider, bracing it with my shoulder, and perch on its sill. It takes only seconds of sawing before I've severed the cord and I am cradling the camera in my lap. It's such a tiny thing, lighter and less bulky than a lipstick tube. So small and so terrible. I take it by the end of the cut cord and smash it against the wall as hard as I can, again and again, until chips of plastic litter the floor around me and I'm suddenly so tired my legs give way. I drop down onto the bed and gather my knees into my chest, letting the wire and the camera slip from my grasp. I'd cry now if I could. If the pills and the drink hadn't killed all the crying parts.

I pull the first beer from the bag. After prying off the cap, I swallow the liquid quickly, medicinally. I follow it with a second and then a third, stalking sleep or stupor, whichever comes first. I shut the window, sending its frame to meet the sill with a shove so hard that the glass shivers in its casing. Then I lie down in the dark, fully clothed, the kitchen knife—silvery, sharp—still clutched tightly in my hand, a hand that feels like someone else's.

17

RAW SPACE

A roiling, too-hot sleep takes me, consigning me to that same recurring dream, of running through the theater district, too close to curtain time, frantic that I will miss my show. And when sleep lets me go again, mind wild and muscles sore as though that run were real, I remember that I am supposed to see Justine's preview tonight. It seems absurd, this idea that I could politely present my ticket, curl into my seat, and abandon myself, defenseless, to the dark, letting the show take me over. That is what I used to crave—more than love, more than sex, more than the icy shock of the day's first drink, more than seeing my name in print, so stark and emphatic against the white of the page. But I don't feel that same desire now. That chief critic's job, which I wanted so fiercely that I could taste it—in my mouth, down my throat—I have barely thought of it in days. Has David Adler ruined me for my work? Have I ruined myself?

That thought levers me from the bed and onto a shard of black plastic. It leaves a laceration, thin and sharp, in the meat of my left foot, more proof that I haven't dreamed or imagined the horrors of the night before. That this has all been real. Or near enough. But while I can see the cut, I can't feel it. Dressing myself is like dressing a mannequin.

At the bodega, I collect coffee and an egg sandwich steaming inside its grubby foil. I'm not afraid to go outside anymore. These people who are watching me, who have watched me for so long, what can they see that they haven't seen already? Then I return to my apartment, even hotter now with the window shut and a pillowcase taped over the glass. As for the sandwich, I can't manage more than a few bites, but I suckle at the vent in the coffee lid until the last gray-brown drops have gone.

One task remains. The same task I set myself a month and a half ago: to find the man I knew as David Adler. There are a dozen ledes I might use, a hundred opening lines. But I begin at the beginning, with the awkward interview at the patisserie. From my nightstand I pluck my current reporter's notebook and flip the pages back and back and back, past plays and musicals and monologues and dance theater until I find it, David Adler's number. Chances are he contacted me through some cheap burner, like the one I bought for Nora. But even though I know that this can't work, I tap in the digits. The phone rings and rings and then a calm, denatured female voice tells me that that I have reached this recording in error. But which error? There have been so many.

Irina's number plays a similar message. When I tap in the number for Jake Levitz, retrieved from my call list, it rings half a dozen times and then emits a shrill beep, like a fax machine, a technical belly flop that somehow feels very Jake. I recall how his office didn't look like a detective's office. How it looked like someone's dingy apartment. Jake's, maybe? Or was it borrowed? And from whom? I dissolve a pill on my tongue as I tug on scarf, hat, and coat, scant protection against the rain that's begun to fall, fast and unremitting, from a sky so gray that it looks black. My umbrella breaks three blocks into my walk, blown inside out, metal spokes dangling like spider's legs. I trudge on without it, barely feeling the water and wind, until I reach the Malaysian restaurant, with its steamed-up windows and spiced scents that turn my stomach sour. As I thrust my shoulder into the protesting glass door, I find I'm wet through, boots squidging at every step of the green runner. When I reach Jake's office, I knock politely and then, when that knock goes unanswered, more savagely, banging my hand against the door until it feels as though something, wood or bone, must splinter.

"Dude," says a voice inside, "seriously. Chill."

The door opens. It isn't Jake. This man is at least forty years younger, even younger than me. Thinner, too, which takes doing. Faded jeans hang from his hips, a T-shirt with a picture of a dolphin sags from his shoulders. Premium weed exudes from the majority of his pores. As he brushes blond hair out of his eyes, he says, "Are you Sadie's friend? You could have, like, called first."

"Yeah," I say. "Sorry about that." He's so slender that it's a simple matter to peer into the apartment beyond him. I see the same room, the same rug, the same unsanitary futon, though the desk is missing now and so is the ficus.

"Does anyone else live here?" I ask. "A roommate?"

"No," he says, waving an arm feebly. "Why? Does she think I have a girl here? 'Cause I don't. Tour is tour, that's what I told her. It meant nothing. I fuckin' swear."

"No. I'm looking for an older guy. Mid-sixties, curly gray hair, heavy smoker. I was here," I say. "In this apartment. Late November or early December. The guy, he said he was a private detective, he had his office here."

"A detective? That's fuckin' weird." From his pocket, he pulls a bag of gummies and places one between his teeth. "You want?"

I shake my head. "So you never met that man?"

"Naw, dude. I mean, before we left for tour, I rented the place out online. But it was a young guy who took the sublet. I met him when I handed him the keys. He didn't say anything about running a fuckin' business. What did you say he was? A detective? The landlord could have kicked me out for that."

"The young guy, what did he look like? Curly dark hair? Glasses?"

"I don't think he had glasses. Maybe his hair was curly. It was like a while ago?"

"Did he give you a name?" I ask. I've slid a toe inside the doorframe so he can't shut me out, not yet.

"David something. You know him?"

"You could say that. Did he give you a credit card number? Or references?"

"Naw. Just cash in hand. There was a check for, like, a security deposit or whatever, but I tore it up when I came back and saw he hadn't trashed the place."

This is the place untrashed?

"Do you have a phone number for him?" I ask. "An email address? Did he leave anything behind?"

"Let me think." He closes his eyes for so long I start to worry he won't open them again. But then he does. "Not much. I guess there were a couple of magazines on the back of the toilet. *Center Stage*? Something like that?"

"*Backstage*?"

"Maybe?" he says with open palms. "But I took them out to recycling like a month ago."

"Okay," I say. "Thank you. If you think of anything else, will you call me?"

"Yeah, okay." He hands me his phone. I enter my name and number and hand it back. He studies the screen, then raises his head. "So you're not, like, Sadie's friend?"

"I'm not."

"Yeah, well, I get that. But if you see her, tell her I'm sorry, okay? Nothing even happened with that girl." There's a pleading, defeated look in his eyes, like a dog waiting to have its nose rubbed in its own mess.

"Sure," I say. He closes the door and I start back down the stairs, but just a few steps in, I slip on the runner and my legs swing out from under me, and for a second, for forever, I'm flying and then I'm falling and then I'm on the ground, crumpled against the landing, windless at first and then rasping, wheezing as air forces itself back in. Tenderly, I lift a hand to my face and inhale sharply when a finger brushes the cut that's opened just below my right eyebrow. The pain is far away. But the hand comes back red.

From above I hear the door opening. A voice drifts down. "Dude, you okay?" I don't answer. I have no answer. The door shuts.

I drag myself up, first onto all fours and then to a hunched version of upright. Making my way more carefully now, holding the banister wherever it's whole, I reach the street and detour into the Malaysian place, where the cashier steps back from the counter when she sees me. I buy a bottle of water and pilfer a stack of napkins, swabbing wetly at my face as the blood comes away in livid pink streaks. Pressing the last napkin against my forehead, I walk back out into the rain.

When the Q train comes, I find a seat, only to have the shalwar kameez–clad woman in the next one snatch a peripheral glance at me and jump from hers, clinging to the center pole for support. One stop later, I switch to the L, then to the A, then out and across to Thirty-ninth and toward the Luck Be a Lady building. I keep my face lowered as I flash the guard my ID. My real ID.

"Wet enough for you?" he asks without looking up. Then he does look up. And abruptly away.

I drift through the security gate, my boots leaving a silvered trail on the floor. At the elevator, the doors' polished brass catches my reflection. Even adjusting for surface distortion, the picture isn't pretty—hair stuck limply to my head, blood smearing my cheek, my right eye swollen half-shut.

The doors open and I squish down the carpeted hall to the Luck Be a Lady office. The sign has gone and a glance under the door suggests that the lights are out, but when I turn the handle, the door swings effortlessly open and the flick of a switch buzzes the fluorescents into life. In the main room, most of the office furniture remains—my desk, my chair, the file cabinets, the phone. But the coffee maker has vanished and so have the posters. And though I would have bet—bet big—that this is what I would find, my stomach drops as though it's taken the elevator without me as I remember my first impression of the place, how it looked like a hastily assembled stage set. Which is exactly what it was. But I was too absorbed in my own role-play to see it. It crushes me, the vain and analytic part of me, to think of all the prompts I missed: the phones that never rang, the meetings that didn't happen. It was all staged for my benefit and staged so poorly. And still I believed it. Some critic.

Were my former colleagues friends of David's? Or simply actors hired for a strange and unusually immersive job? What were Jay and Lana doing with the door closed? Learning lines? Trading memes? What did they do on the day I fled the office? Even now—recognizing that it was all an act, a scene—it is hard to accept Sirko's visit as pure posture. My body carries the memory of the terror I felt, choking and severe, when he walked into the room with Irina beside him. It is here with me in the office now, squeezing my lungs as I think about Sirko's meaty hands emerging from those leather gloves and reaching toward my hair, the tips of the fingers stained yellow.

Those fingers. That yellow.

I had seen them before: Jake Levitz's stubby digits as he fumbled for another cigarette, those same jaundiced whorls. Give Jake a shave, sunglasses, a better class of overcoat, and he reappears as Sirko—just like the messenger in the first act who comes on as a lord in the fourth when you're on a vanishingly slim repertory budget and need to skimp on cast size. David Adler doubled parts. And I never noticed. This last example of my idiocy hits like a blow and I stumble back into the filing cabinet, which sounds a retaliatory clang. I close my eyes, wanting to faint, wanting to fall, but instead easing myself gracelessly to the floor, a marionette with every string snapped.

I don't know if it's the lights or the noise that draws him, but suddenly I'm not alone. Hovering in the doorway is a gangling man in blue janitorial coveralls, with thinning hair barely covering an age-spotted scalp and a face so long that even a horse might diagnose depression.

"Ma'am," he says, "you need help?"

Clearly, I don't know what I need. Maybe I've never known. "I'm fine," I say.

"I've seen fine," he says, leaning against the handle of his mop truck. "Looked different."

"Really. I'm okay. Thank you."

"Ma'am, this may not be my place, but you look like you may have took a beating, which is far away from fine. If you don't mind my saying it, there's a shelter I know over on Eighty-sixth and Amsterdam, basement of a church. A niece of mine stayed there awhile. Said the folks running it are real nice. You want me to take you over there? Help you up, at least?"

He takes a few steps toward me, but I put up a hand to ward him off. "No," I say. "Don't. Please."

"My apologies, ma'am. Probably don't want any man touching you."

"It's not that. And thank you. Really. You're very kind. I know what I must look like, but no one has beaten me. I promise. I had an accident. I fell down some stairs. In a tenement in Chinatown. Introduced myself to the landing forehead first."

He shakes his head as if he doesn't believe me. "All right, ma'am. Well, if you change your mind—"

"Listen. There is something you can do for me. This office, I worked here for a little while. About two weeks ago. Do you know the people who rented it?"

"They weren't here long. Only spoke to them the one time. Some kind of drama club, they said. Landlord gives room to folks like that when the offices don't rent. A donation, like. Keeps the taxman happy."

I know this program. It's called Raw Space. Its officers used to set up storefront theaters in Times Square, back before the mayor's office made those blocks safe and pricey and sterile. They also arranged office space for companies that needed it. I wrote a piece on the organization years back. I hadn't realized it was still operating.

"Thanks," I say. "That helps."

"Excuse my noticing, but if you want to go and tidy yourself, the ladies' room is just down the hall. Doesn't need a key."

"Yes, I remember. And I will. Thank you. But since you mention keys, this file cabinet—" I gesture to the one behind me, the one I failed to open on that last day. "Do you have a key for it, a master?"

"That I don't," he says. "But I've never known it locked. Let me try."

I scramble sideways, like a crab that already smells the can of Old Bay. He sidles in near me, off-gassing artificial pine, and wraps his fingers around the handle. He pulls. The cabinet stays shut. He pulls again.

"Lock's not the problem," he says. "Drawer's gone rusty, maybe if I just twist it a ways . . . and there!" Screeching, the drawer shudders open.

I stumble to my feet, blinking away the clouding black. "Thank you," I say. "Really."

"Happy to oblige. Now maybe you'll oblige me, too. You say it was some stairs that did this. And maybe it was. But it seems to me that my niece said a lot of things about stairs and doors before she left that man. So I'll tell you again, there's a shelter at Eighty-sixth and Amsterdam and it'll be there when you're ready. And no matter what he says—he's sorry, he loves you—you go on and leave. Get right with yourself, get right with God, and you just go."

I think of David Adler, of the times I promised myself I wouldn't look for him anymore, how I blundered on regardless, how even now—bruised and bloodied and with last night's alcohol still singing off-key in my veins—I am blundering still.

"I don't think I can," I say.

"Well, it won't get better from here." He points to my eye. "He will only hurt you worse the next time. Kind of worse could be you don't get up from."

"I know. But I have to see this through."

"No, ma'am. No reason for you to trust me. You don't know me from Adam. I will tell it to you anyway: You don't. But you go on and you take care of yourself, best you can." He walks back out the door, trundling his mop behind him, leaving me alone with the file cabinet.

I don't know what I expect—more surveillance gear, more amateur pornography, my time sheets during my brief LBAL tenure. But here's what I find: a stack of *Playbills*. There's one for *Rosmersholm* on top, then the *Old Yeller* musical, that *Iceman Cometh* revival, that sex comedy. Sorting through the stack, I am reacquainted with every musical and play that I have savaged in print over the last three months.

Two hours later, I'm steaming in a hot bath, fighting to keep my good eye open, not entirely sure how I made it home. The three outer locks are all engaged. The lock on the bathroom door, too. There's vodka beside me, crackling in its glass as the ice melts. I ought to be melting, too, the water is scalding. But I can't feel it. Though the morning's pill has worn away, I'm numb now. Chilled through. How easy it would be to let breath go and just sink down, Ophelia again.

But I have calls to make. And a play to see. So I drag myself from the water, in the manner of a netted fish, and towel off before returning to my laptop, now ringed by *Playbills*. The answer lies somewhere in that stack, with an injured party who found recourse more creative than a social media mob. To find that party, I find the number for Raw Space and I call it, asking to speak to Marianne, the woman I interviewed years ago.

"Hello, Vivian," she says. "Long time!"

I hadn't known what my battered voice would sound like, but it comes over the line relaxed, warm, the words tumbling forth without apparent thought. "I know! Ages. I wasn't even sure you were still operational."

"We were struggling for a while, but the real estate ups and downs and some oversupply means a lot of places aren't selling—some aren't even renting—so it's picked up again. We've been working with some new developers, sourcing outer borough spaces. Were you thinking of a follow-up? I have amazing photos I can get you."

"Actually, I was calling to ask about a specific company," I say, straightening up against the pillows. "Someone at a benefit talked them up to me. He said that they were new and exciting and that you had spotted that before anyone else. Only trouble is, I can't remember the company's name. Blame the open bar, right? The guy said you'd housed them in a building all the way west on Thirty-ninth? Practically in Jersey?"

"Let me call up the database. Thirty-ninth . . . Thirty-ninth . . . Was the address Six thirty-two?"

That's it exactly. "Could be!"

"We had a Romanian company visiting for a couple weeks. They said they needed office space, but I think they might actually have been living there."

"I'm pretty sure this group's local."

"Okay. Let me see. . . . Aha! I bet this is the one you mean. And, yes, they're a new company. New to me, anyway. They're called My Life in Art. Gotta show off that liberal arts degree somehow, I guess. I didn't actually work with them, Suzy did. She said they needed a place to do some table work, hold design meetings, that kind of thing. We arranged a suite for a couple of weeks. But off the record they kind of became an office joke, because they kept throwing around all these terms—post-performative, ultramimetic—and you're like, 'Hey, what even is this project? What if you, like, actually just made a show?' Suzy thought that maybe with a little space and time they'd manage something less pretentious. Is that the group you're looking for?"

"I think it is. Thanks. And ultramimetic doesn't sound great, but I'd love to get in touch with them. Do you have contact information? Phone number? An email address?"

"Let me check." Over the line, I can hear her nails clacking against the keyboard. "Sorry, there's not a lot here. Suzy might have more info, but she's on vacation this week. All I have on the shared database is their website address. Just like the name: mylifeinart—all one word, no caps—dot org."

"Great, Marianne. And thanks for the tip on the new spaces. Send the photos and I'll see if I can talk Roger into assigning me something."

Having put down the phone, I type the site address into the search bar and click the first option. A page loads. On a black screen, letters appear one at a time in icy sapphire until they spell the company's name. Then two tabs emerge in white, "Mission" and "Commission." I click the first.

A quotation, which I recognize from the original *My Life in Art*, Konstantin Stanislavski's memoir, materializes: "Love art in yourself, and not yourself in art." Then it vanishes and more text arrives in its place:

- Theater is ritual. Theater is necessity. For too long we have obscured this with unnecessary trappings—electric lights, recorded sound. These superfluities distract us from catharsis, from communion. And they obscure a vital fact: We are all performers

and we are all spectators, all concerned reciprocally in the great dramatic work that is our shared world.
- My Life in Art explores how theater originates in each of us, in all of us, in the roles we play throughout our lives, both as deliberate actors and as essential observers. This is not the false and forced performance of scripted drama—it is the truth of being.
- Recuperating, reclaiming, and reinventing the theatrical form, My Life in Art conveys theater out of the auditorium and finds it in the street, the boardroom, the bedroom. Without a script, without a director, we perform the theater of our lives. Theater *is* life and we live with art, through art, in art.
- Some participation required.

It's not the most esoteric mission statement I've read, or even the most self-satisfied. It plagiarizes ideas from the Theatre of the Oppressed, with a splash of Artaud and a twist of Grotowski. Plenty of other groups mix that same modern drama cocktail. But there's something in the tone—acrid, smug—that tells me I've found my answer.

I click "Commission." A script reads, "Coming soon," and when that fades away, a photograph appears. It's fuzzy and dim, likely too dim for the average viewer to recognize the face and body, but I know them as my own, sunk into a theater's seat, my head bent over my reporter's notebook as I scribble comments. Below the photo is the legend "Crritic!"

I've seen that spelling before. It's in Beckett's *Waiting for Godot*, from the scene where Didi and Gogo pass the time by playing a game of insults. "Moron!" Didi begins. "Vermin!" Gogo responds. They trade slurs all down the page until Gogo cries, "Crritic!" and Didi, the stage directions say, *wilts, vanquished, and turns away.* To call someone a critic is the last word in verbal abuse, Beckett insists. Some self-hating part of me agrees.

And I can see one thing more, in small type, at the bottom of the page, a countdown clock. The slots for months and weeks have both reset to zero. The remaining columns show two days, sixteen hours, thirty-nine minutes. As I stare—eyes locked, hands a statue above the touch pad—another minute ticks down. Thirty-eight. This must be the time until the site goes live and the New York theater world enjoys an interactive performance with me as its star. After all these years of hiding in the dark, I will be thrust onstage, with every defect spotlighted and no lines memorized. Which is every actor's nightmare. Every critic's terror. This project will mean that I can never do my job again, never exist in the obscurity that has made my life possible. I will be seen in all my imperfections, playing the part of a person and failing, every day, every night.

So that I won't scream, so that I won't run mad, so that I won't take that kitchen knife, still tangled in the blanket, and use it on each wrist—vertical cuts, nothing for show—I shake out my frozen hands and set them to search for some other button or menu or link. But I find none. Other searches return only Stanislavski's book. Which means that I have no further means to reach these people, no other way to stop them.

Helpless, I return to the Luck Be a Lady website, probing for some final hint. The splash page has changed. The animation has disappeared, and gone too are the portals to the various games and the hiring banner. In their place I see an image of a roulette wheel, the game David Adler supposedly rigged. Below it, a red line of text reads, "Give it a spin!" With trembling fingers, I click. The writing fades as the wheel judders to life. A cartoon ball drops with jerky animation, then begins to roll. When the wheel slows, the ball has landed on 00. A total loss. A new legend appears across the screen: "Looks like your luck's run out." Then the screen goes black. I push the power button over and over, but the laptop won't restart. It sits inert, dead, and rapidly cooling.

18

A SAD TALE

As little as I know myself, I know this: at the theater, from the instant the house lights fall until they come on again, I am at my best—generous, capable, engaged. This has been my solace, my communion. The question of whether it remains to me forces me out the door and onto the subway, toward the only wholesome comfort I can name. Besides, Justine dislikes being stood up.

Before I can slink into my seat, Caleb spots me in the lobby and calls out a cheerful greeting. I didn't expect to run into anyone I know. They don't usually let press into such an early preview, so he must be reporting out a feature. His smile falters when he sees the ruin of my face. Then it returns, wider.

"Oh, wow, Vivian. Did you hurt yourself or something?"

"Or something," I say, the words leaden in my mouth.

"Yeah, I can see, but hey, aren't you excited for this? I know they call *Winter's Tale* a problem play," he says, teeth flashing like some one-man signal corps. "But I don't have any problem with it at all!"

It's possible that his aggressive idiocy is a ploy. That he's performing just as I perform. As we all perform. Or maybe Caleb is utterly sincere. Either way, I can conjure no response. He tries again. "Hey! Have you talked to Roger this week, because—"

But then the lights flicker and I murmur something that sounds like an apology even though it isn't and we take our seats. I look up at the stage, my coat still wrapped tight around me in the useless hope of warmth. I have never wanted so much to slip this world and flee into another. But this time, this night, the alchemy fails and transport won't come. Across the aisle I can just make out Caleb's grinning profile as he scribbles into a composition book with an enviably steady hand. But I'm wedged in my seat, unraptured, unmoved, alert to every rustling program, every crinkling candy wrapper, every cell phone set to vibrate. Language turns to nonsense in my ears.

So I concentrate on the images instead, on Justine as Hermione, in a low-cut peach dress and a pregnancy pad that makes her look about eleven months along, making eyes at the Bohemian king. I see the shine of her hair and the swell of her breasts as she laughingly plucks another grape from the stem she holds. But it's not the queen, it's only Justine.

Until suddenly it isn't. Because then the aching wrench of mimesis comes on, lifting me from my seat and onto the stage. And then there I am, lying smooth bellied against those cushions, letting the ripe fruit burst between my sharp white teeth. Beyond my own time as an actor, no embrace has ever held me so completely, no breathless act of love has merged my body with another's quite like this. I can feel what she feels, see what she sees, mouth her lines as she says them. I am not myself anymore. I am this character alone.

The third act arrives, the trial scene, when Hermione, now dressed in rags, stands accused of adultery. Hermione says—softly, tenderly—"Tell me what blessings I have here alive, that I should fear to die?" I whisper the words with her, and the line strikes me with such force that tears—stinging, unbidden—speed down my cheeks, each drop a dark mirror of those that stain Hermione's.

Then a messenger enters, bearing the news that the queen's son is dead. Hermione stands abruptly, then falls back in a faint. Something in the way her body collapses doesn't feel like unconsciousness. It feels like death. My death. Helplessly, I start from my seat, but my legs give out under me. The auditorium darkens further and then collapses into midnight as I plunge toward the purses and programs cluttering the floor.

There is a doctor in the house. Several, as it happens. They let a pediatrician see to me (credit my youthful good looks), and after I explain my syndrome, she checks my pulse and escorts me to a cab. No lollipop. As the car wends its way north and east, I hear a buzzing in my purse and unlock my screen to retrieve a text from Justine so full of expletives that even the app has the decency to look abashed. I let the screen go dark again and then I shut my eyes, reserving strength for the journey out of the car and up the stairs.

At home, in bed, I wake and dream and wake and dream until a cannonade or possibly a smaller species of battering ram thumps at my door, rattling the locks and hinges. I stumble from my bed, wincing. Lifting my shirt, I discover a mosaic of green and yellow bruises arrayed across my ribs, as though I'm trying to camouflage myself from the inside out.

Through the peephole, I see Roger, fist upraised as he drums the door again. Locks undone, I usher him in. His eyes parse the discarded underthings, the beer bottles, the spilled pile of *Playbills*. My mouth is parched, sere, but I bite my tongue—an old actor's trick—until moisture floods back in and I'm able to speak.

"Forgive me," I say, husky from sleep. "My decorator and I had a fatal falling out."

"Come on, Viv," Roger says in a low voice. He's removed the homburg from his head and he kneads it like felted dough. "No jokes now. Word is that you were at *The Winter's Tale* last night. Caleb said that you had some kind of seizure or attack. That they had to stop the play. Is that true?"

"Nothing so dramatic. I have a thing. Neuropathic postural tachycardia syndrome. It's a long and Latinate way of saying that I faint when I stand up too fast. It doesn't happen a lot, but it happens. Don't worry. It's basically harmless as long as I don't hit anything on the way down. A few bruises aside, I'm fine now."

He studies my face. "It's more than a few, kid. And anyway why did it happen last night? In the middle of a show?"

"My best friend was in it. She gave a very convincing fatal swoon and it spooked me. Which I now find very embarrassing. And look, I appreciate the concern, above and beyond the call of line editing. But you could have emailed."

"I did."

"That's right, my laptop died. I have to take it in. Well, you should have phoned."

"Well, guess what? I did that, too."

My eyes dart toward the phone, which I neglected to plug in last night. Also dead.

"Viv," Roger continues, "what's going on with you? You didn't seem all there at Christmas. You drank pretty hard. Okay, so did I. But you barely ate. And look at this—" He gestures vaguely around the studio. "Look at you. Do you even know what day it is?"

"Of course. It's Wednesday."

He shakes his head.

"Thursday," I say, moving to plug in my phone. "Fat Tuesday. Thin Friday. And now that we have our shared calendar sorted, thank you for stopping by, but I really ought to—"

He stops me with a peremptory wave, fanning the air one-handed. "Viv," he says, "take a look at yourself. I mean it." He puts that hand against my shoulder, half marching me into the bathroom with its mirrored medicine cabinet. I try to turn away, but he won't let me. So I look.

One eye appears grossly bloodshot, the other swollen and empurpled below the cut. There are abrasions on the cheek below it and a slash at the corner of my lip. My collarbones jut out too far above my T-shirt collar, and the skin not bruised or reddened looks unnaturally pale. I take a breath, fasten a grin to my face, and catch his eye in the mirror. "So you're saying my pinup days are through?"

"I'm saying you need help, kid. The drinking, it's too much. I had a talk with human resources earlier today and it turns out the company health plan is actually pretty generous when it comes to this sort of thing. It'll pay for a couple weeks at a facility. Cheryl and I can cover the rest if you need it."

"That's kind," I say. I will not return to a facility. Not for Roger. Not for anyone. And drinking? As my troubles go, it barely makes the list. I push past him and perch at the edge of the bed, spine stiff, hands folded in my lap, a plaster saint. "I appreciate your concern," I say. "But you are not my father and you are not my doctor. You have no idea what is going on in my life and you can't sign me in to anywhere that I don't want to go."

"You're right," he says. He slumps into my armchair, frowns, wriggles, then stands up again. "But I am your editor and as your editor I can tell you that the quality of your work is suffering. It's not unprintable, not yet, but over the last months, it's been arriving on my desk more coarse and more cruel. You've never suffered bad art gladly, and I've never asked you to, but you've grown brutal, Viv. Besides, *The Winter's Tale* producers aren't thrilled that you wrecked their preview. I reminded them that you weren't attending in a professional capacity, that you were there as a civilian, but they don't seem to care. There were some donors there, I gather. The *Post* got ahold of the story, photos, too. To kill it, I had to get our editor in chief involved. And she demanded your suspension, effective right now. She says that if you want to work for us again, you need to take the kind of vacation that lasts twelve steps and twenty-eight days. And I don't think she's wrong, Viv."

His cheeks have reddened. As though he's running a race. Running it too fast. He stumbles on. "Besides," he says, "drying out? It's what journalists do. How about we send you somewhere warm? California, maybe? Or the desert? That's where my old boss went in eighty-nine. Came back with a tan and a thing for succulents. Never saw him take a drink again. You're a good writer, Viv. Better than good. I don't want to lose you. But you have to get well."

"And what if I refuse?" I say, mouth like a paper cut.

"Then we'll find another second string," he says with a resigned shrug.

"You'll just pluck some random NYU kid out of a coffee bar on West Fourth and train her up to do what I do?"

Roger smiles in a way that makes his lips disappear into each other. "It worked with you. And before you ask about the lead critic job, I gave it to Caleb yesterday. I'd planned to tell you this morning."

"Get out!" My voice has shriveled into a scream. "Get out! Leave! Go!" And then my body is off the bed and I'm chasing him the very short distance toward the door, even as I'm somewhere slightly removed, watching the scene, aloof, uninvolved, a spectator.

Just before he trundles out, he reaches into his pocket and hands me a folded slip of paper. "Esteban said to give this to you. You take care, kid. And think about it, okay? There are worse things than sober. Even Dorothy Parker got on the wagon sometimes."

Trembling hands refasten each lock, then they open the note, written in swooping purple ink. "Putita," it reads, "what did you do to my cousin? Diego says you went banana daiquiris and now he's too freaked to leave his apartment. I love you, but you can be a crazy little bitch sometimes. Don't ask me for any more favors."

I rip it in half and then in half again and again. Paper fragments scatter the floor until there's nothing left in my hands, but still they go on ripping.

Back on the bed, I crawl atop the *Playbills* toward the pillows. With Roger gone, Esteban estranged, Justine enraged, and Destine and Charlie fled, my world, already so small, has shrunk to a pinprick. Only the man I knew as David Adler remains. His real name must lie among these *Playbills*. But which one?

My swollen eye blurring my vision, I begin to flip through program after program. And blame the possible concussion, but it isn't until I have sorted through nearly the whole of the stack that I realize these programs—from the late fall and early winter—are just set dressing. David interviewed me in early November; the photographs go back at least a month before that. No matter how I wrote about these shows, none of them could have prompted the "Crritic!" project. They aren't clues, just monuments to my unkindness.

So I heave my mind back to the summer, back to those vacant golden months after news of my aunt's death reached me—and there's a feeling of great heaviness, as though gravity has suddenly doubled, crushing me down into the blankets, because after only a moment I know the show to search for. With my laptop still deadweight, I reach for my reporter's notebook and flip back. I find my notes on the show in some pages from late August: *Life/Lesson*, the same show that David Adler had asked me about in the café and one more rabbit-punch reminder that I should have known this all along.

Life/Lesson conjures a Friday evening at summer's end, not long after my aunt's photo albums arrived and I'd been made to reckon with why these women were dead while I remained alive. But this was one of those still, gilded nights that make New York seem like a reasonable place to live, if a person has to live at all. I'd walked to the theater from my apartment, stopping into a Japanese snack stall for a milk tea that I sipped as I strolled. The theater was in a former synagogue and I spent the few minutes before curtain leaning against the metal grate of the shop across the street, watching the last of the sun flash against the temple's rose window as men and women with shining hair and straight-leg jeans passed beneath, losing myself for a moment in the heat and glow, nearly forgetting that I'm not meant for warmth.

When I entered the theater, my mood darkened. For one, there wasn't any stage, just thirty or so chairs arranged in a loose circle under a handful of clamp lights, unsoftened by gels. In place of a program, the grim, poncho-wearing woman at the ticket booth slapped a name tag to my chest, destroying my anonymity and possibly my blouse. Another woman, sapling thin, her hair in pigtail braids, stood behind a table, doling out oatmeal cookies and cups of scorched coffee from a raffia tray.

Other theatergoers stood near me, chatting or toying with their phones as they waited for the lights to fall. But the lights stayed on. A few minutes after eight, a young man with a pale, wispy beard and a name tag reading "Clay" reached out and took me gently by the wrist. I jerked my hand away. He nodded slowly and said, in a voice that had barely broken, "You don't like to be touched? That's cool. I can work with that. Let me show you to your seat."

He led me to a spot in the circle and gestured to a chair. When I took it, he sat down beside me. All around us, people sank down in pairs. In a few cases it was difficult to tell the actors from the audience members, but usually some detail marked the spectator out: a watch, high heels, better grooming.

He stared at me, unblinking, in the way of cats and trainee therapists. "Vivian," he said. "May I call you Vivian?"

The presence of the name tag didn't leave me much choice. "Sure."

"Okay," he said. "I'm Clay."

"According to certain holy books so are we all."

"Yeah? Are you religious? Or spiritual? You seem spiritual."

I reached into my bag for my reporter's notebook, my felt tip jammed in the wire spiral, and I held it between us. "Thank you, Clay. Fabulous EQ. But tell me, when does the play begin?"

"Well, this *is* the play."

I looked around at the pairs, some of them sitting stiff and upright, some of them leaning toward each other, heads bent as if in prayer, the space between their bodies a churchly arch. "Really?"

"I was just about to explain it. After we got to know each other a little bit."

"And do you feel you know me now?"

"Not yet," he said, one hand tugging worriedly at his near beard, "but I want to. See, that's the premise of *Life/Lesson*." His voice changed then—growing deeper, better rehearsed. "We feel that the stories of people's actual lives are way more dramatic than anything the theater offers and a theater that stages those stories becomes more real and present and just, like, closer to life as we live it. And that can make us think about our own lives more. Or like, approach each other with greater empathy, you know? Because we walk around all the time in our own heads, not paying attention to anyone, not paying attention to ourselves. And that's, like, really bad. Because the unexamined life isn't worth living, right?"

"Is the examined one? Socrates died a suicide."

"Really? Wow. That makes me so sad." He tugged at his beard more aggressively. "So the idea here is that we talk to each guest—that's you, you're my guest—for twenty minutes or so. And then together we perform a short scene from your life. Like you could play yourself and I could play your boyfriend or your girlfriend or your mom or whatever. Or if you want, you can play someone else, like your father or your teacher, and I can be you. We'll all watch these stories together and the hope is that maybe we can learn something about each other and about ourselves. How does that sound to you?"

Nauseating. Repulsive. Like the touchy-feely exercises that should have made me abandon a theater major long before a psychotic break forced my hand. In college, I had loved these rehearsal room indulgences—dancing the taste of a lemon, imagining words as colors. But I had grown cooler since. Especially around twentysomethings denying me my chance to sit in the dark and quietly, inconspicuously, commune. Still, Roger had assigned me the review and I had a word count to make. So I played along.

"Fine," I said. I opened my notebook, uncapped my pen, and suspended it just above the blank page. "What do you need to know?"

He looked down at the notebook. "Don't you want to put that away? Like, instead of writing stuff down and being in your analytical mind, you could be here, in the present with me, just experiencing the moment."

"Thanks, but no. Next question."

"Okay, well, how old are you?"

"Thirty-two."

"Oh, cool. I'm twenty-six, practically the same."

"Congratulations." I was sure puberty would kick in for him any day now.

"And where are you from?"

"Massachusetts."

"Boston?"

"Northfield."

"So tell me about your parents. Tell me about your mother."

It was that familiar question, that tired lead-in to every psychiatrist gag, that undid me. Because even when you pretend that nothing matters except solid dramaturgy and a tremendous eleven o'clock number, even when you kill any genuine feeling with casual sex and serious drinking and rationed sedatives, there is a part of you that you keep private: the girl you were and how fiercely that girl was known and loved.

"Thank you, Clay," I said. I made my voice neutral, impassive, wall-to-wall carpeting for the soul. "But that isn't something that I care to discuss. In fact, I think I'm done talking now."

"Hey, no problem," he said, bobbing his chin in an exaggerated nod. "It's part of our process that if there's a question the guest finds awkward or difficult, then we move on. Do you want to tell me about where you went to elementary school?"

"No, not remotely. I told you. I'm through answering."

He tugged at his chin so vigorously that a few of the sparse hairs came free.

"But we have, like, fifteen minutes left."

"I prefer to spend them in quiet contemplation."

He tried to reengage me, but I was lost to him, my face a linen-and-leather mask as I surveyed the room, scribbling observations in my notebook, using the paper as a thin shield to keep the world away.

Once the quarter hour had passed, the woman with braided hair walked to the center of the circle, arms upraised, requesting silence. She turned her head toward all of us, letting her smile fall on everyone in the room like a crop plane spraying pesticide. After an acknowledgment of the ancestral lands the theater stood upon, she gave a brief speech about how we'd now have the opportunity to present scenes from our lives. And if at any time any of us felt that there were fresh ways to resolve a conflict, then he or she or they should feel welcome to clap hands, freeze the scene, and jump right in to try it.

The playlets began. An older woman with purple hair acted out a scene with the father who had never praised her. A young man reimagined a recent breakup, treating the actor playing his boyfriend with pert indignation. Another woman started her scene by apologizing to her younger sister for bullying her. Her sister was in the audience. She froze the scene, stepped in, and then they cried and hugged and the scent of forced catharsis hung heavy in the air. Or maybe that was just patchouli. The odor lingered throughout each new scene—thick, sickening.

It wasn't art. It was group therapy with a pay-what-you-wish jar.

I never liked group therapy.

Inevitably, the circle swung around to me. Clay stood awkwardly, shifting from foot to foot, the fingers of his left hand still yanking awkwardly at his chin. "So I'm Clay," he said. "And this is Vivian. We don't really have a scene for you. Vivian didn't feel comfortable participating and of course this piece only works if we're all brave enough to trust each other, but not everyone's equipped for that and if that's not a choice she can make, then I think we have to be cool and respect that, right?"

At first, an awkward silence threatened, an echo of the tension an audience feels when an actor has forgotten her lines and no one is standing close enough to prompt her. Then one of the sisters started to giggle and laughter flared around the room, swift and bright, like a square of flash paper once it hits the match. The laughter faded; the show resumed. And I sat, an effigy, for the few remaining scenes. At the end, everyone stood and applauded. I applauded, too, slapping my hands together until they stung. Then I fled the theater, but not before the poncho girl shoved a flimsy program at me.

I sped home, walking at a pace that was more properly a jog, taking the steps to my apartment two at a time and then stepping into the bath, where I scrubbed every inch of exposed skin and shampooed my hair twice, trying to slough away the room, those people, the horror of that thin, sad man forcing the jagged contours of my life—my real life—into my only place of safety. Once I was out and dry and newly calm, a drink sliding coolly down my throat, I took out my laptop and I wrote a review as scathing as I could make it. Which is very scathing. Industrial solvents have nothing on me.

So as Oedipus said, I should have known. I rummage through my papers until I find the program and the creator's name. It's Gregory Payne. As my laptop is stilled, I perform a quick image search on my phone, now charged, but already I know whose face I will see: David Adler's. The man who outfoxed me and outfaked me. The best actor I have ever seen.

19

LIGHTS DOWN

I know David Adler's real name now. And I know where he lives. Or at least the place that one of his associates calls home. Looking back on the months since that first interview, I realize Raj's apartment was the rare location that didn't feel like a hastily assembled set. I remember how Raj delayed when I told him to take me home, how he fled to the men's room and then insisted on ordering a burger and another drink that he didn't seem to want. I can imagine him, leaning against a wall near the urinal, jamming his fingers into his smartphone screen, texting that the plan is running way ahead of schedule, promising he'll buy Gregory Payne just enough time to shove his worldly goods into cardboard boxes, to tape a flash drive to the back of a drawer. Was Gregory somewhere in the apartment that night? Or near it? Did he watch me from some shadowed square of pavement? If I had looked harder, if I had acted smarter, if I hadn't impaired myself with pills and drink and low-key sex panic, if I had been a first-rate theater critic rather than a fourth-string detective, would I have found him then?

Gregory Payne had months to organize retribution. I have a day and change. The countdown clock on the My Life in Art site has told me as much. And there's a sensation that comes, a kind of subsonic hum, when a show is nearly over. I feel it now, the weight of a curtain primed to fall. These moments are my last.

Rising from the bed, I begin. A bath first. And then a toweling off, careful of the bruised parts. An Ativan is scored and one half swallowed. It works quickly, but it isn't only the pill working now. I feel distant, unconcerned, as though I'm watching myself from far away—the back row of the mezzanine, say. And then to costume. On go the tights and the black skirt. Then the black mohair sweater that used to be my mother's and the jet beads she gave me when I turned eighteen. My hair is brushed until it gleams and twisted into a low chignon. From the bottle on my night table, each pulse point receives a dab of Je Reviens.

My phone whines and whines again. Justine, as is her way, has texted and texted:

Leaving for the theater

Don't you dare tell me to break a fucking leg with your kind of luck I would break it literally like a compound fucking fracture.

See I do fucking know what literally means

And I asked Craig about this David person and he said he doesn't know any David but he was weird about it

A while ago he was asking about you, about us, college shit or whatever, like I thought he was maybe actually interested in something besides my tits for fucking once

Probably it doesn't mean anything

Also I am so fucking mad at you and once I get through this seven-show week I am going to literally kill you

So don't be dead because I have to murder you first are we very fucking clear

Which is a very Justine way of saying, Wish me luck. And, Forgive me. And, Please be okay.

"I'm sorry," my fingers reply. "For everything. Literally."

It isn't enough. Or it's too much. I have often thought of Justine and me as each other's meager life raft—taking on water, still somehow afloat. Now I wonder if we weren't just two flailing swimmers dragging each other down. But that's a problem for another day. If there is another day. At least I now know how Gregory Payne learned about my past, how he knew to search my college paper for my former name. The phone is replaced in my purse.

In the bathroom, the door of the medicine cabinet is swung wide, turning its mirror to the wall. A tube of concealer is unearthed, followed by other compacts and tubes. The makeup goes on—by touch, not sight—dabbed and patted and smeared. The cabinet swings closed and my eyes want to dart away, but instead they find my face, the bruises still livid beneath the powder, the bright lipstick fooling no one. It looks like someone else's face. Then it's on with the costume: boots, scarf, coat, gloves, and a cloche hat, pulled low over my swollen eye. David Adler's flash drive is retrieved and placed in my purse, alongside other props.

Only downstairs, at the building's front door, do I realize I've left my own door unlocked, an act of impossible carelessness, unimaginable even a week ago. I turn to go back up. But then I stop. What's there? A dead laptop, some half-drunk liquor. I've lost everything already. There's nothing left worth stealing. Except my life, as Hamlet says. Except my life. Except my life.

It's dark outside. Maybe it's been dark for hours. And it's cold—I know it, even if I don't exactly feel it. When I look down I can see my legs moving, hear the sole of each boot smacking the sidewalk, but they look like someone else's boots, someone else's feet and legs. Then I'm standing in front of Raj's building. There's a doorman on duty this time, fingering his cap as he pages through today's *Post*, the paper Roger fought to keep my picture from. I stand at a three-quarter angle, fixing the doorman with my better eye.

"I'm here to see Gregory Payne," a voice says. The voice, I realize, is mine.

"Can I give him a name?" the doorman asks.

"Oh," I say with a glassine trill, "he's expecting me."

The doorman picks up a handset and punches in a code. A murmured conversation follows, though he holds a hand in front of his mouth so I can't make out the words. He replaces the receiver. "Go on up," he says. "Eleven E."

I enter the elevator, ducking to avoid the security cameras and the mirrors, and from far away I sense a lurch in my stomach as the doors close and the car speeds upward. Then I'm back in that immaculate hall with its muted carpet. My feet move toward the door Raj once held for me, now already an inch or two ajar. The flat of my hand presses against the wood, opening into that same living room, that same sofa, that same color field painting, its blues rippling in the glow of the picture light. Beneath it lounges the man I knew as David Adler, his hair shorter now, his glasses vanished, his eyes still black. He looks up from the screen of a sleek laptop and flashes a cold grin. He looks like a cat who's just eaten a bowl of cream. And then the bowl, too.

I can hear my voice say, "Hi, Gregory. Seen anything good lately?" And I'm surprised at how low it sounds, how resonant and clear.

"Vivian," he says, setting the laptop down, "welcome. I wasn't expecting you so soon. Or at all, if I'm being honest. Once you didn't figure out the project in the first couple of weeks, we thought you never would. And even when you found the drive and the site we weren't sure. So, hey. Good job. And, please, call me Greg."

"There are a lot of things I'd like to call you first."

"Funny. And hey, I heard about your accident at the show. Those problem plays can really mess a lady up, huh? I can see the black eye underneath all that makeup. Want to tell me where it hurts?" There's amusement in his voice, dark pleasure.

"I don't feel a thing," I say. "Are we alone?"

"Vivian," he says, his laugh a growl. "So forward! Of course, from watching the video feed I know that already. So let's get to it, right? Or do you need some kind of foreplay first?"

"Answer my question."

"Yes, we're alone. Colby's away for the night."

"Colby?"

"Colby Gupta. My roommate. And the producing director of our humble company. You knew him as Raj, of course. He hasn't acted for years, but I think we can both agree he did pretty well in the part. Any compliments you'd like me to pass along? I'm sure he's sorry to have missed you. After all, you became so close."

"Not that close."

"Yes, and what a relief. When you insisted on coming home with him that night, he called me from the men's room, hysterical. Probably pissing all over his shoes. I told him I'd get the scene ready and that he should just go with it. Improvise. Because we did want to get you over here. But he thought he might actually have to sleep with you. He was petrified. Said he'd never be able to go through with it. But, hey, if it cheers you up at all, Colby said your phone skills were top-notch."

"Thank you. That's very kind. Maybe I'll use him as a reference." My body, nearly weightless now, moves to the bentwood chair and balances at its edge. There's fear, of course, but I'm too numb to really feel it. This is what they said about Ophelia, that she was "incapable of her own distress." That's me, half in the brook already, singing as I drown.

"So Gregory," I continue, "unless my command of dramatic structure fails me, isn't this the moment where you unpack your whole scheme? Take me through just how you planned and executed it?"

"Oh, Vivian. Always so old-fashioned. Melodrama? Really? And besides," he says, gesturing offhandedly to his laptop, "I have work to do. The project is almost ready to go live. So monologues will have to wait, okay?"

Though moisture has fled my mouth, that same cool voice speaks again. "Surely you can answer a few questions about process," I say. "You wouldn't want your audience to think that certain effects were just accidental, would you?"

"Okay," he says, settling back into the couch and knitting his fingers in some complicated stitch. "Fair point. Might as well take credit where it's due. Which effects did you have in mind?"

"Vinnie Mendoza. The body I found in the park. I don't understand what he had to do with any of this. What was he doing in that photo on Raj's desk?" I correct myself. "Colby's desk."

"Oh yeah. Vinnie. That was a good one. We were following you by then. Had been following you for a while. Blake—he played Jay and he's also the one who left the notes under your door when we thought your story needed just a little more tension—he saw you talking to the EMTs and then to the cops, stuck around after you left to ask what had happened. Then we watched the police blotter for a day or two until we found the story. After that, it was just a quick search of his Insta and a little deepfake magic. Freaked you out, didn't it?"

He's probing now, feeling with his eyes and voice for my weak points. I'm weak points through. Bruises all the way down. But my face gives nothing away. "You used a man's death to sex up your performance piece?" I say. "Isn't that perhaps a little sick?"

"Vivian, these chance elements texture the whole exercise. They inject the real into the fictive."

"And that camera. Did you come by to upload the footage? Were you in my building?"

"Only to install it. After that it was all done remotely. Only the best tech for you, Viv. Anything else?"

"Yes," I say. My eyes meet his now, staring into those empty black irises. "Why me? Why go to all of this trouble and care? Yes, I gave *Life/Lesson* an exacting review. But I wasn't alone."

"Most of the reviews were really good," Gregory says. "Very complimentary."

This, of course, is his bruise. "Most? Maybe a few—critics who took you at your word and didn't realize you'd lifted every good idea from a college bookstore copy of *Theatre of the Oppressed* and that Grotowski documentary. I meant what I said in that review, in our chat. The seventies ended a long time ago. Which you must know," I say, sweeping a hand toward the apartment's clean lines. "They weren't building luxury high-rises on St. Mark's back then. By the way, exactly how does the artistic director of an experimental theater company afford a place like this?"

He doesn't respond, but the catlike grin has vanished, replaced by a wrinkling of his forehead.

"Oh good," I say, "just what theater needs. Another trust fund baby."

The wrinkle deepens.

"That also explains the upmarket surveillance equipment. So as to my question, yes, I wrote an unflattering review, but I wasn't alone. And besides, I publish several of those a month. People write surly letters to the editor. They leave unflattering comments online. They don't execute elaborate multimedia vendettas. Indulge me."

"Because you were wrong," he says, his fluting voice, the voice I first knew as David Adler's, straining toward a whine. "That was a great show. Everyone in the room felt it. People were crying and laughing and holding each other and staying in the theater for hours after we'd finished just to talk it through. But some critics savaged it and you were the worst. You called it juvenile and derivative."

"Because it was."

"And then you wrote that essay two weeks later about how our show convinced you that the avant-garde was dead. The show had already closed and you were out there pissing on its grave. So I thought that I would show you," he says. He is leaning more forward now, his black eyes bright like falling stars. "Show you how wrong you were. Show you that the avant-garde was alive and well. On your block. Inside your apartment. And honestly it wasn't even that expensive or hard—a slice of quiche, the sublet, a few cheap costumes and props, a day rate for Brian as the P.I. and Sirko. Everyone else volunteered their services. Seems like you have a lot of fans, Vivian. And honestly, I'm one, too. Because we're a lot alike, you and me. Not in every way, of course. I'm not an alcoholic. I don't give my body away like it's a friend of a friend's cable password. But my most meaningful relationships are with the art I make, the art I see, and that's true for you, too.

"You said that theater needed new forms. And so I made one—a multimedia performance intervention that blurs the boundaries between art and life, built for and around a single spectator. That's you," he says. He says it sweetly, softly, as though murmuring it into a lover's ear. "Everyone will see it, of course. And chances are you'll never work again. Not for any legitimate publication. But this is your show, Vivian. I made it just for you. Don't you like it?"

For Gregory, I now understand, this performance has never been just about revenge. "Crritic!" is intended as a gift, in poisoned wrapping, an offering meant for someone who loves the theater with her shattered heart. Someone like me. And I understand now what he wants from me: praise from the only person who cares about these aesthetic categories as much as he does, who has given the whole of her rickety life to them, who could recognize what he has made as truly, breathlessly new. We are so close to each other in this way, each other's dark mirror. He wants me to see him for what he believes he is—a genius, an innovator. Just as he has seen me, as almost no one else has, with all my wounds and scars, maimed and small and surviving still.

But I am too fine a critic to endure bad art. It's a gift I can't accept.

"Oh, Gregory," I say. I'm standing now, steady on the feet that have sunk into the plush carpet. "That's sweet. Honestly. But do you really think that what you've made is radical, that it counts as innovation? Because I can trace a history from the dadaists and situationists through sixties happenings and more recent solo audience work in Europe. Your piece isn't original, it isn't even—"

"Shut up!" he says, his voice gone high again. "What would you know? You fell for every trick we pulled. Believing that some grad student would bother interviewing you for a thesis. Believing that Colby's girlfriend, Zoë, was some poor Brighton Beach waif. She's from Wisconsin and she learned that crap Russian accent doing Gorky in rep. Polly? That's Zoë's roommate, Maeve, in a pair of contact lenses. She mostly does children's theater. And Brian? Fucking Brian? We got Brian through an ad in *Backstage*. He's spent years doing industrials. Can't act to save his life. We thought we'd have to get another guy for Sirko, but then we thought, Hey, why bother? Bet she's too dumb to notice. And we were right. You could have stopped this so quickly, Vivian. If you'd apologized at the café. If you'd seen through me then. If you'd seen through anything. But you didn't."

I shake my head. Then wait until the room rights itself. "Gregory. You have it all wrong. Credulity doesn't make me a bad critic. In my line, it's called a willing suspension of disbelief and it's a professional necessity. I have to trust that gold gels and a wave sound effect mean I'm at the seaside or that years have elapsed between the first act and the second because a program note tells me so or that a few cheap chairs mean a real room, a real home, a real anything. That's generosity. That's hope. That's love. Every time I step into the theater, every time I sit down on some lumpy plush seat, I make a choice to believe."

"But that's the theater. This is life."

"You seemed so intent on confusing the distinction."

Slowly, ominously, the smile reappears on his face. "Yeah? And how did that make you feel?"

I won't ever tell him. I won't show him either. I'm Diderot's ideal actor, calm in the center of the whirlwind. So far away that I don't even feel a breeze. "Oh," I say, reflecting back his grin. "Is that how you diagrammed the scene? Me breaking down, weeping and pleading and begging you to make it all stop? Did I prostrate myself, Gregory? Did I kneel? Did I offer to fuck you if you would only make it end? The site says that you work without a director, but that's what you are, of course. I'm so sorry, Gregory, but I just don't take direction well. And, that isn't how I want to play this."

"You'll play it however I fucking tell you to," Gregory says. "We have the photos, the videos, everything. Just be glad you figured it out when you did. We had a whole other phase planned. Upping the notes. Being more obvious with the tail. Making you think the Russians were on to you. But if I'm being honest, everyone was a little relieved once you found the drive. There were only so many nights we could watch you drug yourself to sleep clutching the complete prose plays of Ibsen before it just got pretty boring for all involved. So we wrapped and set the launch date. Want to see the template?"

Without waiting for an answer, he reopens the laptop and turns the screen toward me. Under the My Life in Art banner, I see the title "Crritic!" and below it a new image of myself, leaving a Broadway theater, my lips curled into a moue of disgust. Underneath it are two tabs, one labeled "LIFE," the other "ART."

"The LIFE tab takes visitors through the story as you experienced it, with stills and audio and video to supplement. Don't worry. None of the sex stuff is there. That was just for fun. Or we'll make it a paywall extra. But the drinking, the pills, disrupting your friend's show, that's all available. And then the ART tab shows the behind-the-scenes process of how we put it all together—costume, set dressing. Nice, right? The whole thing looks like art—I mean, it *is* art—but it also lets every site visitor know just what a dumb slut you truly are. No one will want you as a reviewer after this. Not even the blogs." He leans back against the sofa, arms crossed against his chest, eyes slitted.

It is no worse than I had imagined. But also no better. The ruin of the life I have made. I can't be a critic anymore, not after this. And without that particular access to art—party to the work and apart from it, present and distanced—I might as well not live at all. The cringing, human part of me should scream now, should run at Gregory or his laptop or both. But he must have uploaded everything to the cloud long ago. So my voice stays low. My hands still.

"Aren't you taking a risk?" I hear myself say. "I could sue."

"You could. You'd lose. We met with an attorney when we were first sketching this out and she said that privacy laws are famously uncertain in their application. Most courts tread lightly on First Amendment stuff. Manhattan courts, especially. And defamation? That's almost impossible to prove. Eventually we might get fined. We might even have to take the site down. But by that time every producer and theatergoer will have screenshot it and you'll never be able to show your face south of Sixty-sixth again.

"But the best part," he continues. "You're just the beta version. We're talking to investors now and the plan is to expand My Life in Art, maybe even franchise it, so anyone can buy a My Life in Art experience for themselves, not knowing when or how it will begin. Or they can tailor a bespoke experience for a friend. Great things are happening, Vivian. A new form of theater, no matter what you say. All because of you."

"Not bad for a dumb slut," I say. There is blood in my mouth—the cut in my lip must have reopened—but I don't move to stanch it, because I'm somewhere else now, sat on the aisle, watching myself watching Gregory Payne smile, the laptop screen lending his face a sickly glow.

"So why not just give up, Vivian?" he says. "Why not admit that you're a little bitch who wouldn't know great art even if it bent you over the dress circle at the Lyric? The theater doesn't need you. It never has."

About this, he is not wrong. And have I needed the theater? I was my best self in its embrace, yet that self was so flimsy, so thin, dissolving as soon as the houselights went on. The theater, I would tell myself, is a laboratory for human life. To sit there—to hear, to see, to feel and feel and feel—was to practice living. But the experiment failed. Practice never made me perfect. I never became a person, I only played one. The act fooled nobody. Not even me. Not anymore. Theater failed me. And I failed it, right back.

But some people can't take criticism.

I am one of those people.

"Oh, Gregory," I say, voice like a silk ribbon. "You've got the casting all wrong. I gave up little bitches years ago. Let's try another role." I open my purse and pull out my kitchen knife. The good one. It glistens in the low light. I point it toward him.

"Hey," he says, backing up on the sofa slightly. "Come on. You're not serious. Put that away."

"I'm very serious, Gregory." I take one step toward him and then another. Until I'm standing right over him, my calves grazing the couch's edge, my knees brushing his. "I love a discussion scene, I really do. Ibsen's great invention. But if we're honest with ourselves and there's no dramaturge here to scold us, then can't we admit that a fifth act murder is just a little more interesting than a chat?"

He swallows and nods toward the knife. "You won't use that."

"Really? I think I probably will. I mean, you don't put a knife in your purse unless you plan on doing some stabbing. Chekhov says so. Besides, I've had several scene study teachers tell me that one has to suffer for one's art. Let's make that happen for you."

"Don't do this, Vivian. Colby knows you're here. I texted him when the doorman said you were coming up."

"No, you didn't. You were too busy dimming the lights and arranging yourself artlessly against the sofa cushions to bother with your phone."

His sucks his lips back into his mouth and I know I've guessed correctly.

"I never gave the doorman my name, and while I'm sure the lobby has a security camera, all the feed will show is a woman in a dark coat with a hat and scarf covering most of her face, a woman who could be anyone. I've kept my gloves on, so no prints in the elevator either." As I speak, I watch his fingers slowly slide toward the pocket of his slacks. I jerk the knife at him. A thread of blood appears just above his collarbone.

"Ow!" he says. "You cut me! I can't believe you fucking cut me!"

"That's what knives do, Gregory. Don't try reaching for your phone again. Hands on your knees where I can see them."

He obliges. But he's frightened. I can sense his terror now, tingling and sharp, like the taste of metal in my mouth.

"There. That wasn't so hard," I say. I lower the knife from his throat. "Do what I say and maybe I'll leave all those pretty arteries alone."

He readies himself for a retort. Then strength leaves him and he slumps back against the pillows. "Okay," he says sulkily. "Fine. What do you want? Do you want me to take the site down?"

"We can start with that."

I perch on the edge of the couch and watch his fingers move in jittery rhythms over the keyboard, executing a command string. Then the "Crritic!" screen fades out.

"There," he says.

"Well done. Take off your pants."

His face is a jigsaw that snaps together to form a picture of complete horror.

"Don't worry, Gregory. You're not my type, either. And if you could manage an erection in this situation I would be absolutely shocked and also in all likelihood extremely unimpressed."

He undoes his buckle and wriggles out of his slacks, which puddle to the floor near the sofa, revealing a pair of gray briefs.

"Underwear as well. . . . And now your shirt."

Then he's standing before me, this bare forked animal, naked except for socks, hands crossed over his pelvis. If I felt anything, I might feel a prickling of compassion, a glint of pity. I don't.

I reach into my bag for my phone, then set it on the coffee table and enable the video function, making sure the screen can see us both. "I want to have a record of this. Performance documentation. So smile for the camera, Gregory. I'm not dumb enough to believe that you won't relaunch the site as soon as I leave, so I have a surprise for you. Another role for me to play. Because revenger? That's not really me either. I trained as an actress—you know this—and back then I always had a type, the kind of woman who never makes it to the final curtain. The Ophelias, the Heddas, the Miss Julies, the Lady Macbeths. I've played them all. Do you know who else I played? All the way back in high school? Juliet. So, Gregory, I'll be brief: 'O happy dagger! This is thy sheath.'"

Before he quite knows what's happening, I've stood up quickly, too quickly, and just before the world goes black, I have plunged the knife into my own breast, just underneath the heart.

As the darkness descends, I can imagine what he sees. The knife, the blood, the smile that flickers on my lips and then fades as my body drops, falling sideways onto the couch and from there onto the floor, where I lie, the blood a flower tinting my black sweater even blacker and trickling to the carpet below.

Gregory Payne struggles to swallow, he struggles to breathe, he struggles not to vomit. As David Adler, he was the best actor I have ever seen, but my body has robbed him of all that pretense. He is not acting now.

"Oh God," he says. And then, "Oh no." And then, "Fuck. Fuck. Fuck. Fuck. Fuck. I can't fucking believe this." And then there aren't any words because he's weeping, crying in an ugly, howling, animal way, so overwhelmed with pity and terror that he doesn't see my hand snake up the table and reach for my phone.

But then he feels the sofa move as I sit back down and it's at least a minute before he can stop screaming long enough for me to get a word in. Of course I record that, too, pausing only when his sniffling has subsided and he has pulled his pants back on.

"Trick knife, Gregory," I say. "A stage prop. Effective, don't you think? I switched it out while you were removing your shirt. It's flimsy looking up close, of course, but in the context of the scene—well, that's the magic of theater for you."

Gregory doesn't reply.

"No ovation? Fine." I pick up my phone and peck at the screen for a moment. "We both know I have a record of your enthusiastic response to the show, a record I've just texted to a few associates and friends. If you ever decide to rescue that site from the cloud, I'll make sure this video goes online just as fast. Yes, it's cheap, overly emotional, and in very bad taste. The nudity is entirely gratuitous. If I know New York theater, that practically guarantees a hit. And, Gregory, just so you know, in the very unlikely event that you persevere anyway, I'll come back here. With a knife that isn't latex."

I return the phone to my purse and take out the flash drive, placing it on the table. "This is yours, I believe. Thanks for the loan. And now, if there's no talk back planned," I say, "I'll see myself out." Which is how I leave him, shirtless on the sofa, still grasping for breath and words.

I glide into the elevator and out of the lobby and onto the street, past the park and the sushi places and the punk rock tribute bars. The kitchen knife falls down into a sewer grate. The trick knife joins it. My body moves without me guiding it, fueled by a sultry glow of pleasure from somewhere deep inside. For the first time in months—years—I'm warm through.

Because an hour or so ago, as I caught my reflection in the bathroom mirror, I expected to see the horror that Roger had shown me. But the depersonalization had spun out so far that I saw someone else instead, a girl, haunted and half-broken, who'd spent years trying to make a life for herself the only way she knew how, turning her face into a mask, her heart into paragraphs, engaging with the art she loved from the safety of an aisle seat.

And there, in that bathroom, I felt that strange mimetic click, that invisible string that joins me to each character onstage. I saw that girl, the girl my mother used to see. I wanted to help her, to save her, in some ridiculous and lunatic and actual way. Have I managed it? I'll know soon. When I return, if I can, to daylight. To treatment, I suppose. To Roger, if he'll have me after. And to Justine, if she'll accept me sober, undisguised. And maybe, one day, months or years from now, I'll call Charlie up and see if he has any new effects to show me. Maybe I will have something to show him, too. A self. My mother's daughter. Fingers, hands, arms, all. A woman who knows how to find her light.

For now, I walk home, through wet, deserted streets, climb the flights of stairs, nudge open my unlocked door, and drape hat, scarf, gloves, and coat over the back of the armchair, the motions smooth, unhurried. I rattle the other half of the Ativan into my palm and swallow it with a long, slow suck from the vodka bottle in the freezer. I turn off the lights and climb into bed, the bottle clutched in my hand, my open eyes staring, held by the dark, which cocoons itself around my body and presses me down into the pillow.

I finish the bottle. Or maybe there's a trickle left when it slips from my hand. Then finally, blessedly, the last stage bulb winks out and the curtain falls. Whatever audience is watching sits stilled now, expectant. And then, from somewhere just beyond my hearing, the applause begins.

ACKNOWLEDGMENTS

I became a professional theater critic at twenty-one, by inclination and by accident. I've stayed one ever since. This book could not have been written without the thousands of nights spent in dozens of theaters all over the city. It's a weird way to organize a life, giving yourself over to other people's stories so many times each week, but it has led me to tell this one. My profound thanks to the editors who have worked with me over the years, first at the *Voice* and then at the *Times*, refining my voice and style, particularly Austin Considine, Jeremy Egner, Scott Heller, Nicole Herrington, Sia Michel, and Brian Parks. I'm also grateful for the friendship and knife-sharp intelligence of my colleagues, especially Helen Shaw and Elisabeth Vincentelli. Thanks, too, for the encouragement of the teachers and professors who started me on this path, Ted Walsh, whom we lost this year, and Marc Robinson, and for Martin Meisel, who thought that it was quite a good idea to keep on it.

Writing a novel has been a lifelong desire. I've written stories since I learned my letters. But it took me many years to trust myself enough to begin this and then many more to find the hours, between work and child care, to complete it. I'm grateful to very early readers—Megan Campisi and Micah Kelber—for their excitement about the book, and to Sophie Nield for lending me the title, a truncated version of her academic essay arguing against immersive theater. My thanks also to somewhat later readers Sarah Weinman, Catherine Ho, Steph Myers, and my sister, Morgan Soloski, for their encouragement. (And to Morgan, once again, for performing a sensitivity read without my even having to ask.)

I could not have dreamed of an agent as superb as Sarah Burnes, who is an absolute cheerleader, in the sense that cheerleaders are elite athletes, with the élan and grace to make all of those jumps and handsprings look easy. I am obliged to her for her boundless support and for the work she did, briskly and lovingly, to bring the book to the auction. Thanks also to her associates at the Gernert Company, Sophie Pugh-Sellers, Rebecca Gardner, Will Roberts, and Nora Gonzalez. And to Sylvie Rabineau at WME for her belief that the book might become a series or film.

If I were a vision board kind of person, I would have made one with Megan Lynch's photo in the center. I'd followed her on social media for years and had quietly fangirled her know-how and taste and humanity. I am beyond thrilled that the book landed with her. Each of her notes has made it better and more urgent and those notes have always been tendered with compassion. Thanks also to Kukuwa Ashun, for holding my hand, via email, as a first-time author, and Sona Vogel, for her alarming precision and her flagging of what would have been a deeply humiliating chronology mistake. I'm grateful to Sara Wood for the tantalizing cover and to Elizabeth Hubbard, Jason Reigal, Frances Sayers, Christopher Smith, Katherine Turro, Sue Walsh, and Emily Walters for publicity, marketing, production, and editorial expertise. And to Elishia Merricks for her passion for the audiobook.

I want to thank my mother, Judy Soloski, for not immediately pointing out every grammar mistake I had made, and for doing so much to make my life easier. My children, Ada Eubank and Thom Eubank, make almost nothing easier and everything gladder with their fierce, instinctive love. My darlings, I am so proud and happy to be your mother. This book, though neither of you is remotely old enough to read it, is for you.

ABOUT THE AUTHOR

ALEXIS SOLOSKI is a prize-winning *New York Times* culture reporter and a former lead theater critic at *The Village Voice*. She has taught at Barnard College and at Columbia University, where she earned her PhD in theater. She lives in Brooklyn with her family. *Here in the Dark* is her first novel.